Toni—
Merry
Christmas—
2019

Rerouting

Bex Jalise

Bex Jalise

This book is a work of fiction. Any references to historical events, real people, or real places are used fictitiously. Other names, characters, places, and events are products of the author's imagination, and any resemblance to actual events or places or persons, living or dead, is entirely coincidental.

ISBN-13: 9781099795930

To JR:

Don't ever be afraid to stand out.

You're marvelous.

Rerouting

ONE

Robbie's finger throbbed from taking her anger out on the dashboard's volume button. The bass thrummed through her seat until she felt it behind her eyes. Nathan had always insisted on keeping the volume at a low hum—barely above audible if he'd ever asked her opinion on it. He'd said it was better for their hearing in the long run, and since he was the doctor and she was only a high school literature teacher, who was she to argue?

But Nathan wasn't here now, was he? He'd opted out of the long run in a decidedly unceremonious fashion. Eight years together deserved more than a simple declaration that they no longer "worked," which was code for "he didn't want to do the work anymore." There should have been a fight or a door slam—something to mark the occasion besides Robbie's stunned silence. Even Rhett Butler had punctuated his famous exit with a "Frankly, my dear, I don't give a damn," before disappearing into the fog. But Robbie hadn't done or said anything, except maybe mumble an apology for nothing.

Nathan had rattled off his reasons for the split in one long breath—clearly, he had been practicing—and hadn't left Robbie much room to argue even if she wanted to. What was there to say after being told that he felt stuck in quicksand?

Robbie cranked the volume until her teeth rattled. She opened the glove compartment and tossed the pebble she'd scooped from the apartment building's flower bed into the plastic box holding the others she'd collected over the years; she'd been gripping it in her palm for the last half hour. The box contained one Robbie had snagged from the high school garden on her first day teaching at Mount Greenwich Academy, as well as stones she'd gathered from her parents' home in San Francisco, her college campus, the restaurant from her first date with Nathan, the beach on the night he'd first said he'd loved her, and other notable moments of her adult life, most of them involving Nathan. She slammed the compartment door shut and leaned against the headrest.

Who was too complacent now, Dr. Tang? Not this girl. Not Robbie Chin. Robbie Chin was a rebel. She was dangerous. Robbie Chin was the type of woman who blatantly ignored decibel warnings and gambled with the health of her eardrums. She was a reckless sort who left dishes crusting on the table and empty wine bottles strewn on the counters. See, Nathan? She took risks.

The passenger door swung open and a head popped in. "Robbie?"

Robbie stared dumbfounded at the piercing eyes peeking out from behind a mop of shaggy hair. "Yes," she stammered, turning the volume down to Nathan-approved levels. "Ernie? Is that you?"

It was a good thing he had found her, because Robbie definitely would not have recognized her best friend's little brother. When she had last seen Ernie Wolfe, he'd been a spindly twenty-year-old with a buzz cut, swiping beers from the bartender her parents had hired for her going away party. He'd filled out over the last few years, adding some healthy bulk to his frame. His hair, if clean, could be considered nice. Though why he wanted it to hang in his eyes like that was anyone's guess, unless he was perpetually stuck in his garage-band days.

When Robbie had called Ivy the night before to tell her the plan, Ivy had insisted that Robbie pick up her freelance photographer brother and drag him along on her drive from Aberbrooke, New York, back home to San Francisco. Two years behind the girls in school, Ernie had been a typical little brother, the kind that ran after them everywhere they went, begging to be included in everything. And though Ivy and Ernie got along now, Robbie remembered a time when Ivy had referred to him solely as The Dork.

The Dork chuckled and tossed a grungy camping backpack and his gear in the half-empty backseat.

"Hey, be careful back there," Robbie said, twisting around in her seat to save a black garment bag from being mangled. "I need this dress for my parents' anniversary party." Robbie's parents expected her home in two weeks—with Nathan—to attend their thirtieth-anniversary party. And because she was ninety-eight percent positive Nathan would come to his senses after a few days without her, when she called the airline, she canceled only her ticket, leaving one waiting for Nathan.

"Sorry," Ernie grunted, moving his bags to a more dignified position before climbing into the passenger seat.

Robbie fingered the ruby pendant hanging at her neck. It had come in a small velvet box. The first of several velvet boxes that had held everything but an engagement ring. She'd thought about leaving the jewelry behind but then changed her mind. Eight years of working toward the end goal of until "death do they part" earned her the jewelry.

She considered it her severance pay.

Cringing, Robbie watched Ernie settle himself in the seat and wondered how much of the dirt on his cargo shorts would rub off on her leather seats. This car had been the first new thing she'd bought herself when she'd started working after college. It was a sign of her independence, of her adulthood. She was obsessive about the maintenance schedule, getting regular oil changes and tune-ups. She never missed a tire rotation, and her Saturday morning routines included a coffee and bagel run, followed by a car wash and interior detailing, which she'd skipped this morning in favor of getting on the road earlier. She eyed his mud-crusted boots on her spotless car mats and silently cursed Ivy for forcing Ernie on her.

"Sorry, if I'm a little dirty," Ernie said. "I was finishing a job this morning when Ivy texted, threatening to do some bad things to me if I made you wait more than twelve seconds. Otherwise, I would have showered in the camp bathrooms. I just made it to the lot when you pulled in. Good timing, huh?"

Robbie fiddled with her dashboard navigation setting, pulling up the route she'd planned to San Francisco, and tried not to think about what might be living in his unwashed hair. "What was the job exactly?"

"I was contracted by a nature magazine to take some shots of the lake. Lakes, actually. The top fifty in the United States, one in each. This was my last one."

"You've been to all fifty states?" Robbie asked, driving them out of the campground and back to the main road, opening a window to air out the odor Ernie had brought with him and the dirt. "Even Alaska and Hawaii?" Robbie had always dreamed of taking a year off and traveling. Visiting all fifty states was a bucket list item, but with Nathan's on-call schedule at the hospital, taking more than a week off at one time was near impossible. Her dreams of being Jack Kerouac had been put on hold.

"Yep. Two of my favorites. I've been on the road for months because of this project. It'll be nice to be home for a bit. At least until the next job." Ernie leaned his head back with a loud yawn that sounded more like a mountain lion than a person. Had she picked up Ernie Wolfe or Mowgli? "Sorry. I don't sleep well on the ground. . . So, Robbie, when was the last time we saw each other? It's been forever."

"Six years ago."

"Right," Ernie said, nodding. "Your going-away party. I remember. Man, I couldn't even drink then."

"Legally, you mean," Robbie said. "I seem to recall you getting your hands on a few behind the garage."

Ernie laughed. "I didn't know anyone saw that. I thought I was so smooth." He brushed the hair off his forehead, and Robbie noticed a faint pink scar over his left eye he hadn't had back then. She thought about asking him how he got it but didn't. "How's your life, Robbie Chin? Married yet?"

Robbie's stomach twisted, the same way it did every time her mother asked if Nathan had proposed yet and what was he waiting for. She never knew how to answer those questions because the truth was: she didn't know. He had to have thought about it. No one lives with another person for six years without the idea crossing their mind at least once. Unless it had crossed his mind, which was what led to her hauling her life across the country for the second time because of him.

"Your sister didn't tell you much, did she?" Robbie asked, pointing her thumb to the back of the Jeep, which depressingly held all of her earthly possessions. Half of which were books.

Ernie looked over his shoulder and let out a low whistle. "I usually only get the highlights when I travel. Not that you getting married, or not, or whatever, wouldn't be a highlight. It's just that—"

"Ernie," Robbie interrupted. The reference to her and Nathan and marriage in any form made her head feel like it was splitting open, and she needed him to stop talking. She twisted the back of one of the diamond stud earrings Nathan had given her for her birthday three years earlier. Another velvet box. "It's okay. It's more of a time-out. You know, to reassess. To make sure we know what we want. The school year ended, so it seemed like a good time to go home and get some perspective, you know?"

Except, she knew what she wanted. She just needed Nathan to realize it, too. Which was why this trip was so important. Let Nathan miss her and see what his world would be like without her. She and Nathan had never been apart for six days since they'd started dating. Six days was a lifetime.

"Sure, right," he said, rubbing the stubble on his chin. "You know, it's just you got everything you own in your car, and—"

"Ernie," Robbie said, more forcefully, her grip tightening on the wheel.

"The timing is pretty good, though. I mean, with your parents' party coming up. You were gonna go home then anyway."

Robbie nodded, blowing out a heavy breath. He needed to stop talking.

"What are you doing about your job? Did you quit?"

"Not yet," she said, scrunching up her nose as her stomach tightened. She technically had a week before she had to let the school's administration know if she accepted their offer of employment for another year. She had already signed the contract and had been ready to send it to the board, but then Nathan had dropped his bombshell. "I have a week to send in my renewed contract."

"So, you're thinking there's a chance this time-out will lead to a reconciliation?"

"I thought you were a photographer, not an investigative reporter," she said, pinning him with a sharp sideways glance.

Ernie mumbled a response Robbie didn't hear before shifting in his seat. "You don't mind if I close my eyes for a while, do you? I was up doing moonlight shots last night."

Mind? Robbie was absolutely giddy over the idea. "Go right ahead. I don't mind at all."

Robbie glanced at the blue dot on the navigation screen, making sure she was still headed in the right direction. They'd pass the turn for the highway entrance ramp soon. Knowing Ivy, her friend had failed to mention to her brother the little fact that they were taking the scenic route home. Ernie would find out soon enough, right about the time he opened his eyes again and discovered they were in the middle of some farmland and not gliding down a highway.

Ernie grumbled, then started snoring. Rolling her eyes, Robbie turned the radio volume up again, not to the crazy eardrum-endangering levels but loud enough to drown out the nasal symphony coming from the seat next to her. Fishing her sunglasses out of her bag on the center console, she remembered why she and Ivy had always tried to ditch him on the playground.

Five minutes later, the electronic tune from Dr. Who's theme song reached her ears. Then again. And then thirty seconds later again. Robbie chuckled. Of course, this was Ernie's ring tone. He had always been a big science fiction fan. The fourth time the song started, Robbie contemplated poking him in the arm to wake him. Someone was really trying to get a hold of him. She wondered if Ernie had a girlfriend waiting for him to come home. It had to be hard to keep up a relationship with his travel schedule.

Hell, she couldn't even keep up a relationship living with the guy. Robbie glanced at her silent phone, willing it to ring. Nathan would call eventually. He probably didn't even know she'd left yet. Nathan had packed an overnight bag and left the apartment after ending things, claiming he would spend the night at the hospital in the on-call room to give her time and space. She knew he had the early shift in the emergency room so he wouldn't make it back to the apartment until later in the afternoon. That was when he'd discover her complete absence. One day, Robbie was there, and then she wasn't. She hoped the sudden removal of her presence punched him in the face when he walked back into the apartment.

Shock and awe. Once he realized she was gone, like for real gone, he would call. He had to. No one threw away eight years of their life because they'd been bored one day. All Robbie had to do was give Nathan the time and space to realize that on his own.

Ernie's phone went off again. This time, Robbie reached across the center console and with just her fingertips pulled Ernie's phone from where it jutted out of his pocket. If he wasn't going to budge to answer it, there was no reason she had to listen to it go off every thirty seconds. The initials M.G. flashed on the screen before Robbie pressed IGNORE CALL. Sorry, M.G., Ernie was unavailable.

TWO

Six years ago. . .

Nathan swung Robbie up into his arms and spun her around.

"What are you doing?" she giggled, wrapping her arms around his neck.

"Carrying you over the threshold," he said before nudging the apartment door—*their* apartment door—open. "Isn't that what you're supposed to do when you move into a new place with someone for the first time?"

"When you get married, you goof," she said as he set her down inside their new shared home. It had been a long drive from San Francisco, especially when they had been driving separately and had to stay off the highways for her sake. They hadn't stopped for lunch, wanting to hurry up and get through the last leg of the trip, and she had a feeling his giddiness was due to low blood sugar. "Did you carry Chris over the threshold when you moved in with him before med school?"

He lifted one side of his mouth into an amused smirk. "Maybe. We promised we'd never tell."

Robbie laughed and walked through their living room and into the kitchen. They'd rented the apartment through a rental service, and Nathan had ordered furniture online that had been delivered the day before. All they had to do was unload their cars and unpack.

"What should we do first? Are you hungry?" She rummaged through the kitchen cabinets, picturing where to store their dishes and cookware eventually.

"Starving," Nathan said, inspecting the couch. "How about this? Let's only bring in from the cars what we absolutely need tonight. You go ahead and shower and get comfortable while I run out and find something to eat."

Robbie narrowed her eyes. "How did you know I wanted a shower?"

"We've been on the road for a week. It's always the first thing you did when we stopped for the night." He placed a quick kiss on her cheek. "Come on; let's get the bags."

Nathan was right. A hot shower was exactly what Robbie had wanted after twelve hours in a car, except she hadn't realized they hadn't unpacked the towels until after Nathan went out to forage for dinner. Even though she promised to wait until the next day to finish unloading their boxes, she found herself digging through the back of her Jeep for the box of bathroom supplies stuffed behind a box of books and suitcases of clothes. And since there was no point in unloading the car to get one box and putting everything back, she emptied her car despite her promises.

She was still standing under the hot water when Nathan returned. She knew he saw her boxes piled in the corner of the living room when he yelled, "Robbie Chin! What did you do?"

She smiled to herself, always amused when he seemed genuinely surprised by something she'd done. He should have known by now: Robbie wasn't the type to wait around for someone to get something done.

"I'll be out in a minute," she yelled back, her stomach growling. When she emerged from the bathroom, scrubbed clean of the car smell and comfortable in her favorite running shorts and tank top, she thought maybe her hunger had caused her to hallucinate. Somehow in the time it took her to find towels and take a shower, Nathan had transformed their living room into a takeout dinner smorgasbord. There were containers from at least six different places spread out on the coffee table, with a plastic cup of flowers serving as a centerpiece. Nathan was pouring wine into two more plastic cups.

"I thought we could sample a bit from different places. See what we like," he said, smiling and offering her a glass.

Whenever Robbie drank anything with the smallest amount of alcohol, red splotches immediately covered her entire body. The Asian flush—a curse of her father's Chinese lineage. She was always careful about the amount she drank in public, hoping to curb the flush. But, at home with Nathan, who was equally afflicted, she could pretend it was perfectly normal to turn into a walking maraschino cherry.

"I think," she said, taking a drink, "we are going to like it here. I can't wait to unpack and really make this place ours."

"Me too," Nathan said, opening a container of pot stickers, then taking the lid off a plate of nachos. "It will be so nice to not live like poor undergrads anymore and finally have an adult home. Don't get me wrong, I liked living with Chris, but Target isn't the only place one can shop."

Robbie nodded and eyed her unopened boxes. She couldn't lie: she loved Target and their affordable home furnishings, just like every other college student with their first apartment. She took another sip of her wine to hide her cringe. Maybe she wouldn't unpack everything she'd brought. Nathan wanted a more grown-up home, more sophisticated. Something befitting the doctor he was. She didn't blame him. He worked his butt off to get through medical school. He deserved to have nice things, quality things. It wouldn't hurt for her to grow up a little, too.

"Come on," he said. "Dig in. I found the DVDs and set up the player. I thought we could watch one of your favorites."

Robbie smiled. "*Pride and Prejudice?* The Colin Firth version?"

Nathan nodded but rolled his eyes.

Robbie squealed and loaded her plate with fried rice and pizza. An odd mix, but it worked. Kind of like her, she thought. She settled on the couch next to Nathan so that her shoulder pressed against his. The sofa could comfortably seat four, but he didn't say anything. Instead, he pulled her legs into his lap and flashed her a toothy grin as he hit the play button.

"Here we go," he said. "Welcome home, Robbie."

THREE

Finding a motel for the night that didn't conjure images of roadside murders was Robbie's top priority. Though the sun wouldn't fully set for another few hours, its lingering presence in her direct line of sight was wearing on her, squashing any hopes she held of putting a few more hundred miles behind them. Getting an earlier start in the morning would make up the difference.

It had been a warmer than usual day for early June, and she was sweaty and sore from sitting in one position for too long. She pulled into the first motel that had an outdoor pool that looked clean—just the thing she needed after a draining first day on the road, replaying her relationship with Nathan and the subsequent breakup in her head against the backdrop of Ernie's constant snoring.

"Where are we?" Ernie asked, stretching like a cat and scratching behind his ears.

"Near Buffalo," Robbie said, killing the engine. "We're stopping here for the night."

Ernie rubbed his eyes and squinted at the dashboard clock. "That can't be right. Is it really after four?"

Robbie nodded, then cracked her neck. That pool was looking better by the second. She considered giving the hot tub a try, but she'd read some pretty nasty statistics about public hot tubs and the thought of becoming one of those numbers made her stomach turn.

"I can't believe I slept that long." Ernie pushed open his door and stuck his legs outside, straightening them with a groan. "You should have woken me." He patted his pockets and felt around the seat beneath him.

Robbie hopped out her side, brushing crumbs from her lap from the sandwich she'd eaten while driving. Earlier in the afternoon, when Ernie had made no indication of waking any time soon, Robbie couldn't endure the hunger pains any longer and had found a fast food place with a drive-through. She'd thought he'd wake for sure when she'd started barking her order into the intercom, but no luck.

"I've got your phone," she said, tossing it to him as they met at the back of the car. "It kept going off, and I couldn't take any more of the Dr. Who theme song, so I silenced it. Sorry."

Ernie squinted as he scrolled through the list of missed calls and messages. "No, I'm sorry. Cell service was spotty for a while in the preserve. Ivy's was the first call I've answered in three days. All the messages and unanswered calls must have finally gotten through."

"But, Dr. Who? Really?" Robbie asked. "Nerd."

"You're the nerd who recognized the theme song," Ernie said, stuffing his phone back in his pocket without listening to even one of the many voicemails he must have gotten. "Did you say we're near Buffalo?" he asked, opening the door to the backseat to retrieve his bags. "We've been driving for, like, seven hours. Shouldn't we be in Pennsylvania by now?"

Robbie shrugged and avoided looking him directly in his eyes, which wasn't difficult with the way his moppy hair hung down in front of his face. "I guess. If were taking the highway."

Ernie closed the door and joined Robbie as she retrieved the overnight bag she'd explicitly packed for motel stays. "We're not taking the highway? Why wouldn't we take the highway?"

Because the thought of merging into speeding traffic made her heart want to burst from her chest. Because no one in their right mind needed to drive that fast while weaving in and out of lanes, cutting off other drivers and risking pissing off the wrong people. Because, sometimes, it didn't matter *how* you reached your destination, only that you did in one piece. Because highways were made for the brave, and not for Robbie Chin.

"I thought the scenic route would be nice. Give me a chance to clear my head," Robbie said, yanking her duffel bag from on top of her few sad cardboard boxes in the trunk. Removing herself from Nathan's life had been as quick and easy as removing a hangnail. It stung for a minute, but then it was as though she'd never been there to begin with. Everything had belonged to Nathan. The furniture. The dishes. Any knick-knacks or pictures. There had been nothing in that apartment anyone could point to and say, "That's Robbie's." Except for her books. The books were all hers. It hadn't struck her as odd until she'd loaded the last box in her car and noticed how much space was left.

Ernie closed the trunk and peered at her with narrowed eyes. He slung his camera bag across his shoulders and grabbed his backpack with one hand and Robbie's duffel with the other. "When it's my turn to drive, can I take the highway? Or is this a strict no highways at all type of policy?"

Robbie shook her head and reached for her bag's handle, but Ernie swung it out of her reach with a laugh. "I can carry my own bag," she said.

"I know you can, but I'm still not letting you," he said, swinging it higher into the air with far less effort than it should take. "Not unless you say I can drive on the highway."

Robbie crossed her arms and scowled. She didn't mind the highway if someone else was behind the wheel, but she wasn't about to give in to Ernie Wolfe and his pesky games. "Fine. Carry my bag. Let's go."

"One room or two?" the older woman behind the counter asked, pointedly looking at each of their hands—for wedding rings, Robbie presumed.

"Two, please," Robbie said as Ernie gasped with mock disbelief.

"Honey," he said, dripping with sarcasm, "don't be that way."

Robbie felt her cheeks flush as heat crept up her neck. "Two rooms," she said again, ignoring Ernie's chuckle. "We're not together. Not like that. He's my friend's little brother. Younger brother, I mean. He's not little. I mean, he grew up, obviously. We're just traveling together, but we're not together-together."

"Two rooms would be great, thanks," Ernie said as the woman slid two faded plastic key rings across the counter with a smirk.

"Have a nice night," she said with a quick wink for Ernie as she pointed toward one of the two halls behind her.

Robbie snatched her key from the counter and led Ernie down the hall to the right, taking note of the sign for the pool on the left. It had been years since she'd used a real key at a hotel instead of a keycard, which made her wonder about the state of the room it opened. Nathan would have held out until he found a Hilton or a Marriott, like on their trip out to New York. But she didn't have Dr. Tang's budget to work with anymore.

"When was the last time you used an actual key in a motel?" Ernie asked as he set Robbie's duffel bag outside her door. "Hope there are no bugs." He cleared his throat and moved the hair out of his eyes at last. "I'm going to wash up, but I'd like to take you dinner, as a thank-you for the ride. Maybe we can try that diner across the street. In about an hour?"

"I was going to hit the pool," Robbie said as though it was a reason to skip dinner, but then his stomach rumbled, and the guilt for not waking him for lunch weighed on her. "But I'll be ready in an hour."

To her surprise, the room was clean and bright and held only a faint odor of staleness in the air. Nothing an open window couldn't take care of. . . if it hadn't been bolted shut. All the more reason to hit the pool. Digging through her bag, she pulled out her swimsuit, grateful she'd decided at the last minute not to throw it in one of the boxes.

She'd been looking forward to having the entire pool to herself since there had been no one in it when they'd checked in, but as she pushed open the sundeck door, she was met with the sounds of those who'd beat her to it. A young couple splashed around in the shallow end, alternating between laughing at each other and kissing. They were children, really. They couldn't have been more than nineteen years old. Nineteen and shameless.

"You don't have any spark anymore." Nathan's voice from the night before rang in her head. Spark this. Marching into the pool area, Robbie tossed her towel on a lounge chair, kicked her shoes off and placed them under the seat of the chair, then strode to the deep end.

She hadn't bothered testing the water before jumping in—sparkless people checked water temperature—and the shock of the initial cold stabbed at her from all directions. She broke the surface of the water gasping for air, causing Romeo and Juliet to stop kissing long enough to stare at her like she'd been the one acting utterly inappropriate in public.

"Are you okay?" the girl asked. She waded closer to Robbie, her tanned skin glistening in the chlorinated water. She was the very picture of what Robbie had grown up thinking an All-American girl looked like. The media's version of the girl next door. A combination of Kelly Kapowski from *Saved by the Bell* and Marcia Brady.

Robbie swiped the tangles of dark hair out of her eyes and glided closer to the middle of the pool until her feet could touch the bottom. "Yep. Thanks. I didn't mean to interrupt you."

The girl glanced sheepishly at her companion and giggled. "I guess we were hogging the pool a little. I'm Holly, and this is Bret, my fiancé."

Bret nodded a hello with a face-splitting grin. Newly engaged, if Robbie had to guess, based on their glow. The drudgery of wedding planning and the never-ending details and decisions hadn't weighed them down yet. They were still in the dreamy, happily-ever-after stage. They were at the beginning while Robbie was at the end—until Nathan called and begged her to come back. Then she would be glowing and happy, too. But more dignified about it.

"I'm Robbie," she said. "Congratulations."

"Robbie?" Bret said, coming up behind Holly and slipping an arm around her waist. "Is that short for Roberta?"

"Robinson, actually." Robbie half-shrugged when he furrowed his eyebrows. "My parents thought they were pretty funny. My dad says he named me after his favorite basketball player, David Robinson. My mom says she chose the name for her favorite fictional character, Robinson Crusoe. Either way, Robinson Chin it is."

"Chin?" Bret asked.

The hairs on the back of Robbie's neck stood up. She could sense what came next the way animals sensed death. It was a special talent she had that had been honed to near perfection after years ignorance—both hers and other people's. First came the chill up the back, followed by the clenched stomach. Then the thoughts raced in: What was the right answer? Depended on the level of rudeness of the tone. Was it a simple question, or was there a silent demand lacing the words? But, wasn't it rude to ask at all? Yes, but they didn't know that. Why was that her problem? It wasn't. He probably meant no harm. But it didn't stop at one question. There were always follow-up questions.

"Are you Asian or something?" Bret asked, peering closer at her with furrowed eyebrows.

And there it was. "Yes, or something," Robbie said. She could feel him mentally dissecting her features one at a time. Her hair. Her eyes. The angles of her face.

A shadow passed behind Bret's eyes—hurt that he'd received such a perfunctory answer. He'd only wanted to show interest in his new acquaintance, and Robbie had to go and burst his little bubble of bliss by being so curt. He stared at Robbie like a puppy dog who'd gotten his paw caught in a fence. He wanted to lick his wound but couldn't reach it. He wanted to run but was stuck. Poor puppy. How could she leave him there whimpering?

"I'm half Chinese."

"What else are you?" Holly's eyes widened. "What's the other half?"

"Italian," Robbie said, diverting her gaze from their curious stares to the parking lot on the other side of the iron fence. How many times in their lives had they been asked *what*, not *who*, they were? Probably none. White was white. Simple. Clean. Not like the muddy types. Robbie hoped they would leave it at that. Let them be the self-absorbed type too caught up in their own whirlwind to notice her blowing by. But it was never that easy. There was always one more.

"Which half is the Chinese half?" Bret asked, keeping up the predictable line of questions.

"The left half," Robbie mumbled, moving to the side of the pool.

"What was that?"

"Nothing." She'd indulged their curiosities long enough and needed to head back to her room to dress for dinner with Ernie. Nathan had grown up answering these questions, too, but he'd never been as put off by them as she was. He always seemed somewhat amused. The funny thing was, people didn't ask her about her background as often when she was with him, like it didn't matter as long as she stood next to someone else like her, or she wasn't such an oddity anymore. If she stayed in her lane, she wouldn't raise any eyebrows. When she dared to swerve, however . . . then there were problems, just like on the highway. "You guys enjoy yourselves."

"You hurt her feelings," Holly whispered to Bret as Robbie walked away. "You should apologize."

"For what?" he asked. They never knew for what. If they did, they wouldn't have asked to begin with.

"You're not supposed to ask about people's nationalities," Holly said.

Robbie shook her head as she opened the door leading back into the hotel. *Ethnicity.* People always got that wrong, too.

The shower did more to cool her off than the pool, thanks to the lack of hot water in the pipes. As Robbie dressed, she pulled her straight, black hair into a ponytail and thought of Holly in the pool, with her honey-colored locks. As a child, Robbie's reflection had always surprised her. People hadn't looked like her growing up, and it had shocked her to see how different she was on the outside when she had been convinced she was the same on the inside. Even in a larger city like San Francisco. Even in her own family.

There was her mother's family with fair, rosy complexions. Hair almost every shade imaginable. Their eyes round and light. Then, there was her father's family. Straight, black hair, all of them. Eyes so dark they were almost black. Olive-toned faces across the board.

Then there was Robinson Chin. The hair and complexion she'd gotten from her father, as well as the shape of her eyes, but her light hazel eyes had come from her mother. She had the stereotypical Chinese, slim body type, but her mother's Italian penchant for hand gestures and love of pasta.

In school, there had been other Asian students—Chinese, Korean, Japanese—but none like Robbie, and she found herself constantly on the outside, with neither the white kids nor the Asian kids knowing which mental bucket to place her in. She was born in *Baywatch* season and grew up on *The O.C.* and *One Tree Hill.* So when she'd looked in the mirror, she'd expected her reflection to resemble what she'd seen around her one way or the other. Instead, she found a strange blend of both.

At the age of twenty-eight, Robbie thought she would have been accustomed to her appearance, but even now, her first reaction was to wonder who that was in the mirror. Was her hair always this straight? She could have sworn she had some auburn highlights. A knock on her door startled her, and she dropped her comb in the sink. Crinkling her nose, she turned away from the mirror and grabbed her bag. Auburn highlights or not, Ernie was waiting for her.

But the man on the other side of her door didn't resemble the Ernie she'd left an hour ago. Freshly showered and shaved, he'd combed back his hair, and he'd put on a clean blue T-shirt and spotless faded jeans. Gone were the crusty hiking boots, replaced by gray and black designer sneakers.

"Ready to go?" Ernie asked, rubbing his stomach. "I'm starving. I haven't had a decent meal in three days."

"Campfire food not your thing?" Robbie asked, keeping her eyes on the ground as they walked. She should have worn one of the emergency sundresses she'd packed instead of her denim cutoffs and cotton tank. And flip-flops? What was she thinking? She could have at least dug out the strappy sandals.

"I'm not much of an outdoorsman," Ernie said, holding open the motel's main door for her. "At least I wasn't when this whole assignment started. I've had enough camping to last me a good long while. Take me back to smog and traffic, please."

"Well, you certainly look the part," Robbie said. "At least you did up to an hour ago."

Ernie glanced at her from the corner of his eye, a grin forming. "Do you miss the stubble?"

Robbie sputtered and concentrated on hurrying across the street, though there was no traffic in either direction. "I didn't say that," she said when Ernie had caught up to her. "I just meant—"

"I know what you meant," Ernie said, leading the way into the diner. "You're just so easy to tease."

Robbie's cheeks burned with annoyance. Stupid Ernie Wolfe.

FOUR

Eighteen years ago . . .

"Go away, Ernie," Ivy yelled from the top of the stairs. "Leave us alone!"

"Mom said you had to play with me," Ernie said, stomping up the stairs holding an armful of Transformers robots.

"But Mom didn't say I had to play Transformers," Ivy said, her arms crossed over her chest.

Robbie sat on Ivy's bed waiting for the latest argument between brother and sister to come to an end so she could play *something*. Mrs. Chin was picking her up in an hour on the way to buy Robbie new shoes, and Robbie didn't want to waste another minute of playtime with this fight. At this point, she didn't care what they played.

"Come on, Ivy," Robbie said. "He's not going to leave us alone unless we play a couple of minutes with him."

Ivy spun around on her heels and glared at Robbie for her betrayal. "But Transformers?"

"I don't have a lot of time," Robbie said, hopping off the bed. "I just want to play something. If we play robots with him now, maybe he'll go away."

"Yeah, Ivy," Ernie said with a lopsided grin. "Just a couple minutes, and maybe I'll go away."

Ivy relented but not without an eye roll and growl in Ernie's direction. "Hurry up and bring them over here."

Ernie dumped his armful of metal robots on Ivy's bedroom floor with a clatter. "Here, Robbie, you can be the red one. He's my favorite."

"Why don't you be the red one then?" Robbie asked. She didn't care which one she was; she only wanted to avoid another meltdown after Ernie realized he'd made a mistake. "I can be the green one."

"I'll be the red one," Ivy said, reaching for the prized robot, but Ernie snatched it away before she could touch it.

"I'm the red one," Ernie said, handing his sister a different toy.

They played for exactly five minutes. Ivy had set the alarm to make sure they didn't go over the allotted Ernie time, and then she pushed him out of her room and closed the door behind him.

"You don't have to be nice to him," Ivy said. "He's just Ernie."

"He's not always bad," Robbie said. She didn't want to tell Ivy, but sometimes Robbie liked playing with Ernie. He liked to play different things than Ivy, and Robbie thought the change was good sometimes. Besides, playing Transformers was still better than sitting at home by herself.

Mrs. Chin fetched Robbie from the Wolfe house an hour later for their shoe shopping excursion. Robbie could hear Ivy and Ernie start up their bickering again before the door closed behind her. "Do those two do anything but fight?" Mrs. Chin asked as Robbie zipped her jacket.

"Not really," Robbie said, sliding her hands in her pockets to avoid having to hold her mother's hand as they crossed the street. Mrs. Chin preferred to shop local, meaning anywhere she could walk to if she could help it. This shoe store they headed to, while a little pricier than the national chains, was only three blocks away. Robbie's fingers brushed against something cold and metallic. Pulling a red truck from her pocket, Robbie let out a small gasp as she gazed at Ernie's favorite Transformer.

"What's that?" Mrs. Chin asked, crinkling her nose.

"It's Ernie's," Robbie said. "He must have put it in my pocket by accident. It's his favorite. He'll have a fit when he finds out it's missing."

Mrs. Chin reached for Robbie's hand as they approached an intersection. Robbie quickly jammed her hands back in her pockets, afraid someone from school would see her and think she was a baby because she still had to hold her mother's hand while crossing the street. Robbie was ten; she knew how to walk without anyone helping her.

Mrs. Chin dropped her hand to her side without a word and proceeded into the street. Robbie followed suit, darting glances back and forth for oncoming traffic. She didn't see her mother stop and look both ways like she usually did, but she couldn't imagine Mrs. Chin being so careless either. So, just in case, she checked for both of them.

"When we're done shopping, you can stop by the Wolfe's on the way home and drop off the truck," Mrs. Chin said. "But just for a minute, then come right home for dinner."

Robbie almost skipped the rest of the way to the shoe store. Even if it was only for a minute, being able to see Ivy twice in one afternoon was a treat. A minute was all they needed to play a quick round of What If or Would You Rather, and it delayed her going home.

True to her word, on the way back from the store, Mrs. Chin nodded to Robbie and said, "Just a minute, remember. Dinner will be ready."

Robbie tossed her bag of new shoes at her mother and took the stairs, two at a time, up to Ivy's front door. She rang the bell and waited, then heard Ernie yell, "Mom, it's Robbie. I'm opening the door!" The door swung open, and Ernie stood there beaming. "Hey, Robbie!"

"Hi, Ernie," Robbie said, almost forgetting he was the reason she'd come back. "Is Ivy here?"

He shook his head. "She went with Dad to pick up the pizza."

Robbie's mouth watered. She didn't know what the Chins were having for dinner, but she knew it wasn't pizza. It was a rare occasion when Mrs. Chin agreed to takeout pizza for dinner. Once in a while, she could be persuaded to make her own, but it had to be Robbie's birthday, or another equally important celebration, to get it from a restaurant.

Disappointed, she reached into her pocket and pulled out his toy. "I think you left this in my pocket by accident."

Ernie furrowed his brow and took the Transformer from her. "It wasn't an accident. I knew you'd bring it back."

"I know it's your favorite." Robbie turned to leave, but Ernie stepped out from the doorway and called her name.

"Can I ask you something?" he said.

Robbie glanced down the street toward her house. It hadn't been a full minute yet—she could spare a few more seconds. "Sure," she said, sitting down on the top step.

Ernie sat next to her, cradling the truck in his hands. "Why does Ivy hate me so much?"

Robbie's chest squeezed. She didn't have siblings, but she knew she'd just walked into a sensitive situation she wasn't sure she could handle. This seemed like the sort of thing a grown-up should handle.

"I don't think she hates you for real," Robbie said, trying to sound more like an adult, or at least someone smarter. "I think she just gets jealous sometimes."

"Of what?"

Robbie shrugged. "Other people getting attention."

"You're nicer to me than she is."

"You're not my brother," Robbie said. "And she's nice to you sometimes. Wasn't she the one who gave you that Transformer?"

"That's why it's my favorite," Ernie said. The seriousness of his tone let Robbie know he'd divulged a secret he'd been holding onto for a while.

"I won't tell her you said that."

"Better not," Ernie said. "Don't be a tattle-tale."

Robbie stood to leave then poked him in the shoulder. "Don't be a brat."

FIVE

The sign greeting them at the diner said to wait to be seated, but the counter was empty, as was almost the rest of the place. "Let's just seat ourselves," Ernie said, scanning the dining area for anyone to help. "I'm sure they won't mind."

"The sign says to wait," Robbie said, pointing to the metal frame in front of them to make a point. "I wasn't raised to be rude." She leaned against the wall and pulled out her phone. "And neither were you. We can give it a minute."

A picture of Robbie and Nathan on vacation greeted her as she pressed the button to wake up her phone screen. They were on the beach, smiling, arms wrapped around each other. Nathan hated selfies, but he'd agreed to this one, for her. When had this been taken? A year and a half ago? She looked at her stupid face smiling back at her, so blind, so—what had Nathan said?—complacent. She'd been elated when he'd consented to the picture, like he'd just crowned her queen of the isle. It was only a picture. There had been no need to be weird about it.

"Is that him?" Ernie said, not hiding the fact that he was staring openly at her phone. "I don't really remember him from before. Did he always look that vacant?"

Robbie stood straighter and shoved the phone in her pocket. Vacant. Who was Ernie to judge? Just because he was a photographer, he thought he could see into people's souls or something? Ernie wasn't a mind-reader. He snapped pictures for a living. She did that almost every day on her phone.

Nathan wasn't vacant. He was brilliant. Top of his medical school class. Sought after by several prestigious hospitals upon his graduation. So he didn't read much, other than news headlines, but when did he have time with the hours he kept? And, okay, his idea of a quality movie required a minimum of three explosions. But the man spent twelve hours a day saving lives—if he didn't deserve a little mindless brain candy entertainment, then who did?

Ernie knew nothing about Nathan. Judging him based on one picture was as bad as all those people who had formed instant opinions of her because of the shape of her eyes, or the sound of her last name.

"He's not vacant," Robbie said through tight lips. "He's brilliant."

"I meant no harm," Ernie said, taking a much-needed step away. "I obviously don't know the guy. Maybe it's a bad picture of him, but it doesn't look like he has any spark in his expression."

Robbie gaped at him. Why did Ernie say that? Why had he chosen those exact words, the ones that mimicked what Nathan had said to her? Did Ivy tell him more than she'd assumed? Was he mocking her? Or was this his twisted version of teasing again?

"Just the two of you?" a waitress asked, finally emerging from the back. "Table or booth?"

"Booth, please," Ernie said, unaware of the right hook he'd just delivered with amazing accuracy.

The waitress smiled at him, the same way the front desk clerk at the motel had, with a combination of wistful dreaming and sympathy. Robbie ducked her head and followed Ernie as he followed the waitress, thinking she should have definitely worn a sundress.

"Here you go," the waitress, Tammy, according to her plastic name tag, said. "I'll be back in a few to take your order." With one last grin for Ernie, that faded when her eyes fell on Robbie, she disappeared again.

Ernie motioned to one side of the booth, waiting for Robbie to pick her seat first. If he thought she was going to smile at him the way Tammy had, he was sorely mistaken. Robbie slid into the booth without even looking at him.

Ernie sat across from her and handed her a menu. He took a cursory glance at the selection, closed the menu, and slapped it down on the table in front of him. Robbie kept her eyes on the list of sandwiches but felt his drilling into her.

"What?" she said without lifting her gaze.

"Are you mad at me or something?" Ernie asked, all innocence and disbelief. As though he didn't have a clue what he could have said to upset her.

"You shouldn't talk about people you don't know." When she heard him chuckle, she snapped her menu closed and narrowed her eyes. "How would you feel if someone did that to you?"

He shrugged. "If I didn't know the person talking, I can't say I would care. I only care about what the people I do know think about me."

Robbie shook her head in disbelief. No one really lived that carefree. "You're lying."

"No, I'm not," Ernie said, leaning forward, a glint in his eye. "Look,

- 30 -

if that guy in the corner walked out of here and told ten people about the pretentious know-it-all with a big nose talking to the pretty girl in the denim shorts, do you think I would care? I'm not pretentious at all."

Robbie felt a smile trying to break through her stern features, but she wouldn't let it. She wouldn't succumb as easily as Tammy or the motel clerk. "You don't have a big nose either. But you are rather a know-it-all."

"And I am talking to a pretty girl."

Robbie returned her eyes to her menu, willing her annoyance with him to stay in place. She wasn't ready to let it go yet. He had insulted the man she fully intended on getting back together with. "It's still not nice to talk about people behind their backs."

Tammy reappeared at the table, paper and pencil in hand, a welcome diversion for their conversation. While Ernie ordered steak and eggs, cornbread, and a bowl of soup, Robbie stuck to her usual diner order: BLT with cheese and a fruit cup.

As Tammy left to place their orders, Robbie leaned back and exhaled, glad they were done talking about Nathan. Ernie wasn't the person she wanted to rehash things with. Robbie saved those conversations for his sister. She and Ivy had already spent three hours on the phone the night before, and Robbie knew there would be many more hours spent in analytical conversation once they reached San Francisco—that is, unless Nathan beat her there and she found him waiting for her on Ivy's doorstep.

"What happened between the two of you anyway, if you don't mind me asking," Ernie said, not picking up on the fact Robbie was done with this topic for the night. "I mean, six years in cohabitation is a long time. There had to be some clues, right, that the end was coming?"

Had there been clues? They never fought, not before last night.

Even then, it wasn't so much a fight as it was a simple declaration on his part and confusion on hers. Their friends had always commented on how in sync they'd always seemed, so in tune with each other, that there was no need for petty arguments.

"I don't really want to talk about it," Robbie said. "Besides, it's not a breakup, breakup. It's a temporary time-out."

"I see," he said, nodding thoughtfully. "So, are you going to call him? Or are you waiting for him? How did you leave it?"

Robbie's chest squeezed along with her fists in her lap. "Are you always this nosy?"

He threw his hands up in front of him. "I'm just trying to help. Thought you could use someone to talk to."

"I have someone. Ivy."

Agreeing to take him along on her road trip had been a colossal mistake. Day one, and he was already digging into her personal life like he belonged there. She didn't need him to analyze and strategize her next steps. She had already done that with his sister.

"Robbie."

Robbie turned toward the sound of her name, grateful for the interruption until she spotted the source. Holly and Bret stood at the counter waiting to be seated, their hands locked so tightly together that when Holly raised her other arm to wave with way too much enthusiasm, Bret's arm shook with the force.

"Friends of yours?" Ernie asked with raised eyebrows.

Robbie threw up a small wave at the young couple and turned back to face Ernie with an eye roll. "They were at the pool earlier."

Either Tammy mistook Holly's enthusiasm for genuine friendship, or she wanted to get under Robbie's skin, because a second later Tammy was at their table with Holly and Bret in tow. "Since you all know each other, do you want to share a table?"

One cursory glance at the sparsely occupied tables behind Tammy confirmed Robbie's suspicions that the woman's sole purpose in bringing these two to their table was to torture her.

"No, it's—" Robbie stammered at the same time Ernie exclaimed, "Sure, that would be great!"

Holly squealed in delight as Ernie vacated his seat, offering the lovebirds the opportunity to sit together. Robbie slid further into the booth, pressing herself against the window, as their new dining companions took their seats across from her without unclasping their hands.

Robbie smiled as politely as she could. "You know what? We already ordered, so—"

"We don't mind," Holly exclaimed, her face frozen in a permanent toothy grin. "We already know what we want."

Only each other, right? Robbie suppressed a gag at the thought.

"I'll have a bacon cheeseburger, fries, and a coke. And she'll have a garden salad and lemonade," Bret announced, puffing out his chest as Holly beamed at her man in control.

While Holly and Bret made their introductions, Robbie slipped her phone from her pocket and checked for messages. None. Nathan was probably picking up dinner for himself since she wasn't there to make it for him. He would call when he got home, not until after he ate, though, since he hated cold takeout. But, still, he was going to call, and Robbie wanted to be sitting alone with some privacy when he did. Which meant they needed to hurry this little party along.

"Nice to meet you," Ernie said beside her, sounding like he actually meant it. "My name's Nick Wolfe."

Robbie jerked her head back and stared open-mouthed at Ernie.

Where had that come from? Nick?

"What is it you do, Nick?" Bret asked.

"I'm a photographer," Ernie said, casting a questioning glance to Robbie who still sat staring.

Nick? Nick Wolfe. Nick Wolfe Photography. The name ran through her head like she should recognize it. When Holly excused herself to wash her hands before their food arrived, and Bret accompanied her— because why wouldn't he?—Robbie used the opportunity to find out what kind of game Ernie was playing.

"Nick?" she asked. "Why the fake name?"

It was Ernie's turn to look taken aback. Arching an eyebrow, he leaned toward her and dropped his voice. "It's not fake. It's my name. Nicholas Andrew Wolfe."

"But, Ernie?"

"Unfortunate nickname. It seems I was very attached to an Ernie doll I had as a toddler. Like, super-attached. Rumor has it, there was a year or two when I would only respond to the name Ernie, and it stuck for the next twenty years." He leaned back, assessing her embarrassment. "You really never knew?"

"How was I supposed to know?" Robbie practically screamed. "Everyone—Ivy, your parents, kids at school, teachers—everyone called you Ernie. They still do."

Nick shrugged. "Some people are more reluctant to change their ways than others. To be fair, I only started using my given name in college. Seemed less confusing that way."

Bret and Holly—Brolly, as Robbie had started thinking of them— returned, hand in hand. Robbie wondered if Bret had let go long enough for Holly to use the facilities by herself, or if he'd accompanied her into the stall.

"Where are you all headed?" Bret asked after they'd settled back into their seats. Holly nodded approvingly at him, apparently pleased with this line of questioning versus his previous one.

"San Francisco," Robbie said as Tammy returned with all four dinners. "When's the big day?"

The pair exchanged glances and toothy grins. "Tomorrow," Holly squealed. "We've eloped. Isn't it romantic?"

Robbie shoved her BLT in her mouth while considering. She was right—Romeo and Juliet. Did Brolly know they both died in the end for no reason? That wasn't romance. It was immaturity and a sure sign they weren't old enough to make that decision on their own, something Robbie drilled into her students every year around prom when the girls got starry-eyed and the boys got horny.

What did Robbie know anyway? She had no spark. And neither did Nathan, according to Ernie, so they were a perfect match. She would never have eloped, though; her mother would kill her.

"How long have you two been together?" Ernie, or Nick, asked.

"Since the first grade," Bret answered, stretching his sinewy arm across the back of the booth and around Holly.

"Wow," Robbie said, "long time. The only person I've known since first grade is my best friend, Ivy."

"And me," Nick said beside her with a wink.

Robbie supposed that was true. Her very first playdate with her very first friend was at Ivy's house after school one day. And there was little Ernie Wolfe, trailing behind the pair of girls wherever they went. "And Nick," Robbie said, tilting her head in his direction. "But you're kind of a package deal with Ivy."

Nick feigned a hurt expression before digging into his meal with gusto. He hadn't been kidding when he'd said he was starving. Holly proceeded in great detail to tell them the story of their entire relationship while they ate, which to Robbie's surprise, she found more entertaining than annoying. At least she wasn't expected to participate in the conversation. Instead, she pretended she was walking the halls of Mount Greenwich Academy in between classes.

When Holly finished in a breathless flush and finally took a bite of her wilting garden salad, Bret wiped the cheeseburger grease from his chin, leaned back, and cleared his throat. Robbie felt the hair on her forearms rise. *Don't do it, man,* she thought. *Stay the course.*

"So, Robbie," Bret said to call her attention away from her dish of berries. "Can you speak Chinese?"

The short answer was no. Robbie couldn't. Neither could her father, who had also been born and raised in the United States. Though, to his credit, he understood a fair amount of Mandarin. Her grandparents had spoken it at home but had always encouraged their children to speak English. When in Rome, or in this case, when in America.

Nevertheless, Robbie had always found this a senseless question. Why Chinese? Why not ask her if she spoke Italian? Which was also no. But the point was, what made it more of a logical question for a stranger to ask about one part of her background and not the other? What made one half of her such an oddity that those around her couldn't contain their curiosity?

She shuddered to think what would happen if the answer was yes. She'd seen it before. Nathan spoke a little Mandarin; his popo had taught him. When Robbie and Nathan had first started dating, he'd taken her to a party with his fellow medical school students. After a few beers, the questions started coming out, and Nathan had admitted to knowing the language. The next forty-five minutes had been spent translating the most idiotic phrases to the delight of infantile intellectuals. Robbie had been glad she'd never learned to speak it and resolved never to try. She never wanted to be treated like a side-show jukebox—have another coin, play me another silly tune.

"Czy bekon jest świeży," Ernie, or Nick—Robbie was really going to have to make an effort to call him that—said without looking up from his plate.

"What was that?" Bret said, furrowing his brows and leaning forward.

"Czy bekon jest świeży," Nick repeated, setting his fork down and looking Bret directly in the eye. "You said your last name is Kubicki? Bret Kubicki? So, you must speak Polish, right?"

"Well, no," Bret stammered, "but—"

Nick shook his head. "It's not different." He wiped his mouth and turned to Robbie, who sat in stunned silence. "We've got an early start tomorrow, don't we?" Robbie nodded, and Nick smiled back at Romeo and Juliet. "Sorry to eat and run, but we really should get going. Dinner's on me. Congratulations on your wedding."

Robbie waited while Nick paid the bill for all four dinners at the counter, barely able to restrain herself from turning around and laughing at the pair of them staring with their mouths hanging open. She'd always wanted to do that but had never found the nerve. Instead, she'd always answered their questions and walked away mumbling to herself and feeling the other party's disappointment cling to her like gum on the bottom of her shoe.

"You speak Polish?" Robbie asked as they headed back to the motel.

"I picked up a phrase or two on assignment in Krakow."

"What did you say?"

Nick broke into a wide smile. "I asked if the bacon was fresh."

Laughter bubbled out of Robbie. "What if he did speak Polish?"

Nick started laughing, too, as they walked through the motel lobby and down the hall to their rooms. "Hey, it was either that or 'is there a fee to use the bathroom?'"

"Well, thank you for that. I've always wanted to call people out," Robbie said, her laughter subsiding.

"Why don't you?"

"Don't have the guts to, I guess. My mom always said to answer politely and move on. Guess I grew up thinking I had to answer all the questions like I owed it to people."

Nick took a deep breath as they stopped outside Robbie's room door. "I was in the seventh grade, and you and Ivy had just started high school. One day, you guys came home and locked yourselves in Ivy's room right away. I wanted to tell Ivy about making the soccer team and went to knock on her door, but I heard crying on the other side."

Robbie gulped. She knew this story, but she didn't know he knew it. "I know what day you're talking about," Robbie whispered.

"I eavesdropped," he continued. "I knew I shouldn't, but I was twelve. I promised myself I would never let anyone make you feel that way again if I could help it."

Robbie didn't know what to say, so she said the only thing that came to mind. "Why?"

"You're Robbie Chin," he said with the same lopsided grin she remembered a boy having once. "Have a good night."

SIX

Fourteen years ago . . .

"Are you really going to make me go to this class alone?" Robbie asked, pulling the heaviest book she could imagine from her locker.

"I have no choice," Ivy said with a shrug. "I didn't get into the super-smart lit class like you did. I'll be slumming it with the regular students."

"I'm sure if you ask the teacher to transfer you, she'd let you in." When Ivy only replied with a doubtful grin, Robbie's heart lodged itself in her throat. She'd known it was a long shot, but she had to try at least. "I don't know anyone. They're all sophomores."

"It's one class. You'll be fine," Ivy said, steering Robbie down the crowded hall to her doom. "I'll meet you outside after. At least my class is just a few doors down."

"Yeah. Your class with everyone we know."

"You'd be bored in there anyway," Ivy continued, trying to bolster Robbie's nerves. "I saw the reading list. It's all stuff you've read. At least

this class will have new books for you. And didn't Mrs. Chin give you
money this morning to go book shopping at Cover to Cover on the way
home, all because of this class?"

"Yes," Robbie said, perking up a little while feeling in her pocket
for the cash from Mrs. Chin. There weren't many things in the world
Mrs. Chin splurged on, but books had always been the one thing Robbie
could count on her mother to loosen the purse strings for. Also an avid
reader, Mrs. Chin understood Robbie's addictive nature when it came to
fictional worlds. "Maybe Drea got some new stuff."

"Since yesterday?" Ivy asked. "Yeah, maybe," she said, noticing
Robbie's spirits dampen again.

Robbie had been lucky with her freshman class schedule. Most of
her classes included Ivy, and the only other one besides literature that
didn't had enough people she'd known in grade school to keep her from
feeling anxious about a crowd of unfamiliar faces. Lit was the last class
before freshman lunch. Fifty minutes. Robbie could handle fifty minutes.
She just had to make it through the first few days, and then she was sure
the rest of the year would fly by after the unfamiliar became mundane.

The crowded hall thinned as more students filtered into their
designated classrooms. Ivy, already half a head taller than Robbie, bent
her head toward her friend's and whispered, "Seriously, you got this."
After a quick squeeze of Robbie's arm, Ivy disappeared into one of the
freshman classes, where Robbie would have been if she hadn't earned a
pass into the advanced honors class.

Steadying herself with a deep breath, Robbie faced her home for the
next fifty minutes. Students were already filling up the seats, with a few
stalling by the doorway, presumably still deciding on where the most
advantageous seats were—not too close to the teacher, but not all the
way in the back, close enough to the door for a quick getaway, but not

directly in front of it. Robbie didn't care where she sat as long as people left her alone.

As she tried to walk through the door, one of the girls loitering at the classroom entrance thrust her arm in front of Robbie, stopping her before she could get through. "This is a sophomore class," she said with a sneer.

Robbie held up her printed schedule. "I'm in this class, too."

The girl narrowed her eyes and inspected the list of classes on Robbie's paper. "Maybe you are," she said, glancing at her friends for their approval. "But to get in this class, you need a password."

Robbie clenched her jaw and crumpled her schedule in her fist. She'd been afraid something like this would happen. Physically, she couldn't push past these three on her own. She could argue and put up a fight, but that would draw more of a crowd, which meant more eyes on her, and that was something Mrs. Chin had always been very clear about avoiding. The safest and quietest thing to do was play along with these assholes.

"I don't have a password," Robbie said through gritted teeth. They had one—something they wanted her to say, something Robbie was certain would be embarrassing. They wouldn't go through all this trouble to make it simple. Robbie glanced behind her down the hall. Where was the teacher? "What is it?"

"It can be anything you want," the girl said, widening her eyes in a show of innocence. But Robbie had seen this look before on the nature channel. This girl with her long limbs was like a swan, beautiful and graceful to look at, but come near her nest, and she'd peck your eyes out. The girl's two friends stood to the side, snickering and darting glances between Robbie and their leader. Robbie recognized one of them from her grade school. She knew the friend had recognized her, too, because she wouldn't make eye contact.

The older girl had said the password could be anything Robbie wanted, but there had to be a catch. It was still too easy, and the three of them were still grinning like fools. Robbie waited. Eventually, the teacher would come in and break up their little party anyway.

The girl must have realized the same thing because she decided to speed up the process. "The password can be anything you want, as long as it's in Japanese."

"I don't know any Japanese," Robbie said, the hair on her arm rising.

"How do you not know any Japanese?" the girl gasped.

"I'm not Japanese."

This little turn of events didn't faze the three of them as they stood there, with their arms crossed, waiting for Robbie to perform like a trained monkey.

"Well, say something in whatever language you speak. Chinese, then," the ringmaster said.

Robbie's grip tightened on her books. "I don't speak Chinese either. I speak English."

"But that's what you are, isn't it? Chinese?" the girl asked, her voicing rising a notch, causing more than one head to turn in their direction. "You don't even know your own language, but you think you can handle advanced lit? I thought your people only liked math."

Robbie bit the inside of her cheek to keep the tears at bay. Too many people were staring now, drilling through her with curious eyes, as though she'd been caught breaking the law. She'd done nothing but walk into class. A class she'd never asked to be in but had been assigned to. It was the first day, and she'd already been accused, tried, and found lacking.

But they wouldn't get her to cry. That's what they wanted, what fueled their little moment of power—to see her cry and hang her head in shame, admit her guilt of not being the same as them. Robbie couldn't control the stares and the gawking, but she could control this much.

"Everyone in your seats," the teacher, Mrs. Brown, announced as she strode into the room just as the bell rang, commencing the class.

The girl's eyes roamed over Robbie one last time with a victorious glint, then with a toss of her wavy hair, she turned and strode to the empty seat in the middle of the classroom flanked by her groupies.

"Let's go," Mrs. Brown said. "In or out."

Robbie flushed and took the desk by the window, counting down the minutes until the next bell released her from this prison that, sadly, should have been her favorite class. She stared at the back of the girl's smug head, hating her more and more as time ticked by.

Ivy knew something was wrong for the rest of the day, especially when Robbie had only purchased one book—one *required* book—from Drea's and nothing else, but she waited until they were safe inside her room at home before asking Robbie about it. "What happened today? You've been super quiet all afternoon, and you didn't make me sit at Drea's for an hour while you looked at all the books."

There, surrounded by Ivy's posters and plush throw pillows, Robbie finally let go of the pent-up emotion from the day. Tears streamed down her face, not out of sadness or damaged feelings, but from a raw anger that had been gnawing on her since before lunch. Ivy's room was Robbie's safe space, the one place she could say the words she wanted to say. Where she could scream and yell and swear (as long as Ivy's parents weren't home) and be herself.

When she finished, she wiped her face and straightened her shirt. Mrs. Chin expected Robbie home for dinner, and not with tears streaking her face. Crying over words wasn't allowed in the Chin house. "You should never give someone else enough power to hurt your feelings," her mother had told her over and over again. "And you never let them see you cry."

SEVEN

Robbie poured herself a complimentary cup of lobby coffee while waiting for the man behind the desk to print her receipt for the night. It must have been a rough night shift because he looked as bleary-eyed as she felt. She had hoped dinner would have been the last she'd have to deal with Brolly. She could never have predicted them staying in the room next to hers, giving her a front row seat to the late-night theatrics. Burying her head in the pillows and blaring the television had done nothing to mask the rapturous sounds coming through the walls, which might as well have been made with cardboard. She'd even considered knocking on Ernie's door across the hall and asking to bunk with him, but she'd gutted it out instead. She just had to suck it up and not make a fuss.

Inhaling the steam from her coffee cup, she grimaced as the metallic twang hit her nose. It was going to hurt going down, but it was there and free. She would have to ask Ernie—damn it, Nick—to stop somewhere on the road for a decent cup later. Right now, she craved the caffeine jolt to jumpstart her day. The clerk slid her receipt across the counter and nodded then walked away without a word. He'd apparently learned his customer service skills from the same person who made the coffee.

Robbie stowed her duffel in the trunk before leaning against the side of the car with her morning sludge, soaking in the early sunshine. Nick still hadn't emerged from his room, though he'd been the one who'd requested her wake-up call the night before without her knowing. Good thing, too, since she completely snoozed through the alarm she'd set on her phone.

Before Brolly's enthusiastic love display had distracted her, Robbie had been obsessing over her lack of messages from Nathan. She wasn't proud of herself, but she'd even resorted to a little cyberstalking. Just a quick perusal of Nathan's social media sites. He wasn't an avid updater. How could he be with his schedule? But it was still reassuring to see he hadn't changed his relationship status. Further proof that this was only a temporary hiccup in their relationship. After the number of fight-free years they had together, they were due. They'd be fine.

Robbie rested her head against the car and let her eyes drift closed. Good thing Nick had offered to drive. She didn't know how long she'd be able to keep her eyes open. Once her eyes shut, Nick's face came to mind. Not the teasing Nick, the one who took too much pleasure in pushing her buttons. Not the judgmental Nick, the one who gave his opinions way too freely. It was the compassionate Nick. The one who'd stepped up and guarded her from yet another round of questions forcing her to justify her existence.

He was not little Ernie the pest anymore. Having him along for the ride might have its perks after all.

Click. "Morning sunshine." Nick's chipper tone confirmed her suspicions that he'd been spared Brolly's after-dinner show. "You ready to hit the road?"

"You didn't just take my picture, did you?" Robbie asked without opening her eyes. She still had a few seconds. She could hear him stashing his bags.

"What? No." The trunk door slammed shut. "I took a picture of the coffee cup. And the car. Come to think of it, you might have gotten caught in the middle. Nothing a little editing can't fix."

Robbie pried one eye open and held out the car keys. "Oh, good. You had me worried I ruined your floating cup in front of the car shot. This is horrible, by the way. We're going to have to find a better place to grab some coffee."

"Will do, boss," Nick said with a salute. "I wouldn't even touch that stuff. You're braver than me."

Robbie slid into the passenger seat as Nick fired up the ignition.

"Stop! Wait for me!" The back door flew open, and Holly jumped into the car, flushed and panting, causing Robbie's heart to leap into her throat. "Hurry up! Before Bret comes!"

"Holly? What are you doing?" Robbie gasped, looking from the frantic girl to Nick.

Tears streamed down the girl's face. "Go, please, go," she sobbed into her hands.

Robbie looked back at the motel, not knowing what to expect. It was like the beginning of a horrible made-for-television movie. "Holly? What did you do?" *Please don't say you killed Bret.* Holly clutched a bag to her chest, and her shoes were hanging off her feet. Robbie' eyes flickered to Nick, who sat with his lips pressed together waiting for direction. Like most men, a woman's tears dumbfounded him.

"I can't," Holly whimpered between gulps, "marry him. I just can't."

"Holly!" A bare-chested Bret ran out of the motel entrance. No blood, so that was a good sign. "Wait!"

"Go! Now!" Holly screamed.

The desperation in Holly's voice wrapped itself around Robbie's chest and squeezed the air from her lungs. Something had to have happened. Something bad. No one went from the sounds from last night to fleeing with strangers without *something* happening, right?

Nick steered the car out of the motel parking lot, and they drove for a few minutes in silence while Robbie glanced behind them every couple seconds to make sure no one followed them. When Holly had regained some composure, enough to catch her breath, Robbie decided it was time to find out why they'd just become the runaway bride's getaway car.

"Did something happen back there?" Robbie asked, turning in her seat to face Holly. She ran her eyes over Holly's crumpled form searching for signs of a struggle. "Did he hurt you?"

Holly shook her head. Mascara ran down her face, leaving two black trails from her eyes to chin. "Lord, no. He would never do anything like that."

"Then . . . why are we running?"

Holly took a steadying breath. "I can't marry him. I don't know what we were thinking. We're only nineteen. What do we know about love and life? He's got a scholarship to the University of Michigan. We were going to get an apartment on campus. I was going to work while he went to school, maybe take some classes at the junior college there."

"Sounds like you had a plan," Robbie said. "What changed?"

"Nothing." Holly burst into tears again.

Nick found a donut shop and turned into the parking lot and killed the engine. "Who wants what?"

"A coffee and a bear claw, please," Robbie said, handing him her now cold cup of motel coffee. "And can you dump this for me?"

Holly held out two soggy bills. "Just a coffee, please."

Nick refused her pitiful offer to pay and leaned closer to Robbie. "I'll give you girls a minute. See if you can figure out what's going on."

"Won't Bret follow us?" Robbie asked as soon as Nick got out of the car.

"I have his keys." Holly held up her hand and jangled the set of keys on a Ford keyring. "He's stuck there for a while. I'll mail them back to the motel at our next stop."

Robbie's stomach clenched. She'd thought of dropping the girl at the closest bus stop, maybe a shopping mall to cool off before she called Bret to pick her up. She certainly didn't expect there to be more stops. "And where are we heading, exactly?"

Holly lifted one shoulder and tilted her head. The tears still rimming her eyes magnified her blue irises, making them appear three times their natural size. Bret, or whoever she ended up with, was a dead man. It was hard enough for Robbie to resist the girl's Precious Moments eyes, how would any testosterone-driven male? "Can you take me home? It's on your way. West from here."

Robbie pulled out her phone and clicked on her navigation app. "Where exactly?"

Holly gave her the address, then Robbie gasped. "That's not quite as on the way as you think. It's almost four hundred miles out of the way!"

Robbie spotted Nick coming out of the donut shop with their breakfast. "Stay here," she said, then slid out of the car to meet him halfway.

"Well?" he asked as Robbie took a fresh cup of coffee from his carrier.

"She wants us to drive her home—to Poppy Grove, four hundred miles out of our way. And get this: she swiped Bret's keys. She says she'll mail them back to him. I say we dump her crazy ass here and let Bret come get her."

"Where's your sense of adventure?" Nick asked, that mischievous glint in his eye reappearing.

"Are you kidding me? What if she's a sociopath? What if she's got a gun?"

Nick chuckled. "I think we'll be fine. I've got a sense about people."

"Crazy people."

"Part of you must want to go, or you wouldn't have let her in the car to begin with," Nick argued.

"First, I didn't *let* her in. She jumped in," Robbie fired back. Her head hurt. She hadn't gotten enough sleep to argue this early in the morning. "Second, I thought maybe he'd hurt her or something. Now I know it's just cold feet."

Nick put a hand on her shoulder and squeezed. "She's only nineteen, right? Young and scared. I promise nothing bad will happen, and if it does, you can hold it over my head until the day we die."

"Which could be today."

Nick nodded. "Yes, life is unpredictable. I'll even take the highway to get there faster. Come on. We can't just leave her here."

"Yes, we can. This isn't our problem."

"No, but she came to you for help for a reason. She obviously trusts you."

"You won't be happy unless we help this girl, will you?"

Nick shrugged, but she recognized the determined set of his jaw. It was the same as when he'd been probing her about her relationship with Nathan and wouldn't stop until he got the answers he wanted.

Robbie grunted. She was too tired to put up more of a fight. He wanted an adventure. "Fine," she said, handing him back her coffee. She took out her earrings and shoved them in her pocket, followed by her ruby necklace.

"What are you doing that for?" he asked, giving her back her cup.

"I don't want little miss weepy to get any ideas."

Holly rambled nonstop for nearly an hour once they'd started driving again. Every time she'd stopped talking long enough for Robbie to think she had finally said all the words known to man, Nick would make some sympathetic noise or cluck of his tongue, and Holly would start up again. When Robbie had glared at him, he simply mouthed the word *adventure* and kept his eyes forward.

"I mean, they say a woman gets only three great loves in her life," Holly said. "I've only ever had Bret. That's one. Just one! What if I'm missing out on another two? What if they're better than Bret? What if I only think I love Bret, but it's not really love, and I won't know that until I find numbers two and three? What if I meet number two and three while married to Bret? Then what?"

Robbie leaned her head against the window. "Then you do what everyone else does and have an affair."

Holly made some little squeaking sound in the back that reminded Robbie of fingernails on a chalkboard, instantly dousing Robbie with regret. "You don't mean that, do you?" Holly asked in a hushed tone.

"Yeah, do you?" Nick asked, small creases forming between his eyes.

Robbie sighed. "No, sorry. I'm having relationship issues of my own, so I may not be the best person to talk to about all this."

"Wait," Holly said, leaning too far forward in her seat. Robbie took the opportunity to make sure she wasn't holding a weapon. "You guys aren't a couple?"

Nick shook his head as Robbie said, "Just old friends."

Holly blew out a sigh. "Really? Because last night, it seemed like maybe—"

"Just friends," Nick said, cutting her off.

Holly leaned back in her seat again and crossed her arms as though Nick had slapped her hand away from the three-tiered chocolate cake. Robbie knew the girl had more to say because she wore the same expression that all girls did when they were biding their time, waiting for the perfect opportunity to bring the topic up again and make her point. It was the expression that screamed Holly thought she was right and she was going to make sure everyone else knew it, too. If Robbie didn't already know how wrong Holly was, she would have been curious to hear her theories.

"Okay, fine," Holly said with a huff. "What's your take on all this, Nick? What do you think I should do?"

"Hard to say," Nick said. "Do you honestly think you only get three loves in your life?"

"That's what I read. Some relationship expert said it," Holly said.

"Maybe you're looking at it wrong. Maybe it's three chances at love, but that doesn't have to mean three different people."

"I'm not following." Holly leaned forward again, and Robbie could tell whatever Nick said next was going to be the most important thing in the world to her.

"You and Bret met in the first grade, right?"

Holly nodded.

"Did you love him?"

"We were friends," she said.

"Okay, so you loved him the way a child loves a friend. That's one. Then what happened?"

"We started dating when we were thirteen. He was my first boyfriend."

"Okay," Nick said, nodding. "There's number two. He went from friend to boyfriend, which is like being two different people, because he took two different roles in your life."

"What about number three?" Robbie couldn't help asking, finding herself sucked into his theory right along with Holly.

"We did break up for a bit in high school, then got back together senior year," Holly said, sounding hopeful.

"Bingo. Older and wiser Bret is love number three," Nick said with a triumphant smile.

Holly yelped and clapped her hands together. "Oh my goodness, it is number three. He's my three. I'm such an idiot. He'll never forgive me."

"Sure he will," Nick said. "Just call him."

"I can't," Holly whined. "I took his phone, too."

Robbie watched Nick struggle to hold in his laughter. When she saw his shoulders shake, and his face turn red from the restraint, she lost her own control and let out a loud peal that set the other two off as well. Of course, Holly had taken his phone too. Robbie was a little surprised Holly had left Bret with his shoes.

When the laughter subsided, Robbie returned her head to the window and closed her eyes as she thought about Holly's revelation. Three loves. How would Nick count her and Nathan?

She'd had boyfriends before Nathan, two to be exact, though she'd never claimed to love either one of them—which was the reason number two had broken up with her. He'd said it right away, three weeks into their courtship. Robbie had tried to get there. She'd even practiced saying it in the mirror. She'd made sure to take special note of the sweet things he'd done for her, hoping something would spark a feeling close to love inside her. But after six months of him waiting to hear her say those three little words, he'd had enough and moved on to greener, more verbal, pastures.

So technically, did that make Nathan her first love? And if Holly and her expert were right, did that mean Robbie had two more loves somewhere out there in the world waiting for her, too?

Robbie pressed her eyes tighter. All this three-loves thing was nonsense. There's no controlling love. Love doesn't take a number and wait its turn. It's there, or it's not. She'd had it with Nathan. *Still* had it, she reminded herself.

But what if Holly was right? The idea that there could be someone better out in the world for Robbie was ludicrous. Nathan was perfect for her. Though they'd met in college, they both hailed from the Bay Area, making travel to visit family easy. They both came from mixed families. Hers—Chinese and Italian. His—Chinese and Irish. With Nathan, she never had to explain why she received tiny red envelopes in the mail every February, or why family dinners on Sundays were a must when in town. He never questioned why she refused to order Chop Suey in a Chinese restaurant or mocked those who clamored for the fortune cookies at the end of a meal. And he never once asked her if she ate her spaghetti with chopsticks. (There was that one time, but she'd been in college, and it would have taken too long to wash the dishes first.)

And the most essential item on the checklist: Mrs. Chin adored him.

Cara Spinosi Chin was a hard nut to crack. Many had tried. Many had failed. There were few people in Mrs. Chin's world she allowed to refer to her as anything other than Mrs. Chin. There was Robbie, of course, who only referred to her as Mom when she was in earshot. Robbie's father. Mrs. Chin's two closest friends.

And Nathan.

Not even Ivy, who had known Mrs. Chin since the girls had been in kindergarten, was allowed to call her anything other than Mrs. Chin.

The fact that Mrs. Chin had asked Nathan to refer to her as Cara had been the final check mark on the list of qualifications. Though, to his credit, in eight years, Nathan had never once called Robbie's mother Cara. But it was nice to know he could.

The day Mrs. Chin had made that earth-shattering proclamation, she'd made it clear what she'd expected of them. Robbie had decided then and there that Nathan was the one she would marry, and she'd been working toward that day ever since. She'd made compromises and adjustments, given up old dreams to make new ones. She'd adjusted and molded herself to fit into the Nathan Tang puzzle. Every extra penny that Robbie hadn't spent on car washes or her addiction to store-bought coffee and books, she had saved with the intention of putting toward their future. A nice wedding—one her parents would offer to pay for, but she would never accept—and a house for the family they were sure to have.

She felt hollow inside at the thought of having to do it all over again. She didn't have the energy twenty-year-old Robbie had. Where would she even meet someone these days? In a bar? Online? How did Ivy do it? She had a new boyfriend every few months. But she'd always been the outgoing one. Ivy, like Nathan, had an ease with people that Robbie lacked. Maybe that's why Robbie had gravitated toward them—they each had something Robbie needed.

Three loves. It was a beautiful story from some therapist wanting to sell books. It might have worked on Holly, but this was one book Robbie wasn't buying.

EIGHT

Twelve years ago . . .

Robbie slammed her history book shut and shoved it in her backpack. Her high school's parents' association meeting had drawn to a close, and she couldn't wait to get out of there. Mrs. Chin had promised Robbie she could practice driving after the meeting so long as Robbie waited in the hall outside the assembly room. She had a history test the next day, so Robbie used the time to get her studying done. That way, Mrs. Chin couldn't argue a shorter driving time in favor of Robbie's exam preparations.

One of the women cracked the door open as the association members, mostly mothers, said their goodbyes.

"Lisa, great to see you. We should get together for lunch."

"Molly, how's the baby? He's in kindergarten now, isn't he?"

"Great shoes, Danielle. Where'd you get them?"

"This meeting was shorter than the others. Good thing Erin couldn't make it today. It would have gone on forever."

"So, you'll get the numbers together for the Christmas Carnival, right, Mrs. Chin?"

Robbie cringed.

"Let me know if you need any help."

Robbie turned her back to the door so her mother's friends didn't see her eyes roll halfway out of her head. Why did her mother have to be so weird about things? It was one thing to demand Robbie's friends call her Mrs. Chin, but to expect other adults—her mother's peers—to do the same was embarrassing. Even Ivy's parents referred to the Chins as Tom and Mrs. Chin.

"I think I'll be fine, Sara. I'll use the template and budget from last year unless I hear anything's changed," Mrs. Chin said, strutting out of the assembly room. Since being elected the vice president of the association, she'd had a certain amount of swagger in her steps around these women. And Robbie found it wholly irritating.

"Are you ready, Mom?" she asked, slinging her backpack on her shoulder. Robbie's skin felt two sizes too small on her slender frame. It was time to go. "You said I could drive, remember?"

"I remember, Robbie," her mother said. "Don't be rude, though, or you'll never get behind the wheel."

Robbie plastered a smile on her face and turned to the other women. "Hi, Mrs. Sanders. Mrs. Walker. Mrs. O'Brien. Mrs. Leonard. It's nice to see you all again."

"It's good to see you, too," Sara Sanders said as her eyes flickered between Robbie and her mother.

Mrs. Chin turned her attention to something one of the other women was saying, but Robbie's focus remained on Mrs. Sanders, whose eyes had narrowed slightly, and her grin twitched as though the force used to hold up her expression was faltering. Robbie did nothing to conceal her open stare. If Mrs. Sanders wanted a look, then she could have it, but that didn't mean Robbie had to make it easy for her.

"Come on, Robbie. Let's get your practice in before it gets too dark. And you have a test tomorrow, don't you?" Mrs. Chin said, finally walking away from her entourage.

"I finished studying already. That's how long your meeting was," Robbie said, picking up her pace.

Mrs. Chin let her go. Robbie knew she would. If there was one thing her mother hated more than anything, it was causing a scene in public. She'd never been one of those mothers who would yell and scold her child in a store or restaurant, which Robbie had quickly learned hadn't meant she could get away with anything. It did mean, however, that there was a grace period built into their arguments. And the sooner Robbie distanced herself, the longer her grace period lasted. Besides, she couldn't go anywhere without her mother—Mrs. Chin had the keys and the license.

"I'm not sure you should drive," Mrs. Chin said, meeting Robbie at the car. "You're a little too emotional about something."

"I'm fine, Mom," Robbie said, uncrossing her arms to reach for the keys. "You promised."

"Driving is a privilege, not a right."

"Wouldn't you rather you teach me than me learning it on the street?"

Mrs. Chin smirked but handed over the keys and walked around to the passenger door. "You want to tell me what's gotten you in such a snit?" she asked once the car doors were securely closed. Robbie noted how her mother's grin hadn't slipped from its place, in case anyone walked by. Others might not be able to hear their conversation, but she could at least make it appear pleasant.

"Not really."

"I can't help if you don't tell me."

Robbie grunted and curled her lip then adjusted the mirrors and checked her blind spots. "Did you see the way Mrs. Sanders looked at us in there?"

Mrs. Chin stiffened in her seat, not a lot, but enough that Robbie, who had spent years studying her mother's expressions and mannerisms as a way to crack the secret code that was Cara Chin, noticed. "I don't know what you're talking about."

Liar. "Yes, you do. You saw it. The way she kept looking from me to you, trying to find a resemblance or any other physical proof that I really am your daughter."

"Oh, Robbie. You're so dramatic. She just hadn't seen you in a while."

"I saw her last week, Mom. At the game."

"Well, I'm sure it wasn't what you think," Mrs. Chin said. "Turn right at the next street."

Robbie's palms grew slick against the leather of the steering wheel. Why couldn't her mother ever admit it? Why wouldn't she ever talk about the way people looked at them? Or the things people had said to her or asked her about her family?

Ivy was compassionate and empathetic, quick to take Robbie's side, but she didn't get it, not really. For once, Robbie wanted someone to *understand*. She wanted someone to get angry with her, someone to tell her it wasn't her fault. That her existence wasn't wrong or a mistake.

She refused to believe that her mother—a woman in charge of multiple charity events and a member of several boards in the community—could be so blind. Mrs. Chin lived in the details. Nothing got past her. Except for this.

"You missed the turn," Mrs. Chin said, pointing to a street on the right they flew past. "Slow down."

"Sorry," Robbie mumbled as she maneuvered to the next street to turn around. "Why do you make everyone call you Mrs. Chin?"

"That's my name."

"You have a first name. All the other moms refer to each other by their first names. Even you use their first names. Why do you make them call you Mrs. Chin?" Robbie turned right, then lightly applied the brake as she let the car coast down a hill. As though people like Sara Sanders didn't already look at them with confusion, Mrs. Chin had to add in the extra incentive of being *that* mom. The one who had to be different. She couldn't, for once, be like the other moms?

"Why does it bother you so much?"

"Because it's weird," Robbie said, taking another right, then aiming the car toward home. Maybe driving practice hadn't been the best idea, after all. "It sounds so stuck up. Like you think you're better than everyone. It's embarrassing."

"I'm embarrassing?" her mother gasped next to her. "You think I'm embarrassing?"

Robbie's face burned. She'd gone a step too far, and she knew her words hurt her mother. But there was no going back now. Just like driving, she just had to make the next turn and hope for the best. "I think the way it can be perceived is embarrassing. You see these women all the time. Some of them are your friends. Why can't you just let them use your first name?"

"I like being called Mrs. Chin," her mother said. She clasped her hands neatly in her lap and focused her eyes on the road ahead. "I don't have to justify my decisions to you. I'm the mother, remember?"

"Oh, I remember," Robbie said before she swung the car into her driveway. She killed the engine, slid the keys from the ignition, and handed them to Mrs. Chin. "I'm going to Ivy's. She wanted to borrow my notes for the test tomorrow."

"You're not staying there."

"Fifteen minutes."

Robbie fumed the whole way to Ivy's house. She'd made up the bit about Ivy needing her notes. Ivy took better notes than Robbie. Robbie just needed to be somewhere Mrs. Chin wasn't. The woman had no clue. No clue at all.

NINE

Holly snored softly in the back seat, a droplet of drool collecting in the corner of her mouth. The exit for Poppy Grove, Pennsylvania, loomed ahead. Two miles. Two miles, then Robbie and Nick could be on their way again. Robbie had calculated the distance while Holly slumbered, and even if they stopped long enough to eat somewhere, they could make it to Columbus, Ohio, before stopping for the night, maybe farther if Nick stayed on the highway as promised.

"Do you want to wake up Sleeping Beauty?" Nick whispered as he silenced his ringing phone and clicked on the turn signal then merged onto the exit ramp. Robbie appreciated the soft click of her blinker light. So many people merged traffic lanes without signaling as though it was everyone else's responsibility to know where they were going. She had enough to worry about when she was behind the wheel. She didn't need to try reading minds, too.

"Do I have to?" Robbie asked, watching him from the corner of his eye as he checked the missed call on his phone screen. This wasn't the first time he ignored an incoming call. She could chalk it up to driver safety, but a niggling feeling in the pit of her stomach told her it was something more than that. She found it ironic that while she'd been hoping for her phone to ring, he'd been ignoring his. "It's been so peaceful since she fell asleep. Couldn't we leave her somewhere? These small towns are friendly, right? Someone she knows is bound to find her."

"We could do that," Nick said, approaching what must have been the main commerce area.

Robbie sat up straighter and stared out her window at the quaint town that must have stepped right off a postcard. None of the buildings were over three stories high. The shops lining the main street were painted clapboard, with a few brick structures interspersed, but even those had been painted with bright colors. A basket of blooming poppies—what else?—hung from every street lamp, and squat flower pots sat on every corner. People on the street smiled and waved to each other and gawked at the strange car parking in front of Junior Bear's Pizza.

"Or we could stop and have some lunch," Nick continued.

Robbie saw the gleam in his eye and knew he'd already decided where to point his camera first. Hell, she might even snap a few pictures with her phone, too. She felt like Dorothy looking at Oz for the very first time.

"I have a feeling we're not in Kansas anymore," Robbie whispered.

Nick chuckled. "Does that make me the Scarecrow?"

Robbie smiled. She hadn't meant to say it out loud, but at least he understood the reference. Nathan never got her references. Sometimes she thought he'd grown up under a rock. "I was thinking more like Toto."

"Does that mean you'll rub my belly?"

A stinging heat crept up Robbie's neck and washed over her cheeks. "Hey, Holly," she said, turning in her seat and nudging the girl's knees to avoid having to look at Nick. "Holly, we're here."

Holly shifted in her seat and rubbed her eyes. "Where? Poppy Grove already?"

"Yep. How's that for door-to-door service?" Nick said, straining to reach into the seat behind him where he'd stowed his camera bag, and in the process, leaned too close to Robbie, who pressed herself against the door to give him as much space as possible. "Why Junior Bear's Pizza?"

"It's my family's restaurant," Holly squealed. "Come on in."

As hungry as Robbie was, the thought of meeting a whole family of Hollys washed away any desire to eat. Drop and go, that was what she'd been planning. Food they could get anywhere. It didn't have to be here. And it didn't have to be now. "Oh, I don't think we should—"

"Nonsense," Holly said, cutting her off. "You drove me all the way here. The least I could do is get you a free lunch. And they're less likely to lose their shit when I tell them I ran away to get married if a stranger is with me."

"Come on, Robbie," Nick said, fiddling with the setting on his camera. "We do need to eat."

"Another adventure?" Robbie asked with a raised eyebrow.

"Now you're getting it." Before she had the time to turn her head away, Nick raised the camera and snapped her picture. "Let's stretch our legs. I promise to speed the rest of the afternoon."

Robbie grunted and pushed open the car door. Why couldn't

anybody follow the damn plan? First Nathan, then Holly, now Nick.

Their little stowaway was already on the sidewalk in front of the car waving them in. "You're gonna love our pizza," Holly said, swinging the restaurant door open. "JB's is the best in the whole county."

The three of them stepped inside to a round of applause, halting Robbie in her tracks. She'd seen this before. This was the reveal portion of an elaborate reality prank show. To capture every angle of their surprise, hidden cameras were probably stashed in odd places, like maybe in the eyes of the stuffed bear wearing a T-shirt in the corner. Robbie waited for a member of the crowd of strangers to yell, "Gotcha!" When no one stepped forward to relieve her, she turned to Holly for an explanation, but it seemed as though Holly was a target of her own reality show moment. Her eyes locked on someone in the middle of the crowd. Turning a questioning glance to Nick, Robbie hoped for an explanation, but he had his camera aimed in the same direction.

Bret stepped forward, his grin blinding even in the midday sun. "What took you so long?" he asked. The clapping died down, and as one unit, the crowd stepped back, giving the couple center stage. Not knowing what else to do, Robbie took a step toward the door, hoping to make a quick getaway before things got weirder, but Nick remained frozen, clicking his camera.

"What? How?" Holly said, grabbing Robbie's arm and taking a step forward, dragging Robbie and the weirdness she'd hoped to avoid with her.

Robbie held her breath as a fluttering stirred in her chest. The hero had come back to declare his undying love and fight for his lady. A sappy soundtrack played in her head while she watched a scene from a teen love story play out in front of her.

Bret held up a single key. "You know I keep a spare in my wallet.

And I figured you wouldn't remember about the short cut. I told them everything," he said, motioning to the teary-eyed crowd around them. "They've given us their blessing. All I need now is yours."

Young love was so theatrical. This was why angst-filled teen romance books and films made millions. Adults running around like this, making grand declarations in front of a whole town, chasing each other for hundreds of miles, was embarrassing. This kind of love required the unique mix of egoism and bravado only inexperienced youth possessed. Even Shakespeare had cast Romeo and Juliet as teenagers. Robbie was glad Nathan wouldn't think of doing something so outrageous. He'd plan on something more private, so they could talk things out like adults who don't thrive on making a scene.

Robbie knew what Holly would do even as the girl pretended to hesitate and consider. Holly would do what every other teenage girl in love would do. She ran into Bret's open arms and hung on to him while sobbing into his shoulder. Robbie didn't mean to, but even she teared up a little at the sweetness of it. She wished she wasn't standing right next to it, though.

"Thank you for taking care of my girl, Robbie," Bret said once Holly had loosened her death grip from his neck. "Our parents are throwing an engagement party for us tonight. I hope you'll stay for it."

"Oh, no—" Robbie started to say.

"We'd love to," Nick chimed in.

Everyone else was so focused on Brolly, they didn't notice the steely-eyed, murderous glare she shot Nick. What was he thinking? They were already half a day behind schedule. This would put them a full day behind in driving. She couldn't expect Nathan to wait around San Francisco for her forever. He had patients to get back to. Besides, she didn't want Nathan wasting his money on a hotel room for a night because of Brolly's party.

Robbie brushed her hand against the phone in her pocket—her silent phone. No message from Nathan at all. He was going to call. He had to. His last words to her were not going to be, "It's time we moved on."

"What wrong?" Nick asked.

"Haven't we had enough adventure for one day?" Robbie hissed. "We have places to get to."

Nick stepped closer and placed his hand on Robbie's back, presumably to keep her from running away. "Ivy's not going anywhere. And you're done teaching for the summer, right? So it's not like you have a job to rush back to. Live a little, Robbie Chin."

It *would* serve Nathan right to have to wait around for her after making her wait this long to hear from him. She should let him be the one wondering for once.

"Is there someplace we can get rooms for the night?" Robbie asked.

"That's what I'm talking about," Nick said with a victor's grin.

"I know just the place," Bret said. "But let's eat first."

To Brolly's credit, the pizza was delicious. Not at all what Robbie had expected from a place called Junior Bear's in the middle of nowhere Pennsylvania. Also to their credit, when Brolly made up, they made up like champions. Huddled in a corner booth, they resumed their public make-out sessions, which oddly enough, no one seemed to mind. Not their parents, friends, or even the one old grandmother, who may or may not have been blind anyway. But there they were, their love on full display. Robbie was grateful nothing else was on display, and that she sat out of earshot.

As a high school teacher, Robbie had grown accustomed to amorous displays. Teenagers, in general, had no shame, and making out with your significant other was equivalent to wearing a badge of honor. One that said, "Look, everyone. Someone likes me. I'm worth something!" For most teenagers, anyway.

Robbie's first real boyfriend, Josh McKenna, had hung with a crowd that wasn't exactly the popular crowd but was popular crowd-adjacent. A definite step up in social standing for Robbie and Ivy, who were firmly situated in the middle-of-the-road group. Josh had also been a fan of the public make-out session, which had always made Robbie's skin crawl.

"Think they'll make the long haul? 'Death do they part' and all that?" Nick asked, wiping pizza sauce from his hands.

Robbie shrugged. "Does anyone ever know?"

Thousands, if not millions, of books have been written about love and all its aspects. The thrill and romance of new love. The steady predictability of long-term love. Even the heartbreaking end of it. And yet, no one ever seemed to know for certain what created it and how to determine its viability. Robbie bet not even Holly's love expert with all her theories on the number of loves in one's life could predict a couple's lifespan. All the best romance stories had been written around the one central question: will they or won't they?

Robbie had first studied, then taught, literature for years, and always the story ended there. Rarely, if ever, was the next question asked—the "now what?" There was either a happily ever after, or there wasn't. And if there was, then what? And for how long?

Nick tilted his head and peered at her as though looking through his camera lens. Instinctively, Robbie leaned away and crossed her arms. "Don't you know?" he asked. His tone lost the teasing quality it usually held when he asked her personal questions and had been replaced with genuine curiosity. "Isn't that why you keep checking your phone?

Because you know you're supposed to be with that Nathan guy?"

There was that word *know* again. Robbie taught her students that all literature followed a particular structure, a formula. There were only a handful of formulas in existence and every story—good story—followed one of those formulas. As a student of literature, once the formula was determined, predicting outcomes for the story became fairly easy. And since art, like literature, imitated life, shouldn't predicting outcomes like successful relationships be easy, as well?

Robbie had thought it had been once. She'd followed the formula. She'd met a boy she'd liked who'd liked her back. They'd dated and progressed their relationship in any normal, healthy way. They'd been committed. They'd shared a life and a home. The next step in the formula was marriage. It had always been marriage. This separation was nothing but a plot point. An obstacle to overcome that would make them stronger.

She had to know, right? Yet something about the way Nick asked if she *knew* unsettled her.

"Yes, *I* know," Robbie said, her cheeks flushing, not only because of this line of questioning but also because she didn't realize he'd caught her checking her phone as much as she had in the car. "I meant you could never know for certain about other people."

Nick furrowed his brow. "Even the one you're with?"

Robbie set down her drink with a thud and glared at him over their shared pizza.

"I didn't mean *you* you," he said quickly. "I meant the universal 'you.' Like, the only person you can ever be sure about is yourself. Unless you're a mind-reader or something."

"I suppose," Robbie said slowly, not sure if he was setting her up for a trap, or just thinking out loud. "But, if you're at that point where you're thinking long term, generally you know enough of the other person to tell if they're thinking the same thing."

Robbie stopped talking and swallowed the lump forming in her throat. She'd been thinking long term. She'd been making her plans. She'd done research and made lists. She'd scrimped and saved what she could, for six years, all in the name of the long term. And she'd thought Nathan had been on track with her until he'd announced he was on a completely different train. She didn't know anything.

Nick lowered his head. "You would like to think so," he mumbled, a shadow passing through his normally bright eyes. "Never mind. Just a stupid thought I had." He wiped his mouth and rose from his seat. "I'll be outside."

Robbie watched him leave, not quite sure what had just happened. They'd started out talking about Holly and Bret, then her and Nathan, and now Ernie was upset? That's right, Robbie had downgraded him back to Ernie. After spending all night and all day readjusting her thinking of him as a full-grown man, he'd blown it with his pouting. It was her life he'd been questioning. Where did he get off acting all put out?

"Everything okay?" Bret asked, appearing at the side of her table. He had a twinkle in his eye, and Holly's lip gloss smeared in the corner of his mouth. "I saw Nick leave . . ."

"I think he needed to stretch his legs after the long ride." Robbie recognized the signs of a kid wanting to ask for a favor. Like a student asking for a paper extension, he shifted from one foot to the other and tried to make stilted small talk to soften her up. She'd already delivered his Juliet back to him, what more did he want? Robbie motioned to the seat across from her. "What's up, Bret?"

"Nick said he was a photographer," Bret said, clasping his hands together on the table in front of him, pleading his case. "I was hoping he'd maybe take some pictures for us at the party?"

Robbie smiled her *you're so special* smile, the one she saved for the star athletes who thought they could get away with missing an exam or two if they scored enough points on the field or court. "That's really up to him," Robbie said as she saw Ernie outside the window focusing his camera on something across the street. "Do you want me to ask him for you?"

"That would be great. Thanks so much!" Bret bounced away from the table and back to Holly's lips.

Robbie chuckled at his overt display of eagerness as her phone buzzed on the table next to her. In her eagerness to answer, she almost didn't look to see who the caller was, but divine intervention was on her side, and she stopped, her fingertips brushing the screen as her mother's name flashed in front of her. Snatching her hand back as though Mrs. Chin could reach through the phone and grab her, Robbie counted the number of rings before her voicemail picked up. Then, to be sure, she counted to sixty after the high-pitched trill of her phone alerted her to a new message.

"Hi, hon," Mrs. Chin's voice sounded in her ear. "It's Mom. Just wanted to make sure you were still coming home for the party." A weight sat on Robbie's chest as she listened to her mother. Of course, she was still coming. She said she would. She never went back on a promise. "And if you are, don't forget it's a nice event. So a dress. Nothing flashy. You know, something you would wear to a function with Nathan."

Robbie groaned. She had definitely done the right thing in letting Mrs. Chin go to voicemail. Robbie was a grown woman living across the country, and her mother still had to have a say in her wardrobe.

"Maybe the party will spark some ideas of his own," Mrs. Chin continued. How much could this woman squeeze into a two-minute recording? The weight pressing down on her grew heavier the more her mother spoke. "That would make the weekend perfect. Okay, hon. Let us know your plans. Bye."

If Robbie didn't respond in a timely manner, Mrs. Chin would call again, and again, with variations of the same themes: subtle guilt trips, a touch controlling, and apparent attempts at marrying her off. Instead of returning the call, she sent her mother a quick text.

"Got your message. Sorry, super busy, but yes, still coming to the party. See you soon."

She tossed her phone in her bag with a sigh. Determined not to speak directly to her mother until things with Nathan were back to normal, even if that meant hiding out in Ivy's house for a week, she slid out of the booth and headed for the door in desperate need of fresh air. Ernie stood on the curb, aiming his lens at a row of buildings across the street that looked so much like the end of a rainbow, Robbie wondered where they'd stashed the pot of gold.

"So, Bret wants to know if you'll take pictures for them tonight at the party," Robbie said, staying behind his shoulder so she didn't block the light, eager to think about anything other than her mother's message. "I think he was too scared to ask you himself."

Ernie lowered the camera and smirked at her. "I'll do it."

"You will?"

"Sure," he said, returning to his focus on the buildings. "If he asks me himself."

"Are you trying to be mean, Ernie?"

"First," he said, pressing the shutter button. "It's not mean. I think if he's man enough to get married, then he's man enough to ask me himself for something he wants. What good will he be to Holly if he can't ask a simple question? Second . . . Ernie?"

"Does it bother you if I call you Ernie?"

He let the camera hang across his chest by the worn leather strap. Robbie wondered how many cities around the world that strap had seen. How many countries had it passed through? "No, it doesn't bother me," he said, his frown from earlier disappearing and his teasing smile peeking through. "An elite few are allowed to call me that these days, and you happen to be one of them."

"How did I get such an honor?" Robbie asked.

"You've seen me without pants on," he said with a wink.

Robbie's face burned. When? How? Why wouldn't she remember this? Had she been drunk?

"Ivy's sixth birthday," he said with a laugh at her speechless expression. "And my four-year-old self stripped down to run through the sprinklers on the lawn."

Robbie covered her mouth with her hands, stifling her laughter. "I remember that! Ivy was so mad at you. You took all the attention off her when she was blowing out the candles. You were such a brat."

A man in an apron stepped out of the shop on the corner with a hose in hand and began spraying down the sidewalk in front of his building. "Would you like a re-enactment?" Nick asked. "Or, is it your turn?"

"Neither!" Robbie gasped as he took her elbow and tried to lead her in the direction of the hose. "You'd better behave, or I'm calling your sister."

Nick dropped her arm and threw his hands in the air. "Tattle-tale."

"Brat."

TEN

Twelve years ago . . .

"Why won't you ever kiss me in public?" Josh asked Robbie one afternoon as they left the mall where they'd been hanging out with their friends.

"I kiss you in public," she argued as she reached for his hand. "I'll kiss you right now."

He rolled his eyes and pulled his hand away from hers. "That's not what I mean. I mean, in there, around people we know. Not out here by ourselves."

"Do we have to put on a show for everyone? It's rude and weird." Robbie folded her arms across her chest, stung by his refusal to hold her hand. Josh had been doing that more lately, pushing for more public displays and refusing the private ones. Unless he wanted something. Then he was all sweetness and petting.

"People think you don't want to touch me." He unlocked the car door for her but didn't open it like he usually did. Instead, he sulked around to his side of the car. "Like there's something wrong with me. With us."

They'd been going out for months and seen each other every day. They'd walked through the halls at school with his arm around her. "That's ridiculous. No one thinks that," Robbie said, refusing to fall for his bait.

"Prove it," he said, revving his engine. "Next time we're out with everyone, make out with me. It doesn't have to be a long one, but you have to let me squeeze your ass."

Robbie hated ultimatums and being told what to do. She scratched at her neck, sure she'd broken out with hives. But healthy relationships required trust and compromise. And she wanted to prove they had a healthy relationship. She swallowed down the part of her screaming to punch him in the face. "Fine. Next time we all hang out, we'll make out."

Josh reached over to rub her knee. "Good. We don't want them to think Chinese girls are frigid."

Later that night, Robbie sat at her kitchen table using her trigonometry homework as an excuse to watch her parents clean up together after dinner. She noticed the way her father always found little ways to touch Mrs. Chin. A brush of the hand as he handed her a dirty dish to wash. The way he moved the hair out of her eyes while she scrubbed a pot. The way their bodies leaned toward each other when they spoke and how he rested his hand on her back as he moved past her.

Chinese people weren't frigid.

She'd grown up watching her father kiss Mrs. Chin every morning and every night. When they went out at night, it wasn't uncommon for her father to wrap an arm around Mrs. Chin's shoulders—something Robbie pretended to be mortified about, but in reality, thought was kind of sweet.

So, what was wrong with her that she couldn't kiss her boyfriend in front of other people?

"You almost done, kiddo?" her father asked, wiping down the counter.

Robbie hadn't noticed that while she pondered the likelihood of inheriting a frigid gene from a distant Chinese relative, her parents had finished the dishes, and Mrs. Chin had already disappeared into the living room, probably to warm up the television for her parents' nightly ritual of tea and something on the DVR.

"Yeah, almost," she said, pushing her book aside. "Dad, can I ask you something?"

His eyes lit up as he took a seat at the table. It had been a few years since Robbie had asked him for homework help, and he seemed eager to prove himself her hero again. "What are we working on?" he asked, peering at the equations and symbols in her book.

"Actually," she said, then cleared her throat. "I wanted to get your opinion on something about Josh."

Her father blushed deeper than if he'd just downed a beer. "Teen relationships," he said. "That's more your mother's area of expertise."

"You were a teen once, weren't you?"

"Yes." He fiddled with the edges of Robbie's math book. "But I was never a teen girl, and that's a whole other beast." He coughed and shook his head. "Not that you're a beast. You're a lovely girl, pretty well-behaved compared to the horror stories I hear from other fathers. But still, teen girl issues are well above my pay grade."

He rose from his seat and motioned to the living room. "Do you want me to get your mother?"

That was the last thing Robbie wanted. Robbie wanted to talk about being different with someone who actually was different. What would Mrs. Chin know about being different?

ELEVEN

Robbie sat in the bay window of her room at the Poppy Grove Inn watching the party preparations take place in the street below. The whole town had gathered to pitch in for the party, a hive of worker bees, each with a job of their own. One group of fine citizens erected tents in the town square. Another carried out tables and mismatched chairs from local establishments. The kitchen staff at Junior Bear's Pizza operated in overdrive, churning out enough food to feed all of Poppy Grove for days.

Somehow, Holly's family had become convinced that Robbie and Nick were responsible for the couple's reconciliation. Though Robbie had protested, saying they'd only driven Holly home, no one would give in to her arguments, and they insisted on putting up her and Nick in the Inn's nicest rooms for the night at no charge. If they'd known she'd been betting on Brolly losing, their reception would have been much different. They probably would have been run out of town by a pitchfork-wielding mob.

Statistically speaking, the young couple wouldn't make it. They had everything going against them—age, maturity levels, lack of financial security. Everything except the love, support, and encouragement of their entire world. And that counted for something, right? Should they crash and burn, they would both land softly in the warm embrace of their families. And should they succeed? Then they would do so with fanfare and applause.

Robbie wondered what kind of landing awaited her in San Francisco. Mrs. Chin wasn't known for her warm cups of tea or comforting hugs. And she'd made it known on more than one occasion how deep her disappointment would run if Robbie blew things with Dr. Nathan Tang. The words *rip my heart out in pieces* had been said with such solemnity Robbie had believed it could happen.

Robbie's phone pinged, and like Pavlov's dog, her thoughts turned to Nathan. But it wasn't Nathan, it was Ivy, checking on her progress across the country.

"Gotten lost yet?" the text read.

Robbie blew out a heavy breath, figuring out where to begin. She needed more than a few text messages to explain their detour. Instead of opening that Pandora's box, she replied, "Doing some sightseeing. Will be a day late." She snapped a photo of her quaint room with its four-poster bed and sent it for good measure, to prove they hadn't driven into a ditch.

"Ernie and his adventures," Ivy replied. Then, "Separate rooms, right?"

"YES," Robbie fired back.

"Have fun and be careful," Ivy texted before sending a picture of her at the beach, leaning against a man's shoulder.

Robbie chuckled. As a fellow teacher, Ivy was also done with the school year and had a few weeks to herself before the summer school session she taught began. Robbie assumed the man with her was the principal she'd been dating on the sly to avoid stirring up trouble with the rest of the faculty. Though Robbie wasn't confident in how low-key Ivy could be.

"Make good choices," Robbie typed.

Robbie returned to her people-watching and spotted Nick, camera in hand, near the town square. And then she saw Bret walk out of Junior Bear's and join him. *Good for you*, Robbie thought. *Way to man up*. She watched their exchange until she was convinced it was going well, as evidenced by the handshake and Nick's clap on Bret's shoulder. It looked like Bret got his photographer.

"How come you never told me Ernie's name was Nick?" Robbie texted Ivy.

"You didn't know?" the answer came back. "Haha. Just always figured you did."

Robbie waited for the next part of the message as three dots floated across her screen. "He's not making you call him Nick, is he? He can be so pretentious sometimes. Nick Wolfe, big time photographer."

Big time? Robbie thought he worked freelance jobs, which in her world meant whatever he could get. "No, he's fine. Just wondering."

But now Ivy's comments had piqued her interest. Robbie may be one of the privileged few allowed to call Nick by his childhood nickname, but what did she know about Nick, the man?

She pulled her laptop from her bag and settled onto her bed for a little cyber-sleuthing. Bringing up a search engine, she typed in "Nick Wolfe, photographer," and hit enter. At once, a page of thumbnail pictures popped up in front of her, as well as a list of news articles, press releases, and magazines with his name.

Big-time photographer was right. And boy had Robbie been wrong.

Nick wasn't a freelancer scraping by on any job he could book; he was a freelancer because no one could afford to keep him on staff full-time. Her old friend, Ernie, was a full-fledged, highly sought-after artist. He'd worked for every major fashion publication, politicians, celebrities, news magazines—you name it, he'd done it. One article named him one of the country's top thirty under thirty to watch in the arts and entertainment field.

Ernie. Little Ernie who had stripped down to nothing and run through sprinklers at his sister's birthday party. Ernie, who had followed them around begging to be played with. Ernie who used to blackmail Ivy into letting him tag along to high school parties. Scrawny, awkward, pesky Ernie. Though, he wasn't that scrawny and awkward-looking with those models hanging on him at the Oscars. Or when shaking hands with Grammy award winners. Or standing next to those astronauts.

It was official. Ernie was gone for good. Nick was here to stay.

A sudden cold sweat slicked her palms. For the past two days, she'd been operating under the assumption that she'd been traveling with one person when, in reality, she had no idea who she'd been riding next to. What must he think of her in her T-shirts and cut offs? Hair in a ponytail and no makeup?

She flung herself off the bed and dug through her travel bag searching for something appropriate to wear to the party. Nothing but shorts and tank tops—not the cute club kind, the utilitarian ones built for comfort and bloating. She had stuffed a sundress into the corner of her bag when she'd packed, but it was a wrinkled mess and more of a beachy daytime dress, not evening engagement party dress.

They'd passed a cute boutique with interesting clothes in the window on their way from Junior Bear's to the Inn. She was sure to find something party-perfect there. When she and Nathan had started dating,

Robbie had gradually weeded out her more colorful and daring outfits—the ones Mrs. Chin couldn't hide her disapproval of—in favor of items more conservative than her usual taste, playing it safe with muted solid colors. Black, gray, navy. Anything that blended into the background and made Mrs. Chin grin with satisfaction.

"Dress like you deserve him," her mother had told Robbie numerous times early in her relationship when she'd realized how successful Nathan Tang was destined to become.

While Robbie wasn't vying to deserve Nick, she certainly didn't want to cause him any embarrassment. He was used to models and celebrities. The least she could do was make sure she wore something clean and wrinkle-free. He was making this absurd trip across the country as a favor to her, after all. He could have easily hopped a plane and been home in a matter of hours instead of days.

The scent of roses slapped her in the face as she stepped into the breezy, pink shop. The residents of Poppy Grove took their flowers seriously. Buckets of fresh-cut blooms stood in every corner of the boutique, and a gray stone, waist-high planter ran the length of the shop, dividing it in half. Overflowing with roses and peonies, and dripping with lily of the valleys, it gave the store a fairy garden aura.

The bright dresses and flowing fabrics reminded Robbie of the shops in the San Francisco Mission District, a favorite splurging spot for pre-Nathan Robbie. The floral patterns and geometric prints called to her, like a beacon guiding her home. She grabbed an armful of clothes and headed to the dressing stall that opened to the shop with a curtain.

The first three dresses lost their luster before she had them on all the way. She was swimming in the skirt of the third one, a green-and-white-striped maxi dress with yards of fabric hanging from the waist when a voice on the other side of the curtain called to her. "Are you doing alright in there, miss?" The shop's owner, a plump redhead, rattled the curtain without opening it.

Robbie grunted. "Yes. Fine." Giving up on getting the dress to drape gracefully over her barely-there hips, she yanked it off and thrust it out the curtain. "Actually, I'm done with this one."

The woman clucked her tongue, and Robbie imagined her shaking her head at the wadded-up material shoved into her hands. "This dress was a mistake for me to order. No one has ever had good luck trying this on. I should pull it off the rack, but I keep thinking someone will get it to work for them."

Robbie appreciated the woman's attempts at soothing her ego. No matter how good the store smelled or how pretty the floral decor, there was simply not enough magic in the world to stretch her frame another six inches or add curves where nature had never intended them.

"Are you looking for something special, hon?" the owner asked.

Robbie surveyed the pile of dresses she hadn't tried on yet. She'd been too hopeful. Every single one of them was meant for her dream version of herself. The one she pictured in her head before surprising herself with her reflection. "I was looking for something for the party tonight," Robbie said, running her finger along the neckline of her favorite, a silky strapless dress in teal. She laughed to herself. She'd never be able to hold the thing up. The comfort of her tank tops and shorts tempted her to give in already. Who was she fooling?

"May I suggest something?" Before Robbie answered, a hand appeared inside the curtain holding a dress. "I thought of this dress as soon as you walked through the door. I think it will be adorable on you."

Adorable wasn't the image Robbie strove for. Flirty. Sexy. Effortlessly stunning. But she'd take adorable over resembling a ten-year-old boy wearing his mother's clothes. Robbie took the dress from the woman and held it up to inspect it. She hadn't noticed this one as she'd perused the racks, probably because it was shorter than the ones she'd picked for herself. The cherry pleated skirt had enough flair to give it bounce. The hem was embroidered with a peacock feather pattern that climbed up one side to the banded waist. The chiffon bodice was of the same color, with a mandarin collar and a dramatic keyhole opening. Robbie crinkled her nose. Of course, the woman thought of her. There was a decided Asian feel to the dress. Who else in this town would she think of wearing it? Her first impulse was to pass on it without even trying, but she slipped it on anyway to appease the woman's curiosity.

Robbie stared at herself in the mirror. The color brought out her early summer tan and made her dark eyes warm like embers instead of cold like flint. The embroidery was fun and light, just like she wanted to be at the party. The short skirt accentuated her legs, giving them the illusion of length. And the way the chiffon draped over her, then tucked in at the banded skirt, softened her figure by highlighting her narrow waist and adding volume to her hips and bust.

"Well?"

Robbie pushed the curtain aside and stepped out of the dressing stall. "What do you think?"

The woman clasped her hands at her chest and sighed. "It's just perfect."

Robbie's wide grin made her cheeks ache. "I think so, too. I'll take it." Nathan would never have seen that one coming. No spark. Yeah, right.

Back in her room at the inn, Robbie stood in front of the mirror and smoothed her skirt. She'd taken her hair out of her ponytail and had slipped on a pair of sandals she'd fished out of the trunk of her car that gave her an extra two inches in height. She had also dug out her jewelry and found the ruby earrings Nathan had gotten for her the previous Christmas to go with her necklace. They went beautifully with the dress. The music had started in the town square, and the sounds of people gathering in the street floated through her open window. The party had officially begun, and she was stalling. Maybe this dress wasn't a good idea after all.

She started to change out of the dress. It was too much. Too short. Too bright. Too Chinese. What would Mrs. Chin say? Her mother, who on World Day in grammar school had always dressed Robbie in red, white, and blue when everyone else had gone dressed as leprechauns or in lederhosen.

"You're supposed to dress like where you came from," Robbie had complained, thinking she'd been breaking the rules.

"You come from America. You were born here. You will die here," her mother had said. "Besides, no one else will be wearing Chinese clothes."

"What about Italian?" Robbie had argued. "I could wear Italian clothes." Her mother had narrowed her eyes, possibly considering.

"No one would believe you," she'd said with a stern finality. Red, white, and blue. Every year.

Nathan would have expected her to change, and Mrs. Chin would curl up her nose at the obvious embroidery and brightness of the red. Once upon a time, Robbie wouldn't have cared what anyone thought, and the fact that it drove her mother crazy had been all the fuel she'd needed. Had she matured over the years, or had she weeded out more than her clothes?

Forcing both Mrs. Chin's and Nathan's voices out of her head, Robbie marched out of her room and down the stairs. She didn't know anyone here, nor would she be likely to see any of them again after leaving town in the morning. She had nothing to lose.

"Robbie, there you are," Holly squealed as Robbie approached the center of the town, scanning the crowd for Nick. He'd gone down early to take pictures before he completely lost the light, he'd said. Holly ran up and embraced her as though they were old friends. "Come on. I want to introduce you to some people."

Robbie steeled herself, the heavy weight of doubt creeping over her again as the little hairs on her arm prickled. Walking through a crowd of people she didn't know was one thing, but mingling and making small talk had never been her strong suit. Growing up, whenever her parents had taken her to a social event, her mother had always told her to stand in the back and look pleasant. Don't draw too much attention. Don't make a scene. As she got older, if she went to a party, she had Ivy, then Nathan, to act as a buffer between her and the other party-goers.

She didn't trust Holly to act as a suitable buffer and Nick had disappeared somewhere. She blamed the dress. It was too bright, making it too easy for Holly to spot her in the crowd. If she'd worn her denim shorts, she would have blended into the background and would have slipped by unnoticed.

Holly dragged her to a group of young women, all about Holly's age, and introduced her as the one who'd saved her relationship with Bret. Robbie waited for the arched eyebrows, the wide, confused eyes, the hesitant questions. But none came. At least none about her background. Holly's friends wanted to know one thing: how she'd gotten roped into the whole Holly and Bret drama.

Robbie told the story a dozen times and even found herself laughing along with the *Thelma and Louise* references. She flitted from one group to another, and it wasn't until two hours later she realized she'd made her way through a party of strangers without a buffer. No best friend and no boyfriend to hide behind when the questioning glances became too pointed. Maybe the new dress did have some magic in it after all.

"You've been busy," Nick said, joining her at the dessert table. "I don't think you've had one minute to yourself all night."

She met his eyes, emboldened by the power of the dress, or the third cocktail. "You've been stalking me?"

He quirked a half smile. "I wouldn't put it like that."

"Have you been getting good pictures?" Robbie picked a cookie off a silver tray, needing something to do with her hands other than letting them shake her plastic cup, sloshing its contents over the side. Knowing Nick's level of fame in the photography world, and her ignorance of it, made her more nervous than she should have been.

"Some," he said. "See?" He held out the camera and showed her an image of Holly and Bret dancing and gazing at each other as though no one else in the world existed. They looked the way every couple in love should look, and Robbie's heart clenched. She thought about the picture on her phone, the one of her and Nathan. They didn't look like Holly and Bret in a way that didn't have to do with the shape of their eyes or the color of their skin.

"It's beautiful," Robbie said because it was, and they were. Young and shiny and beautiful. Also, naive and idealistic, and dreamy. She and Nathan were none of those things.

"Dance?" Nick asked, slinging his camera across his shoulders and holding out his hand.

Robbie glanced to the left then the right, not sure what or who she searched for, but certain it had to be lurking there somewhere. When nothing popped out of the shadows to stop her, she ditched the cookie that had turned to mush in her hands and brushed the crumbs from her fingers.

"It's been a while. I'm not very good at this," Robbie said, placing her hand in Nick's.

He pulled her close and wrapped an arm around her waist. "Me neither."

She glanced up at his grin and felt his sure hand on her waist and knew he was lying. He was going to be excellent at this.

TWELVE

Robbie received little satisfaction in the knowledge she'd been right. Nick's confidence on the dance floor compounded her anxiety. All left feet and no grace, she was certain everyone noticed how he dragged her around the dance floor.

"You seem tense," he said close to her ear. "Everything okay? Did something happen?"

Robbie shook her head to clear the web of thoughts she'd gotten stuck in. "Sorry. Not used to dancing, I guess." She glanced over his shoulder, happy she had those extra two inches from her shoes, and checked to see who was watching. "So, what's next for you? After you get home, I mean?"

"Rest, hopefully. Then, I don't know. Go wherever the next job takes me."

Robbie couldn't imagine not knowing where she would be week after week. She liked reliability and stability. One of the reasons she liked teaching was because she could plan an entire nine months at a time. "Do you like that kind of nomadic lifestyle?" She scrunched up her nose as though the thought carried a foul odor with it.

"It's certainly interesting," Nick said before twirling her under his arm. "When else in my life will I have the opportunity to travel and explore without worrying about other things?"

"Other things, like what?"

"Family. Kids. Whether or not I can maintain a healthy relationship."

Robbie watched his expression change from amused to thoughtful from under hooded eyes. His tone had lost the lightness again, like it had in the pizza place, and she wondered what weighed it down. "Doesn't traveling all the time kind of get in the way of the healthy relationship?"

He didn't look at her but set his mouth in a straight line. She'd struck a chord. "That's what I've been told."

"By whom?" Robbie asked softly. She thought of his buzzing phone and the slew of unanswered calls and messages. Someone somewhere missed him. Nick's eyes flickered in her direction as he pressed his lips together. "Come on. I've kept your secrets before."

Nick's shoulders stiffened under her hand while he took a deep breath. "Her name was Megan. College girlfriend."

Robbie nodded. She had a vague memory of Ivy mentioning her little brother's girlfriend once or twice after she'd moved.

"I thought I was going to marry her," he continued. "Had the ring and everything."

"What happened?"

"I got offered a photography fellowship working with one of the top photographers in London after graduation."

"I remember that," Robbie said. "Ivy was proud of you. She told everyone you were going to be the next Annie Leibovitz, only a dude." Robbie had already moved to New York by then, and because her school year hadn't ended yet by the time he'd had to leave, she hadn't been able to return home for his going-away party. But, her parents had gone, and Ivy had sent pictures.

Nick smiled down at her without the warmth behind it. "It was only for a year, and I thought with all the technology these days, long-distance relationships had a much higher survival rate than they used to."

Robbie's stomach twisted, knowing what came next. It was an inevitable ending. If it had a different one, they wouldn't be standing where they were. They wouldn't be dancing. And he wouldn't have such a wounded expression in his eyes that reawakened in her the urge to soothe. She didn't have a Transformer in her pocket this time.

"Long distance relationships are hard no matter what," he said. "I just wish I found out before turning down a permanent job in London and coming home with a ring in my hand like an idiot."

"She cheated?" Robbie asked. He nodded, and Robbie understood his shock at her offhand comment to Holly about infidelity. It had hit closer to home than she had known.

"That's when I decided I was going to do what I wanted and go where I wanted. I would see everything I want to see. I've busted my butt, taking every job that came my way, no matter where it was."

"Sounds like you're running away."

Nick shook his head. "Not running away. Getting ready. I fully intend on having a family one day. Wife, kids, picket fence, all that. And when that day comes, I'll be in, all in. I'll be the dad that hears about his kids' day every night at dinner. I'll be the one who coaches little league or football."

"What if you have a girl?" Robbie asked with a smile. She liked his grown-up version of himself.

"Hey, girls can play sports. Or I guess I'll have to learn ballet lingo.

Whatever she needs. The point is, when I settle down, I'm really settling down. I'm never letting distance get in the way again. So, I'm doing it all now."

"Hence all your adventures."

"Hence, indeed," Nick said, his mocking tone returning. "What about you? You do any traveling?"

Robbie shrugged. "I'd love to, but with Nathan's work schedule, he could never get more than four days off at a time. So, we never get very far. Couple days back home. A long weekend in Florida."

"You could always go by yourself," Nick said, then pressed a firm hand in her back and dipped her backward. "You do get summers off."

Robbie flushed when she returned right side up, her heart humming. "Please. I can't even eat in a restaurant alone. Or drive on the highway. How am I supposed to go halfway around the world by myself?"

The music started to die down, and couples trickled off the dance floor, leaving Robbie and Nick almost secluded in the middle of the town square. They'd stopped their swaying, but Nick still had his arm around her waist. He gazed down at her, his eyes holding steady with hers. "I think you're more capable than you give yourself credit for. You were going to drive cross-country by yourself until my sister forced my company on you."

"That's different," Robbie whispered, a lump forming in the back of her throat.

"Why?"

Because the trip was a way to get Nathan back. Because she'd never thought she would get this far without him begging her to turn around and come home.

"It just is," she said, dropping her hand from Nick's shoulder and lowering her eyes to the ground. A pang of guilt struck her in the chest at the thought of Nathan. When they reconciled, he wouldn't be happy finding out she'd danced with another man this way. Or that the man had looked at her the way Nick had. Or that she'd like it.

"Nick," Holly called from the edge of the dance floor. "Can you please take just one more picture? I want one of everyone! The whole party before everyone goes home."

Nick tipped his head to Robbie. "Duty calls," he said with an eye roll. "Time to pay the bills—if they were paying me, that is."

The sun had barely broken over the horizon when Robbie threw her bag in the car. She hadn't been able to sleep again, watching the moonlight trace a path across her ceiling until a decent time finally arrived in which to call Ivy without facing her wrath at an "ungodly" hour. She'd stopped and listened outside Nick's door on her way out of the inn, but there were no sounds of movement, and no light coming from under the door, so she let him be. A café down the street was already open, and after Robbie left a note for Nick with the innkeeper, she went for breakfast.

Though Ivy had never said it, Robbie could tell every time Ivy and Nathan had been in the same room that Ivy wasn't completely on board with their relationship. There had never been any fights or outward tension between them; it had been something only Robbie had felt and had chalked up mostly to protective best friend stuff. Maybe even a little jealousy that Robbie had someone else in her life occupying space that had used to belong to only Ivy. But it was precisely because of Ivy's supportive restraint of her distaste that Robbie knew she could trust her friend to be honest with her now.

"Am I completely crazy?" Robbie asked, settling into a seat near the window with a coffee and the largest blueberry muffin she'd ever seen.

"Yes," Ivy yawned. "About what?"

"Nathan. Is it totally nuts to think we'll get back together?"

There was some rustling on Ivy's end, and Robbie envisioned her best friend propping herself up and bracing herself for a conversation better had with a bottle of wine and a cheesecake between them instead of a few thousand miles and two time zones. "Is it out of the realm of possibility? Absolutely not. Plenty of couples have their ups and downs, and their breakups and make-ups. No relationship is perfect."

"Except for ours, you mean," Robbie said, feeling better about her prospects with Nathan. Ivy would have laid it out flat for her if she thought Robbie was chasing ghosts.

Ivy yawned again as she laughed. "Well, yes, but we're transcendent, my love. If one of us were a dude, I'd totally marry you."

"Please, we'd have like eight babies already and be bitching about taxes and the cost of fueling up the minivan."

"Hurry up and come home. I miss you."

"Tell your brother to stop trying to save every damsel in distress. We're a whole day behind now."

"Ugh. He's annoying like that. Get on the highway," Ivy said, using her stern teacher voice.

Robbie grunted. "It's my turn to drive. Sorry, honey." Nick had emerged from the inn with clean clothes, but underneath his baseball cap, she could see he'd decided not to comb his hair. He stowed his bags in Robbie's car then squinted in her direction, where she waved to him from inside the coffee shop. "Your brother finally woke up."

"Let me talk to him," Ivy said as Nick entered the shop and joined Robbie.

Robbie held out the phone. "Here. It's Ivy."

Nick put the phone to his ear with a questioning look. "What's up?"

The hum of the coffee machines behind the counter combined with the music piped through the speakers prevented Robbie from hearing what Ivy said, but judging by Nick's furrowed brow and constant "mm-hmm"-ing, Robbie guessed he was getting an earful. After another minute, he wished Ivy a good day and hung up.

"You told on me?" he said, handing Robbie back her phone and sinking into the seat across from her.

"She wanted to know why we were running late," Robbie said with all innocence.

"You had breakfast without me? I thought you said you couldn't eat in restaurants alone?"

"I wasn't alone," Robbie said, with a sunny smile. "I was with Ivy. You want something to eat before we go?"

"Yes, I do," Nick said with a tilted grin and standing again. "I'll get it to go, so I don't make you even later, tattle-tale."

"Great," Robbie said, slapping her hands on her legs as she stood. "I'll meet you at the car, brat."

Robbie hummed to herself. Ivy was right. All couples had their ups and downs in the course of their relationships. This down just felt so much worse because they hadn't had any before. People called it quits then changed their minds daily. As long as one of them stayed strong and steady, they'd make it through this mess. She glanced at the phone she still held in her hand and stared at the glaring lack of any new messages or calls.

It was taking Nathan a lot longer than she had expected for him to realize his horrible mistake. Or maybe he had, but he was too embarrassed to admit it. Nathan hated being wrong. It wasn't something he was accustomed to. She would have to be strong and steady for a while longer. Maybe if he didn't reach out before the end of the day, she would figure out a good way to break the ice with him. Let him know it was okay to admit his mistakes and that she didn't hold it against him.

"You ready, slowpoke?" Nick asked, sauntering up to the car with a paper bag and two coffees.

"Double fisting this morning?" Robbie asked, jealous she hadn't thought of getting another cup.

He held out one of the cups. "This one's for you. I don't need you falling asleep at the wheel today driving down all those country lanes."

"You're a lot funnier than you used to be, Ernie," Robbie said, thankfully accepting the extra jolt of caffeine and getting into the car. After their talk on the dance floor, Robbie had lost the jitters she'd had around Nick Wolfe, the photographer, and slid into comfort with Nick Wolfe, her childhood friend. He'd been hurt, like her. No matter what kind of brave face he painted, she knew he was still running from his pain—something she could relate to.

"I will take that as a compliment," he said before climbing into the passenger seat.

Robbie adjusted the seat. She'd had it at the perfect setting until Nick had driven the day before and moved its position all the way back to fit his tall frame. Robbie couldn't even reach the pedals from where he'd left it. Looking over her shoulder out the back window, she put the car in reverse and lightly stepped on the gas.

"I don't know if—"

She registered the sound of metal crunching before the car lurched sideways with such a force, she banged her head first against the headrest, then into the side airbag instead of the window. Someone screamed. It took her a minute to realize it had been her, but when she stopped, the Jeep had come to a rest as well. Tires squealed, and Robbie made out the tail lights of a black pickup as it sped through the town square, then out of sight.

"Are you okay?" Nick asked, one hand bracing against the dashboard, the other outstretched in front of her, the only thing that had kept her from flying forward into the wheel.

"What the hell was that?" Robbie said, clutching her head. "I didn't even see him coming."

"Me neither." He reached over and killed the stalled engine. "Can you get out?"

"I don't think I can open the door from this side."

"Hang on." Nick climbed out of the car and made his way around the back, pausing to inspect the damage before opening Robbie's door from the outside. "Brace yourself."

"That bad?" But he didn't have to answer. She saw it on his face.

This could not be happening. She took excruciatingly good care of her car. She'd never had a driving accident. Ever.

"No, no, no," Robbie muttered, rubbing the sore spot on her head. "What am I going to do?"

Nick placed his cool hand over her heated one. "It happens. It'll be fine. We'll just walk across the square to the auto shop and see if anyone's in yet. The important thing is that we're okay, right?"

Robbie lowered her head and sighed. "We're so screwed."

Nick smiled. "Come on. We'll file a police report and check the auto shop. Look at it this way: it's—"

"Don't say it."

"Just another adventure."

"Give me a minute," she said, sitting down on the curb and resting her head in her hands. The reality of the situation had set in, sending her head into a tailspin. She'd been in a hit-and-run. The entire driver's side of her precious Jeep, her only means of transportation, had been crumpled like a sheet of tin foil, leaving them stuck in Poppy Grove.

"Hey, Robbie," Nick said, crouching in front of her, his hands on her shoulders. "Are you sure you're okay? Do I need to call an ambulance?"

"I'm fine," she said, covering her face with her hands. "I'm . . . processing."

"Processing. Okay." He stood again and took a deep breath. "So, the first thing we should do—"

"Stop," Robbie snapped, her jaw clenching. She shifted to keep her legs from twitching. "I'm not your newest damsel. I know this is bad for you, too, that you're stuck here with me, but I just need to figure this out and wrap my head around this mess. Can you give me a minute?"

His eyes dimmed as he pressed his lips together to keep from frowning. "Sure," he said, backing away from her. "Let me know when you're ready."

She hadn't meant to blow up at Nick. He was only trying to help; she knew that. But she couldn't stomach the idea of him thinking of her the same way he thought of Holly. Like a lost little girl, far from home, who needed to be taken care of. She didn't want him to fix things for her. She didn't need a hero. She had thought Nathan was her hero, saving her from a life of always being the outcast, of always having to justify herself. But look where that got her. She was done with heroes.

THIRTEEN

"You want the good news or the bad news?" the coverall-clad mechanic asked, wiping his hands on a greasy rag.

It was a trick question. If someone felt the need to ask which one Robbie wanted first, it was because there was no good news. Or the bad news was so bad it eclipsed whatever goodness may have been found in any other circumstance. There was no winning here.

"Just tell me," Robbie said, pinching the bridge of her nose to stave off a looming headache with one hand and playing with her ruby pendant with the other.

"Engine is shot from the impact. You'll need a new one. That will run you about three grand. You've got some substantial body damage and will need wheel realignment. About another six grand. And that's just for parts. Labor will run about two to three grand," Sam, according to the name stitched to his chest, said.

"But I take such good care of the car. Regular tune-ups and oil changes, I swear," Robbie said, as though she could argue away the damages.

Sam nodded almost sympathetically. "Unfortunately, tune-ups don't prevent collisions from happening. You're lucky you didn't sustain more damage to yourselves."

Robbie's grip tightened around her pendant, and she narrowed her eyes to menacing slits. She didn't care for the way he'd implied the accident had been her fault. Partially, maybe, but she wasn't about to take all the blame. She hadn't sped out of the parking space by any means. The other driver should have seen her and stopped.

"You said good news?" Nick asked, placing a steadying hand on Robbie's shoulder with a gentle squeeze.

"It won't take long at all to get it fixed," Sam said with a smile as he shoved his rag into his back pocket. "Once we get all the parts sent over from Penn Run, it should only take about a week."

Robbie knew it. Her heart thudded against her ribs, trying to escape this nightmare. There was never good news. There was always some catch the messenger tried to sugarcoat to avoid getting shot. "And how is that good news?" she asked through gritted teeth.

"There is another option," Sam said, appearing genuinely pleased with himself. "My cousin owns a car dealership on the edge of town. I'm sure he'll give you a real good deal on a trade-in, even with it all busted. There are some good, salvageable parts here. He opens up at noon. How about I give him a call and let him know to expect you?"

Robbie stared slack-jawed, marveling over the fact that Sam fathomed this good news. Turning to face Nick, she jabbed her finger in his chest and said, "This is your fault." Then back to Sam. "I don't have a choice, do I? Go ahead and make your call. I'll be back later to get my bags."

Robbie stormed out of the garage and down the street in no particular direction. Nick hesitated and said a few more words to the mechanic, then trotted after her.

"How is this my fault?" he asked when he'd caught up to her.

"You were the one who wanted the adventure. I was perfectly fine leaving Holly at a bus stop. But no, you just *had to* come all this way to bring her yourself. Then, we just *had to* stay for the party." Somewhere deep inside, buried beneath the annoyance of her disrupted plans, and the anxiety over what the cost of a new car would do to her savings, and the worry that Nathan might not come around after all of this, she knew it wasn't Nick's fault. But she needed someone to be angry at, and it was more fun being angry at someone else than herself, or worst of all—no one.

"You heard what he said," Nick said, keeping up with her clipped pace, which wasn't hard since his legs were almost twice as long as hers. "You have options. We can ship your stuff to San Francisco and get a flight back. Isn't it better that it happened here, rather than somewhere in the middle of nowhere?"

Robbie spread her arms wide. "What do you call this place? I have no idea where we are right now."

"Trust me," Nick said, putting both his hands on her shoulders and forcing her to look at him. "We're far from nowhere. We have a place to stay the night and plenty of food options. Plus, we've got each other, so we're not stranded alone."

Robbie wanted to punch his carefree face. Not because she was still mad at him about the car—she knew she couldn't stay angry for something not really his fault. She wanted to punch him because he was just so smug about it. He was much too confident in his abilities to turn a crap day into something fun and enjoyable. She hadn't wanted to come to Poppy Grove to begin with, but he'd convinced her. She certainly hadn't wanted to stay, but they had. And she'd ended up enjoying herself far more than she'd ever thought she would have.

And he was about to do it again.

"You've got something up your sleeve, don't you?" she asked, narrowing her eyes.

Nick let out a low rumble of a laugh. "It's not like I planned this. But, look, we're up and dressed and caffeinated, with no job to go to, no errands to run, and a whole morning stretched out in front of us before we have to decide what to do about the car. Let's make the most of it."

Robbie swung her head around and gazed longingly at the garage where her precious Jeep sat six feet in the air holding hostage what little of her coffee that hadn't spilled, while Sam poked around underneath it.

"What's wrong?" Nick asked, noticing her frown.

Robbie pointed at the garage. "I left my coffee in the car." With a sigh, she gave in. "Come on. Let's go."

"Where to?"

"We're starting this day over. You left your breakfast in the car, too. Back to the coffee shop, then we'll figure something out."

An hour later, fed and aimless, Robbie strolled down the Poppy Grove streets with Nick looking for something to do. They'd debated seeing a movie, but the theater wasn't open yet. Neither one of them were up to antique shopping, or shopping of any kind. Especially Robbie, now that she had to figure out what to do about the car. So instead, they found themselves walking toward a small wooded area on the edge of town.

The woman working at the coffee shop had heard them trying to decide how to spend their time, and she'd mentioned a path cutting through the trees, leading to a small lake. After a quick stop at Sam's auto shop to retrieve Nick's camera bag, and to make sure that nothing had changed about the car, they were on their way.

They walked in silence until they reached the woods. Robbie had been mentally calculating the balance in her bank account and felt the color rise in her face as she thought about their living arrangements. Nathan paid the rent—all of it, which included most utilities, while Robbie handled the smaller living expenses, like groceries and the cable and internet bills. Clearly, she hadn't wasted money on buying anything for the apartment, as evidenced by her lack of belongings. And while she had a tidy sum in her savings, enough to live off of for a little while if she needed to, she was hesitant to dip too deep into her nest egg.

The money she'd been putting away, like a little squirrel storing nuts for the winter, had been earmarked for their future. A wedding. A home. She'd planned on saying her vows while standing on equal footing, so Nathan didn't think she was dead weight, a drain on his finances.

"It's a lot of pressure to be the bread-winner and provide for a family," Mrs. Chin had told her soon after Robbie had moved to New York with Nathan. "I'm sure he's waiting to make sure you're both financially stable before proposing."

Robbie had started saving with her very next paycheck. If curbing her shopping impulses meant helping contribute to their future family's well-being, she was more than willing to relegate her book-buying to second-hand stores only, mostly.

And while she was still eighty-seven percent certain Nathan would call and beg forgiveness, that small thirteen percent of her needed to make a plan. She couldn't spend the rest of her life in Poppy Grove, but the thought of throwing away a substantial chunk of money on a new car when just an hour ago her Jeep was pristine and all hers, sent a sharp pain between her eyes.

Robbie hadn't even noticed that Nick was also rooted in his own thoughts until he brushed her elbow, startling her out of her mental calculations (contrary to popular belief in high school, not all Asians were math whizzes), and gazed down at her with a frown.

"Hey, Robbie," he said. "Can I ask you a favor?"

"Sure," she said with a furrowed brow. What could he possibly need from her?

"I never told my family what happened with Megan." Nick paused while Robbie nodded in understanding. "Could you please not tell Ivy?"

"You want me to keep a secret from my best friend?" Robbie meant it as a joke, but his frown didn't budge. "Of course, I'll keep it quiet if you want."

"Thanks," he said. The shy grin Robbie remembered from his youth emerged. "It's just kind of embarrassing."

"I don't think there's anything to be embarrassed about, but I understand," Robbie said, picking her way over a fallen branch. "Your secret is safe with me."

They broke through the tree line and stepped out on a small rocky beach. It was an early summer day, and the breeze coming off the water was refreshing. Nick immediately put his eye to his camera and focused the lens on the landscape around them. Robbie found a smooth patch on the ground and sat down with her phone in hand.

"Still nothing?" Nick asked without taking his eyes off the horizon.

"No, but—"

"I'm sure he'll call."

Today was Nathan's late day. He didn't have to be at the hospital until three in the afternoon. He slept in on his late days. Robbie was certain that was it. He was still sleeping. "He's probably not awake yet."

"So," Nick said, lowering the camera, "you want to tell me what happened yet?"

Robbie arched an eyebrow and pretended not to understand. She hadn't told anyone but Ivy what had happened, but she'd told Ivy everything since they'd been six years old. As long as it was a secret kept between Robbie and her best friend, she could imagine this whole situation as another one of their What If games. *What if* they won the lottery? *What if* they had to eat only one food for the rest of their lives? *What if* they woke up one day with superpowers? *What if* it was really over with Nathan?

"I told you my sordid tale," Nick said, his eyes drilling into her. "I think it's fair."

Fair or not, it had been a few days since she'd rehashed the break up with Ivy, and the urge to go over it again, in a more sober light, bubbled up inside her, and Ivy was still thousands of miles away. *What if* she pretended Nick was an extension of Ivy?

While Nick pointed his camera at everything but her, Robbie told him how she'd made Nathan's favorite dinner, lit some candles, and opened a bottle of wine as a little celebration for the end of the school year. She'd made it through another year of teenage drama and hormones. She described how Nathan had come home, sullen and quiet, not too unusual after a long day in the emergency room. He'd sat and ate half his dinner, letting Robbie prattle on about her plans for the summer break, then he'd put his fork down and said, "Robbie, I think we need to break up."

When pressed for reasons why, Nathan had said, "We've lost our spark." To elaborate further, he'd followed it up with other justifications, like how Robbie had become too complacent and too predictable. Which could only mean that he'd thought *she'd* lost her spark.

"But, isn't that what happens after being in a relationship for that long? When you really know the other person?" Robbie asked, her voice rising in pitch. "Doesn't everybody become predictable after a time?"

Nick shrugged. "I've never been in a relationship for that long, but I would think so. I mean, I can pretty much predict what Ivy will do. Or my longest friends. So, I would assume it's the same in a romantic relationship."

"Right. It is. And you wouldn't dump your sister or your friends and go out and get new ones because of that, would you?"

"Did he get a new girlfriend?" Nick asked, letting the camera hang around his neck for the first time since they'd stepped onto the beach. "Is there someone else?"

"No," Robbie gasped. Though, in all honesty, she hadn't thought about it until now. Could there be someone else? The idea that he'd found her too boring had lodged itself in the forefront of her thoughts, and she hadn't made that leap to think he'd found her boring *compared to someone else*. Someone new. Someone bright and shiny around him—the way she used to be, back when he'd hadn't been allowed to see her without makeup, or when she'd refused to use the public bathroom when out on a date. When she'd always smelled like some flowers and the ocean, and not like bathroom cleaner and dish soap. "Do you think there could be?"

"I don't know, Robbie," Nick said, taking a seat next to her on the rocks. "Maybe I'm just projecting some of my own experience here, but I think the possibility is always there. Even if nothing has happened yet, maybe he just wants the door open so it could."

Robbie felt the wind punched out of her. Nick was right. Of course, he was. Nathan was a handsome, successful doctor. Women would be crazy not to throw themselves at him. Nathan wouldn't have any problems finding someone more exciting to fill her shoes. Maybe he already had, which explained why he hadn't called. Tears formed in the corner of her eyes, but she wouldn't release him. Not yet. She didn't know anything for sure. There was still an eighty percent chance he'd call and want to make amends.

"I didn't mean to upset you," Nick said, hanging his head.

"You didn't," Robbie said, nudging his arm with her elbow. "I needed to hear that. Even if I didn't want to." She dabbed her eyes and offered him a smile. "Go on. Take your pictures."

Robbie walked along the shore, collecting interesting rocks, while Nick seemed to find an endless array of subjects to photograph. Out of what was rapidly becoming an obsessive habit, she scrolled through her phone again. Her throat went dry when she saw she had one new email. This was it. Finally. But when she opened the email app, she saw the message was not from Nathan but the wife of one of his coworkers, Beth Rochelle. Beth and her husband, Patrick, had invited Robbie and Nathan to their annual cookout the following weekend. Robbie checked the list of email addresses Beth had included on the email and didn't see Nathan's at all. Beth had assumed, as most people had, that Nathan would get the message through her.

Obviously, Beth didn't know they'd split, or she would have sent Nathan the invitation and not Robbie. Patrick was someone Nathan spoke to rather often, so if Nathan were going to tell someone at work, this guy would have been a top contender for getting the news.

This backyard barbecue invitation stirred up more questions than was intended, but they all deserved an answer. If Nathan didn't call her, was she obligated to call him and tell him about this email? Was she duty-bound by their not too distant past to forward this message? And why should she? Wasn't Beth just as much Robbie's friend as Patrick was Nathan's? Robbie knew in the technical world of breakups, Beth and Patrick belonged to Nathan. He'd met them first and brought them into her world. Nathan worked with the guy. They couldn't not talk. But did that automatically mean Robbie had to give up her friendship with the wife?

There should be a breakup instruction manual. If there were prenuptial agreements and divorce settlements, why couldn't there be breakup contracts? They'd been together for just as long as a lot of couples who divorced. They'd been living together and sharing their lives. Why were there no set terms to their breakup to abide by? Life would be a hell of a lot easier if they'd established clear rules and custody agreements regarding friends.

"Hey, Nick," she called over her shoulder. Getting a man's point of view would be nice. What had he done after his breakup? "Nick," she called again, louder when he didn't answer.

Robbie turned around and scanned the shoreline expecting to find Nick absorbed in his camera lens. Instead, he was absorbed in a group of young twenty-somethings circling him the way a pride of hungry lions circled a gazelle. Robbie recognized them from the party—Holly's friends. All former high school cheerleaders. All pretty in that "I don't need any makeup, my thick hair naturally looks this wavy and full" way. They reminded Robbie of the models she'd seen with Nick on the internet. Robbie ran a hand through her straight-as-a-broom-handle hair. Only an act of God could bend her hair like that. Never mind convincing it to hold a curl for longer than twenty minutes.

Nick laughed at something the voluptuous brunette said. Great. They were clever, too. It wasn't enough they'd been blessed with smooth skin and curves. They had to be engaging, as well. Confident and witty in a way that Robbie had always envied. In a way that maybe Nathan wished she was.

Robbie had pretended to be that girl at the party the night before.

And for a hot minute, she'd believed it. But it hadn't been real. It had been a figment of imagination conjured up by the combination of the dress and the drinks. Though, it had felt real at the time. So real, in fact, she'd hardly recognized herself. Nathan would have been surprised if he had seen her. She was usually the quiet one at parties and dinners, letting him take the lead.

She put her phone with the email from Beth away. Her question about Nathan could wait. Nick was busy.

FOURTEEN

Six years ago . . .

"Whose house is this again?" Robbie asked as Nathan helped her from the car. They'd only been in New York for a few weeks, and she was still trying to remember the names of all Nathan's new colleagues.

"Patrick Rochelle," Nathan said. "His wife is Beth. He works in the emergency department with me."

"Right. Patrick and Beth," Robbie repeated, hoping to drill their hosts' names into her memory. They'd been invited to the Rochelle's annual barbecue, and Nathan had been eager to attend and make a good impression on his new coworkers who were sure to be there. In her desire to please Nathan and make him proud, she'd dressed somewhat more formally than she would have for any other barbecue, opting for a skirt and pumps instead of anything else that would have been more comfortable. After all, Oscar Wilde had once said, "You can never be overdressed or overeducated."

She envied the pair of strappy flats another woman walking into the party was wearing. *Next year*, she promised herself, when she wasn't the new one to the group anymore, and the verdict had come back as acceptable.

"You look beautiful," Nathan whispered in her ear as they approached the front door. "It'll be fun. I'll be right by your side."

Both Patrick and Beth greeted them with warmth, welcoming them to their home and introducing them to the guests Nathan hadn't yet met at the hospital. The whole scene reminded Robbie of a Victorian novel, one where no one was allowed to talk to anyone else unless introduced by a third party, and Robbie was grateful for it. Like the infamous Mr. Darcy, she wasn't any good at recommending herself to strangers, and Beth seemed to take some enjoyment in bringing around the new people.

"How are you liking Aberbrooke?" Beth asked her after Patrick had whisked Nathan away to marvel over their new home theater system. Robbie darted glances in the direction they'd gone, hoping to see Nathan rounding the corner. "Are you settling in okay?"

"I think so," Robbie said, feeling less pressured to say the right thing when it was just Beth. "It's different than San Francisco, but so far the people we've met are all very nice. I got a job at Mount Greenwich Academy, so I'm a little anxious to start that."

"Oh, Mount Greenwich. Very impressive. They're the best school in the area with a waiting list as long as my arm."

Robbie raised her chin a fraction of an inch and tried to hide her smile behind her glass of iced tea. *It was impressive.* There had to have been over a hundred applicants for the job, and Robbie got it. When she thought about it, there had only been about twelve applicants for Nathan's position. His odds were much better than hers going into the job hunt. Why had everyone made such a big deal about how grueling his job search had to have been?

"Don't tell me—it's all about Nathan right now, isn't it?" Beth asked, a knowing and compassionate light shining behind her eyes. "It was the same for Patrick and me. To hear our families talk, you'd think he walked on water. All I did was write a small little computer code that secures every transaction made through PayNow."

"You code for PayNow?" Way more impressive than Mount Greenwich Academy.

"I worked for months writing and rewriting the software that protects millions of dollars in transactions daily, and you know what Patrick tells people I do? 'Something with computers.'"

"I would be shouting it from the rooftops. In fact, I think I will. Do you mind if I tell people I know the genius behind the revolutionary app?" Robbie asked with a wink.

"I knew I liked you," Beth said. "Let's make a pact. I'll tell everyone how great you are if you tell everyone how great I am."

"Deal."

"There you are," Nathan said, coming up behind Robbie with Patrick and sliding his arm around her waist. "Having fun?"

"I am," Robbie said, turning to Nathan with a wide smile. "Did you know that Beth codes the PayNow app? She wrote the whole security code."

Nathan nodded and took a drink of his beer. She watched the blood rush to the surface of his cheeks. "Patrick said you worked with computers."

The one simple statement sent the women into a fit of giggles, eliciting confused looks from their respective partners. Robbie may not have Ivy in Aberbrooke, but she had Beth Rochelle now, and in a pinch, Robbie felt that Beth would do as a suitable replacement.

Later that night, Nathan stopped at a burger place on the way home. "Wait here a minute," he said with a wink. Confused, Robbie sat in the idling car as Nathan ran inside the restaurant and emerged again a minute later with a white box in his hand. "Here you go," he said, handing her the box as he buckled his seatbelt.

"What is this?" Robbie asked. But she already knew. She smelled the cinnamon and nutmeg wafting out from under the lid.

"Patrick said this place had some of the best apple pie in the area. I thought you could give it a try. I know you've been missing DeLucca's Bakery."

Robbie leaned back and smiled, reaching over to take Nathan's hand in hers. Yes, she was settling in just fine.

FIFTEEN

Robbie sorted through the pile of rocks she'd collected to pass the time until Nick finished flirting with his bevy of beauties. Judging by the lilting giggles ebbing like the tide, there was no immediate end in sight. As though sensing her need to talk to someone, her phone buzzed next to her with an incoming call. She knew it would be Ivy. The chances of Nathan contacting her had dwindled to a mere seventy-five percent.

"Making good time?" Ivy asked.

Robbie cringed. She hadn't broken the news to Ivy yet, hoping for some miracle that would have returned them to the road. "Still in Poppy Grove. We've had a minor car issue. We're probably stuck until tomorrow."

"That sucks!" Ivy replied. "But good news. Ernie's friend at San Fran University High called and said there's an opening in their lit department that's yours if you want it. Perfect timing, right?"

"What do you mean, Ernie's friend called? Why would Ernie's friend tell you about a job opening *for me*?" Robbie's eyes sought out Nick on the beach, while small beads of sweat formed on her back. "Ivy, what did he do?"

"What?" Ivy stammered. "Nothing. I mean, not much. He made a phone call, that's all. I assumed you knew. He didn't tell you?"

Scooping up a pink-and brown-striped stone, Robbie gripped it in her hand, digging the jagged edges into her palm. "No," she said, hurling the rock as far as she could, a moment of satisfaction brushing against her as it hit the water. "He did not tell me."

Ivy let out a heavy sigh. "Oh, Ernie," she muttered. "He's only trying to help—not that I condone him going behind your back. But he seriously thinks he's doing the right thing. You know that, right?"

Robbie curled her upper lip and rolled her eyes. She couldn't be too mad at Ivy. He was her little brother, after all, so of course Ivy would stick up for him. "I know," she said more to maintain peace than anything. "But I'm not even one hundred percent sure I'm staying in San Francisco yet. Hell, I haven't even officially quit Mount Greenwich. How could I possibly consider a job somewhere else right now?"

"Speaking of Mount Greenwich," Ivy said, with a careful steer away from the topic of her brother. "When do you owe them an answer?"

"End of the week." Robbie squinted up at the sky. She would have an answer about Nathan then, too. If he went all week without calling her, then she knew for sure it was over. As it was, she was only sixty-eight and a half percent sure he'd call.

"What are you up to since you're not driving?" Ivy asked.

Robbie sneaked a picture of Nick and the girls and sent it to Ivy. "Waiting."

"Oh, man. Good luck with that." There was a pause followed by a shuffle. "Listen, I've got to run. But call me later, okay? And don't be too mad at Ernie."

"Got a hot date with your secret boyfriend?"

"Something like that," Ivy said before they said their goodbyes.

Robbie sat staring out at the lake. Even though Ivy had done her best to keep Robbie from dwelling on what Nick had done, Robbie couldn't stop the irritation from mounting the more she thought about it. Not only had he been talking to someone about her behind her back, but he had also taken her life and her future into his hands without her permission. She never asked him to help her find a job, and she certainly never said it was okay to go blabbing her situation all over the Bay Area. Nick the Fixer at it again.

"Hey," Nick blurted, making her jump. He lowered himself with a thud in the rocks beside her. "What are you doing over here?"

She lifted one shoulder. "Killing time. How are things going over there?" Holly's friends were still clustered on the beach, casting wary glances in their direction, no doubt wondering how long it would take Nick to return to them.

"You met Holly's friends last night, right?"

"I did. Nice girls."

"They're okay," he said, taking his cap off and brushing back the hair that had worked its way out from underneath. "A little silly, I think. Why don't you come over and hang out?"

Why didn't she poke her eye out with a fork? "I'm a little tired and not really in the making nice mood. Besides," she said, noticing how their glances had progressed into outright stares, "I don't think it's me they want to hang out with. Maybe you could call some friends and get them some jobs while you're at it."

Nick stiffened beside her, his clasped hands tightening. "Who—"

"Ivy," Robbie said. "Your friend called her. Good news. There's a job opening."

"Isn't that good news?" he asked, his words rolling off his tongue in slow motion.

"I didn't ask you to make any calls."

"I know you didn't," he said, "I just thought—"

"You made an assumption about me and my life without speaking to me first. How do you even know I want to continue teaching? I don't even know that."

"Don't you?"

Robbie shrugged. "Maybe not. I love literature and all, but maybe a school setting isn't the place for me. Maybe I want to be a book reviewer. Or I could get a job as a copy editor, or even a book agent. The point is: I don't know, so you can't possibly know."

Nick took off his cap and ran a hand through his uncombed hair. "You're right," he said, at last. "I shouldn't have gotten involved like that without asking you first. It was presumptuous of me, and I overstepped. I apologize. It won't happen again."

Drawing her knees up to her chest, she wrapped her arms around her legs. "Yes, it probably will. You can't help it."

Nick chuckled and replaced the cap on his head. "Forgive me?"

"Nick," the girl who'd made him laugh called. "Nick, take a walk with us."

He arched a questioning brow at Robbie. "Forgive me?" he asked again.

"This time," she said, bumping her shoulder against his. Then, motioning to his fan club, "You're being beckoned." When he didn't make a move to leave but continued to look with the same sad eyes he'd had as a kid when he'd gotten hurt on the playground, she willed her arms to stay where they were instead of wrapping around him instead. "I'm fine. I promise. I have some car research to do." She waved her phone in his face as proof of her busyness. "Seriously, go," she said, nudging him with her elbow.

Nick looked back at the former cheerleaders, then turned to Robbie, as though there was an actual choice to make. "Fifteen minutes. Twenty tops. Then we go back, get some lunch, and you can tell me about your car research. Deal?"

"You got it."

Nick squeezed her shoulder and got up, brushing the dirt from his shorts. "Oh, hey, I almost forgot," he said, digging into his pocket. "I found these over there and thought you might like them for your collection. Hold out your hand." She did, and he dropped three rocks into her palm, all smooth as glass and in various shades of purple. "Cool, huh?"

"How'd you know about my collection?" she asked, marveling over the color of the stones. She hadn't come across any like these in her hunt.

"I don't remember a time in my life when we've been at a beach together, and you didn't collect rocks," he said, backing away from her with a grin. "Ivy had a whole bucket of them in her room, and I'm guessing you did, too."

"Nick, come on," a different girl yelled.

"Fifteen minutes," he said, then turned and walked away.

Robbie closed her hand around the rocks. She didn't have a bucket—she had a cardboard box. She'd snagged it from the recycling pile before her mother had a chance to take out the garbage and stashed it under her bed. It was still there, or at least it was the last time she'd visited her parents, full of colorful and interesting rocks she'd collected while growing up that were too heavy to move to New York. She uncurled her fingers and studied the lavender and purple stones, already picturing what a nice addition they would make to her pile.

"Robbie. Robbie, wake up."

Robbie blinked, opened her eyes, then squeezed them shut again. The sun hung overhead, and she feared she'd just been blinded. "Has it been fifteen minutes already?"

"More like forty-five," Nick said, helping her to a sitting position. "I'm sorry. So, so sorry. Things got crazy. Are you hungry?"

Robbie's stomach grumbled. "I could eat."

He pulled her to her feet and waited while she got her bearings. "I should have been more careful about the time."

"Apparently, I needed the nap," she said, putting a hand on his arm to get him to stop making excuses.

"Are you gonna burn laying out like that for so long?" he asked, concern written in the lines creasing his forehead.

Robbie shook her head. "It's the one good thing about being half Italian and half Chinese. Something about the combination of skin tones makes it nearly impossible to get a sunburn."

"You've never had a sunburn? Ever?" he asked as they started making their way back to the path in the trees.

In the distance, further down the beach, Robbie heard the high-pitched laughter of a group of girls. "Not once. Everyone else got red as lobsters in the summer, and I always tanned beautifully, in my opinion."

"Not just your opinion," Nick said, staring at her a little too long.

The heat trailing over her skin had nothing to do with the sun. "Tell me about your morning. Did you walk far?"

Nick groaned and ran a hand over his face. "It's such a long, stupid story," he said. "It's better saved for when we're bored on the road. Lunch is on me for making you wait so long."

"I won't turn down a free meal," Robbie said. "Especially now with this whole car thing."

They stopped at Sam's auto shop to tell him to go ahead and call his car-dealing cousin. As much as she hated to say good-bye to her precious Jeep, Robbie couldn't wait another week to get it fixed. And since she'd have to get a new car anyway, it seemed a waste to pay for airfare and shipping, too. Sam rubbed his stomach in delight and delivered another round of "good news."

"I priced out the parts of your vehicle for you, and it looks like you'll be able to get about seven grand for it," Sam said. "More than enough to find something on the lot. Isn't that good news?"

"Sam really needs to work on his definition of good news," Robbie said as they walked to Junior Bear's Pizza from the garage, lugging their overnight luggage. Sam had been gracious enough to allow her to stow the rest of her belongings in the corner of his shop until she picked them up in whatever "new" car she returned with. In the meantime, he was going to tow her Jeep to his cousin's. "I think he thinks it means something else. And seven grand is more than enough? What kind of cars are they selling at this dealership?"

"We'll find out soon," Nick said, swinging open the restaurant door. "Everything will be okay. We'll make up the time."

"And no more stowaways, no matter how much they cry," Robbie said, pointing a finger in his face.

"Cross my heart," he said, crisscrossing his finger over his chest.

They placed their orders from behind their respective laptops. Nick wanted to touch up the photos from the party and send them to Bret before he started working on the nature pictures for his magazine client. Robbie, who had called her insurance agent on the beach, waited to see what her accident would do to her premiums. She already knew there was nothing from Nathan in her inbox because she'd checked on her phone while Nick had been pulling their bags from the car.

One look at her agent's email and Robbie's suspicions were confirmed. There was no way she was filing a claim. Because it had been a hit-and-run, there was no one for her to demand reparations from. Her bank account benefited more from selling her paid-off car for parts than trying to go through insurance.

Robbie was reminded, however, about the pending invitation sitting in her inbox. She'd forgotten to ask Nick his opinion, but when she glanced at him from across computer screens, he seemed so focused on the task at hand, she hated to interrupt him with more of her relationship issues. Besides, with his penchant for taking over things, she didn't want to give him the impression that she was open to more of his brand of "helping."

She reread the email for the tenth time, determined to wring every drop of meaning and nuance from each syllable. But, try as she might, dissecting a cookout invitation was nothing like analyzing *Lord of the Flies* in her third period European Literature class. She'd started and deleted five different responses, ranging from the simple, "I regret not being able to attend as I will be out of town," to the more complicated, "I regret not being able to attend as I will be out of town at my parents' anniversary party, and may possibly be there forever. I don't speak for Nathan, however, as, you may or may not have heard, we are no longer together. You will need to contact him directly regarding his availability that day."

"Crap," Nick said, shutting his computer. "Battery died."

Robbie looked up from her email quandary. "Just plug it in," she said, pointing to the outlet on the wall beside them.

"My cord is buried on the bottom of my pack," he said.

Robbie glanced at his behemoth orange camping pack. Whatever he had in there stretched the aching seams as far as they could go without busting. She imagined the pack exploding, firing dirt-stained clothes in every direction at the slightest provocation. Never mind trying to dig out the plug for the computer in the middle of a pizza joint.

"Can you use my computer?" she asked. She wasn't getting anything useful done anyway. Someone might as well be productive. "I don't have any photo software, but if you need a search engine or email?"

"You don't mind? It will only be a minute. I just need to get to my email and my online file server."

"Not at all. I'm done anyway. I'm going to use the washroom." Robbie handed Nick her laptop and excused herself. She'd stared at Beth's email long enough she had it memorized.

When she returned to the table, Nick sat with her laptop closed in front of him, and his hat pulled low over his brow. "Everything okay? Get the pictures sent off?" she asked.

"Yep. All done." Nick rose from the table, bumping it with his knee and almost causing a glass of water to topple over the side. He had a hard time shoving his dead laptop into his bag and then wrestled with the zipper to get it close. "We should drop our bags off at the inn and see about getting a ride to the dealership."

Robbie scooped up her computer and shoved it back in her bag while glaring at Nick from the corner of her eye. He was acting weird. He seemed jumpy. Nervous. He didn't even wait for her, pushing his way out of the restaurant while Robbie was still gathering her things.

Robbie broke into a jog to catch up to him, her duffel bag banging against her legs. He was already on the sidewalk and heading toward the inn by the time she came up beside him, panting. "Why are you being so weird? Did something happen while I was in the bathroom?"

It wasn't like he stumbled on her hidden porn collection on her computer—if she had one—or anything else so off-putting he had to race to get away from her. Finally, taking pity on her short legs and strained lungs, Nick slowed down and let her catch her breath.

"I'm not being weird. Am I?"

"Yes. Totally weird. What happened? Did I say something or do something wrong?"

Nick's eyes widened. "No, not at all." He set his pack on the ground and rubbed the back of his neck. "I got a text from my client, and they're anxious to get the lake pictures, so I'm on a pretty tight deadline. I guess I'm just stressed."

"Well, let's get you a room so you can dig out your power cord and get to work," Robbie said, trying to lift Nick's pack. The thing had to weigh more than her. She didn't know how he walked through forests carrying it on his back without causing some severe damage.

He took the pack from her and eased it onto his shoulder as though it weighed nothing more than a sack of pillows, and Robbie found herself wondering if he could lift her that easily. Feeling her cheeks burn, she hurried ahead before he could see her thoughts written across her reddened face.

"Unfortunately, we don't have both rooms available any longer," the innkeeper informed them as they stood in the lobby, bags in hand. "We have one of the rooms if you'd like to share."

Robbie shifted from one foot to the other. The image of Nick scooping her up like his backpack still dancing in her head. "Are there any other motels near here? Like walking distance?" she asked.

"No, ma'am," the innkeeper said, barely looking in her direction. There was something different than the day before about his smile, too. "The next closest one is out on Route 43. About seventeen miles from here."

"I slept in the woods for almost a whole year," Nick said. "I can bunker down anywhere."

Robbie stopped her nervous fidgeting. She couldn't allow Nick to sleep on the ground somewhere while she stayed in the suite all by herself. The room was easily large enough for two people.

"That's silly," Robbie said and turned to the innkeeper. "We'll share. Thank you."

Robbie unlocked the door to the same room she'd had the night before. The bed had been made, and there was a fresh scent in the air. She stowed her bags in the closet and grabbed her purse. "I'll leave you alone to get some work done," she said. "I'm going to the dealership."

"You don't have to go by yourself. I'll go with," Nick said, one arm deep into the orange pack. It was already late afternoon, so if Nick wanted to make some headway on his photos, he didn't need her in the background distracting him. Her future employment might be in question, but she didn't want to put Nick in the same position.

"I'm going to get this mess taken care of. You get some work done since you can't work and drive at the same time tomorrow. I'll text you in a bit. If you're hungry, I can stop somewhere and pick up some food on the way back."

"Are you sure?" he asked, plugging in his laptop and popping his camera's memory card into its slot.

"Totally. I think I need to do this by myself." She'd bought the Jeep by herself. It seemed fitting that she said good-bye to it by herself, especially if she cried like she suspected she might. Don't make a scene, Robbie heard Mrs. Chin say in her head. Nick didn't need to see her blubber like an idiot over a car. "I'll see you in a bit." She turned to leave but paused when he called her name.

"Thanks for understanding," he said, tossing his baseball cap on the sofa and brushing his hair back from his eyes.

Robbie smiled. "Get to work. I don't care how good a

photographer you are—those pictures won't edit themselves."

SIXTEEN

Robbie returned to Poppy Grove Inn four hours later carrying greasy burger bags and two slices of apple pie, her favorite childhood dessert. Nick rose from the small desk at the window when she walked in and relieved her of her cargo. "You've been gone for a while," he said, the corners of his mouth turned down. "I thought you were going to check in."

"Yeah, sorry," Robbie said. "Good news—well, sort of, more like Sam good news—I got a new car. It's all gassed up, and I picked up my stuff from the auto shop so we can leave first thing in the morning. Then I noticed they were showing *Pretty in Pink* at the theater. It's been years since I've seen it, so I caught the afternoon show. By the time the movie ended, I was starving and figured you would be, too." Robbie paused and took a breath, noticing Nick's furrowed brow. "You weren't worried, were you?"

"No," he said. "Maybe. I mean, you're walking around a strange town by yourself."

"You could have called or something, too." Robbie emptied the contents of the bags on the small table by the sofa. Though she was sorry he'd worried, she wasn't going to let that damper her lightened mood. In addition to never eating in a restaurant alone, she'd also never been to the movies alone. Robbie had left the theater victorious—something had gone right that day, and she'd thought cheeseburgers and pie made a fitting celebration. Though, it was nice to know *someone* worried about her well-being. Nathan didn't seem to care to know where she was or who she was with.

"You're right," Nick said, picking up a burger and inspecting it. "But I didn't want you to think I was stalking you or, you know, trying to tell you what to do."

Robbie handed him a can of soda from the bag, choosing to ignore the latter comment. Molly Ringwald had helped her move past that part of her morning with her delightful resolve to stay exactly who she was— homemade prom dress and all. "You used to follow Ivy and me around for hours, hiding behind trees and rocks, while we pretended we couldn't see you, and now you're worried about being a stalker?"

"I was just a kid then," he said.

Robbie noticed they were somehow a step closer to each other. Had he moved, or had she? She didn't remember taking that step, but she hadn't seen him do it either.

"I'm not little Ernie anymore." He took the can from her hand, his fingertips brushing hers. "Should we go take a look at your new car?"

Robbie swallowed hard. He wasn't little Ernie, but he was still Ivy's little brother. Stepping away, she diverted her attention back to the food and scrunched her nose. "How about you let it be a surprise in the morning? Did you get a lot of work done?"

"Fine. We'll do it your way," he said, picking up a burger. "Though now I'm sufficiently curious. And, yes, I did get a lot done. Thanks," he said, plopping down on the sofa and turning on the television. "What time do you want to head out of here tomorrow? I was thinking to hit the road by six. What do you think?"

Robbie sat as far from him on the small couch, love seat really, as she could manage to avoid any more accidental body part brushing. "You just can't wait to see my sweet new ride. But six sounds good. Be careful you don't spill anything on my bed."

"You're not sleeping on the sofa," Nick said, wiping the grease off his hands. "You take the bed."

Robbie sized up the six-foot-plus man and the four-foot couch. "There's no way you'll fit on this thing. I'd be much more comfortable on this than you. Go ahead and take the bed."

"I knew you would argue with me. You never go down without a fight."

"I'm not arguing. It's just logical. And, what do you mean I don't go down without a fight?"

Nick took a large swig of his soda then wiped his mouth. "All those years growing up, any time anyone questioned you or tried to tell you what they thought you should be doing, you always shot them down. I remember you and Ivy took me to the park, and that kid from down the street, John O'Brien, started giving you a hard time. He was saying something about you being stupid."

"Oh, yeah. He was mad because we beat him in tetherball."

"He was getting louder, and all these other kids started gathering around. And then he said, 'You're so stupid, it was probably your grandfather who bombed Pearl Harbor.' Now, we had just learned about it in school, so I was shocked at the accusation. But you stood there, calm and quiet while he ranted. Then finally, you said, 'First, my grandfather was eight when that happened. Second, we're Chinese, not Japanese. If you're going to make racist comments, at least make sure they're about the right group of people.' And then you walked away." He chuckled and shook his head. "You always knew who you were and spoke your mind."

"You remember that?" Robbie set her dinner on the table and leaned back. "That's how you saw me?"

"Robbie Chin. The girl who didn't take anyone's crap," he said, nodding and taking a huge bite of his burger.

Robbie stared at the back of his head while he ate. He had to have been about ten when that incident at the park happened, and it stuck with him all these years later? Funny how someone else's perception of her could be so different from her own. She'd just been trying to survive another day with another bully. She hadn't been trying to make a statement or set an example. And she definitely didn't see herself as the girl who knew who she was. Then or now.

"What's the matter?" Nick asked, pausing in his meal, and turning to look over his shoulder at Robbie who still sat staring.

"I just don't see myself as anything resembling what you described," Robbie said. "If anything, I'm the opposite. I never knew who I was supposed to be. I never felt at home in my skin. Everyone else was one thing or the other. I was both and neither at the same time. No one knew what bucket to put me in, including me. What you saw was an illusion."

"I don't believe that."

"Well, it's true. I never felt comfortable until I met Nathan. It was like someone finally understood. I didn't have to explain things to him. He got it. He got me."

"Are you telling me that girl I grew up seeing every single day of my life wasn't the real you? That you weren't the real you until Nathan Tang came along?"

"That's what I'm telling you," Robbie said, leaning forward again.

"I call bullshit," Nick said, crumpling his burger wrapper and launching it across the room to the garbage can next to the desk. "I'm not denying you put up with a ton of crap. I witnessed it. But you can't tell me the Robbie I remember, the one who spent countless hours in my home with my sister, never felt comfortable there. I refuse to believe the Robbie who returned my favorite toy to me after Ivy and I had one of our fights—"

"You left it in my coat."

"Of course, I did," Nick said. "I wanted you to come to our house and ask to see me and not Ivy. For once, I wanted you to ask for me."

"To get back at Ivy?"

"No," he said, leaning toward her so his shoulder grazed hers despite her best efforts to maintain space between them. "Because I wanted to see you. I always wanted to see you." He paused, then quickly cleared his throat. "You were also the one who told a bunch of senior football players to leave the scrawny, moppy-headed freshman alone my first week of high school."

"They were giving me a hard time, and I knew they had their sights set on you loser freshmen, too. I was trying to kill two birds with one stone."

"And weren't you also the one, who although you were a student at the time, gave me way too generous of a graduation gift when I finished high school?"

"Ivy told me you were saving up for a new camera for college. I was tutoring at the time; I had extra pocket money."

"Make all the excuses you want," Nick said, leaning back and throwing his arm over the back of the sofa. "That was the real Robinson Chin. And none of those things had anything to do with Dr. Nathan Tang."

Robbie sighed. "Yeah, well, things sure felt easier with him."

"So people magically stopped asking about your background and making ignorant remarks because you were dating him?"

"No," Robbie said. "Those never stop. But I didn't feel like I owed them an answer anymore."

"Why not?"

Robbie shrugged. She thought about all the times she'd been with Nathan, and they'd faced all the questions about their backgrounds. Nathan had always taken the lead, answering question after question with a patience and politeness Robbie never had. "I guess because Nathan usually answered for us." Robbie saw the skepticism Nick tried to hide. "It's tiring, you know, having to justify your existence and explain how you came into this world, how your parents could have possibly met. Do you know there was a girl in college who called me a liar? She said I couldn't possibly be half Italian because my last name was Chin. And she was pre-med! I had to explain how it took two people to procreate."

Nick snickered. "I didn't know people were that dumb."

"You have no idea."

Robbie sipped her soda and propped her feet up on the table as a reality dating television show started. They each fell silent while the opening credits played. Then, as a bouncy scantily clad woman came on screen, Robbie turned her head and said, "Hey, are you going to tell me what happened on the beach?"

Nick smiled and reached for his slice of apple pie. "I told you. I'll tell you in the car. Hey, you know what this pie reminds me of?"

Robbie narrowed her eyes and scrunched her nose, going along with his topic change. They had a long day of driving ahead of them. It might be better to save the entertainment until then. "DeLucca's Bakery back home."

"Exactly," he said while shoving an overflowing forkful in his mouth.

"It's my favorite. Whenever I had a bad day as a kid, my mom would get me a slice. I can't have a proper crisis without apple pie now. It's my number one comfort food."

After the show ended, Nick decided to work some more while Robbie crawled into bed with her laptop. Opening her computer, she stared at the still unanswered email from Beth Rochelle. Watching Nick across the room over the top of her screen, she debated bringing Nick into her decision-making. They seemed to have reached a place of understanding. There was still a chance Nick would overstep, but there was at least an equal chance he wouldn't now. "Hey, Nick, can I ask you something?"

"Mm-hmm," he mumbled, clicking away on his keyboard.

"I got an email from one of Nathan's coworker's wives. It's an invitation for both of us to a cookout this weekend. Should I forward it to Nathan? Reply just for me? Tell her to ask him herself? I mean, if she sent me the email, obviously she doesn't know about our temporary split, so he must not have told anyone. That's some sort of sign, isn't it?"

Nick stiffened in his chair but didn't turn to look at her. "Sign of what?"

"That he isn't ready to be broken up for real?"

"Honestly, Robbie, I don't know the guy, so I haven't a clue what it means to him."

Robbie slumped against the headboard with a grunt. It wasn't the enthusiastic encouragement she'd hoped for.

"Is this woman someone you would stay friends with if the breakup turns out to be permanent?"

The only times Robbie saw Beth Rochelle was with Nathan, either as part of a couple outing or a hospital function. Their only interaction outside those events involved email invitations and an occasional social media post, despite their pledge years ago to have each other's backs. "No, probably not."

"Then, I would just tell her you're out of town and leave it at that."

Robbie considered his advice. It sounded reasonable enough, but his body language was so stiff, almost like he had to force himself to remain calm. It was the posture of a student caught cheating but trying to deny it. She typed out a quick reply to Beth, as Nick suggested, but didn't leave it at that. Instead, she hit forward and sent the invitation to Nathan.

It took only five minutes before she received a direct message back from him.

"You're alive?" Nathan typed. Did he sound pleased at the thought, or annoyed?

Robbie took a deep breath and glanced at Nick across the room; he had gone back to editing a new batch of pictures. "Yes, I'm alive. And I see you are, too."

"Where are you?"

"On my way to San Francisco." She purposely didn't use the word *home*. She didn't want to give Nathan the impression that she thought of anywhere other than with him as home. Just in case. "For my parents' anniversary party."

"Right. I almost forgot."

The blood rushed through Robbie's veins, pounding in her temples. How could he forget? She'd been talking about it for months. She'd bought plane tickets, reminded him to take the weekend off work, and she'd even brought his suit to the cleaners in preparation for the event.

"I'm going to be out of town," he added.

Robbie pressed her lips together to keep from squealing and

checked to make sure Nick remained engrossed with his project. Nathan was going to be out of town because he'd be in San Francisco, making up with her. "Out of town?" she typed with shaking hands.

"Vegas. There's a conference this weekend. Starts Thursday," Nathan replied.

Robbie's racing heart skidded to a stop. A conference? She didn't remember him ever talking about a conference. How long had he been planning on going to Vegas? He was supposed to be heading back to San Francisco with her for her parents' party. They'd just broken up three days ago. Didn't conference registration and preparation take longer than three days? Her face burned. She knew why she hadn't heard about this conference before, but she didn't want to say it. If she said it, it would be true. And it couldn't be true.

"When did you decide on going to this conference?" She stared at the messenger window waiting for a reply that was taking too long in coming. He didn't want to say it, either.

"Eight weeks ago. I put a deposit down."

Eight weeks? He'd known he'd be going to Vegas the weekend before of her parents' party for eight weeks and hadn't said one word to her? He knew he couldn't take off two weekends in a row, and he'd let her make plans and talk about itineraries, all the while knowing none of it was going to happen. He'd never had any intention of going home with her. Had this been what their entire relationship had been? Robbie making plans for the two of them while Nathan had always known they weren't going to happen?

"When did you decide you wanted to break up?" The words came out before she could stop them, but they were in black and white now, staring up at her from her computer screen, and there was no taking them back.

Nick's phone vibrated on the desk next to him. He answered with a smooth "Nick Wolfe" and a half smile to Robbie. She forced herself to smile back so he wouldn't suspect she was sitting there getting her heart ripped out again after he'd warned her to leave it alone.

"About the same time," Nathan finally replied.

In her heart, Robbie had known that was the answer. How could it be anything different? But the truth of it still knocked the breath from her lungs. Nick was talking faster now, and he'd started pacing, but Robbie was too preoccupied with her chest imploding to register anything he said. He must have mistaken her anguish for annoyance because he gave a small wave and walked into the hall to finish his phone call.

"Why didn't you say anything earlier? Why didn't you tell me you were unhappy?" Robbie asked when the door closed behind Nick. "We could've talked about it."

"There was nothing really to talk about," Nathan answered. "It wasn't like you did something. It was just . . ."

"Just me," Robbie finished for him.

"Not just you. Me, too. We weren't the same people we used to be. We used to have fun."

Robbie chuckled, though it wasn't a humorous moment by any means. "I wanted to do new things. I wanted to have fun with you. You were always too busy and tired when you got home. I thought asking you to do something with me would be too much." Her stomach hardened. "What else?" Robbie asked. Now that this conversation had started, she was hungry for more. She wouldn't be satisfied until she squeezed every last drop of honesty from him.

"It was too easy," he said. "You always made it too easy to get my way."

"So, you wanted me to bitch and complain?" This had to be a first.

"Not all the time. But maybe once in a while put up a little fight, yeah."

What was it Nick had said earlier about the real Robbie? That she'd never gone down without a fight? Nathan seemed to think she hadn't fought enough. And all this time, Robbie had thought that was a good thing, something other couples had been envious of. She never in a million years would have guessed their problem had been they hadn't fought enough.

Nick came back into the room, rubbing the back of his neck. Robbie glanced up at him and angled the computer screen away from his view when he stopped by the side of the bed.

"Can I ask you a favor now?" Nick asked, shoving the phone back in his pocket.

She hadn't thought of a response yet for Nathan, but she knew she had to make it quick if they were going to keep talking. If she waited too long, he would assume the conversation was over, and she wasn't ready to end it like this. "Sure," she said, willing to agree to anything as long as it was fast.

"Do you mind if we stop in Vegas on the way? A client of mine is pretty adamant about meeting up. It's a little over thirty hours from here, but I can do most of the driving. I figure we can get there sometime Wednesday night?"

"Vegas?" Robbie asked, a glimmer of hope returning. "So we'd be there Thursday?"

"Yeah," Nick said. "It will only be another nine hours or so to San Francisco from there—"

"Let's do it," Robbie said. This was perfect. Exactly what she needed. It wouldn't be difficult to track down what conference Nathan was attending. She could surprise him. Show him she still knew how to have fun and be spontaneous. Maybe he'd get a little mad. Even better. They could have that fight he'd been itching for.

"Are you sure? You wouldn't get to Mrs. Chin's until Friday night then," Nick said.

True. But if there were a chance she'd be arriving still known as Dr. Nathan Tang's girlfriend, she was taking it. Besides, her parents weren't expecting her for another week. "Just another adventure, right? We'll be home in plenty of time for the party." She cringed at the use of the word *home* slipping out.

Nick beamed at her. "There's the Robbie I've been looking for!"

Robbie watched him return to his work with a lightness in his movements. She had to tell Nick about her plan. It was only fair. It didn't change anything, though. He got to go to Vegas and meet his client with or without her plan. She glanced at the last message from Nathan, still unanswered as Nick hummed to himself at the desk, so happy and peaceful at that moment, lost in his work, doing the thing he'd been passionate about for years. It would be a shame to interrupt him while he was clearly in his groove. They had thirty hours in the car to look forward to. She'd tell him somewhere in Nebraska.

Another message popped up. "Good night, Robbie. Have a good trip."

See you soon, she thought. "You, too."

SEVENTEEN

Two years ago . . .

"You're sure you can't make it home this year for Christmas?" Mrs. Chin asked for the third time in the same phone call.

Robbie pinched the bridge of her nose and held her breath until her lungs burned. How many times could she give the same answer? "Yes, Mom, I'm sure. Nathan is on-call this year."

"You can come home."

"And leave him to celebrate Christmas by himself?" Robbie was shocked Mrs. Chin would even suggest such a thing. Usually, Nathan's comfort was her primary concern.

"No, of course, you're right," Mrs. Chin said, returning to her normal self. "He shouldn't be alone at Christmas. It's right that you stay with him."

"Yeah, I mean, someone has to do the laundry, right?" Robbie clamped her mouth shut. She'd momentarily forgotten who she was talking to. A comment like that one, one that hinted at displeasure with her boyfriend, was not for Mrs. Chin's ears, because if Mrs. Chin suspected there was trouble in paradise, then—

"You two aren't fighting, are you? I heard a tone. Are you using that same tone when you talk to Nathan? He's not in the room, is he?" Mrs. Chin said.

"No, Mom. Nathan went to the gym. But he should be home any minute."

"What's with the tone of voice?"

"Nothing." Robbie couldn't keep the annoyance from her voice. With her aggravation at Nathan being compounded by her aggravation at Mrs. Chin knowing she felt this way, keeping it from spilling out was a herculean feat she was not prepared for. "It's just that we were supposed to go to my staff's Christmas party tomorrow. I RSVP'd and everything. And then today, Nathan comes home and tells me how the hospital staff threw together a holiday dinner at the same time, and he wants me to cancel my party to go to his."

"So?"

"So . . . we agreed to go to mine first. Weeks ago. And because someone at the hospital made a dinner reservation, last minute might I add, I have to cancel our already agreed upon plans?"

"It is the hospital, Robbie. It's his job."

Never had Robbie made as big of a mistake as she had when she'd decided to tell Mrs. Chin about her issue with Saint Nathan. "It's my job, too, Mother."

"Yes, I know, but it's not the same. He deals with life and death in a very high-pressure atmosphere. He needs to be able to rely and depend on his coworkers. And one way to build that type of trust is through social bonding. Plus, it wouldn't hurt for his superiors to get to know him better."

"He's been there for four years," Robbie said through tight lips. "They know him."

"Look, all I'm saying is that it's unfortunate they're both scheduled at the same time. But part of being a couple is doing what's best for the team. And if going to Nathan's dinner will help his career, in the long run, that will benefit you, too."

If they ever got married, she meant. Mrs. Chin used to be a lot more veiled in her attempts at pushing the issue, but over the last few months, she'd grown more aggressive. There was only one way to diffuse this situation before it got out of hand. "Okay, Mom. You're right. I'll talk to Nathan when he gets home."

"And remember to be nice. Don't use that tone."

"I don't have a tone." She did. "I'll talk to you in a few days. Tell Dad hi for me."

When Nathan arrived home, he dropped his gym bag at the door, blew Robbie a kiss, and went straight to the shower, like he did after every visit to the gym. Robbie used to think it was cute, the way he wanted to be clean and fresh smelling before interacting with her. Now, she saw it as a way to rub in how perfect he was compared to her, who was still wearing her yoga outfit from her class earlier in the day. To be fair, she hadn't sweat during class, and her workout clothes cost a fortune from one of those boutique places, so she was going to get as much use out of them as she could.

She waited for him in the kitchen, which she knew would be his next stop to make one of those nutrition shakes. Some days, she had it ready for him when he emerged from the bathroom. Not today.

"Hey, do you mind if we don't go out tonight? I've got the early shift in the morning, and then tomorrow night. . ." Nathan said, gathering his health drink supplies.

"That's fine," Robbie said. She'd lost the desire to go out when he'd dropped his news about the hospital party. "Can we talk about tomorrow?"

He paused, his hand holding a scoop of brown powder over the blender, "Sure. Everything okay?"

"Not really," Robbie said, wiping her hands on her thighs, trying to keep the lightness in her voice instead of the dreaded tone. "I was thinking, what if we do both? Have dinner with the hospital staff, and leave early to go to the school's party? They're not serving a full dinner, so if we arrived late, we could slide in for drinks and mingling. Best of both worlds."

Nathan furrowed his brow. "Isn't it rude to leave the dinner like that? A dine and dash?"

"We could explain the issue. People will understand. Holidays are busy for everyone."

Nathan's throaty grumble, the one he made when he was stuck with a difficult choice, grated on Robbie's nerves. She'd argued a perfectly logical point. This shouldn't be hard. Two parties. Split the evening. Plenty of people did it, especially during a heavy party season like Christmas.

"It's just that the restaurant is one of those nicer places with, like, seven courses," he said, dumping his scoop, then digging for another. "It could end up being a long dinner. I wouldn't want you worrying the whole time about when we'd be able to leave. And they may understand leaving after dinner but in the middle of it? And if we went to the school party first, we'd miss half the dinner."

Of course, he would have another equally logical argument—one that held slightly more weight.

He switched the blender on which offered enough camouflage for her sigh. They couldn't be rude. Not to a room full of people who could make or break Nathan's career. The school's party was much more informal: drinks and finger foods at a local bar, nothing fancy like the five-star steaks and lobster they were sure to have with the doctors.

"Beth will be there," Nathan said when the blending finished. "You like her."

With his back to her, he didn't see her curl her lip. At one time, the thought of seeing Beth would have been reason enough to go to a stuffy doctor party. When they'd first met, she'd been witty and engaging, talking to Robbie as though they'd been friends for ages. But after the first few social gatherings, their interactions, while still friendly, were not as warm or any deeper in bond. They were surface friends. Or friends by circumstance. Better than nothing friends.

"What do you want for dinner tonight?" Robbie asked. Mrs. Chin would be so happy.

EIGHTEEN

Robbie had set her alarm for five thirty in the morning. When she'd tiptoed into the bathroom without making a sound, Nick had still been snoring on the couch, his legs thrown up over the side. She emerged fifteen minutes later, planning to run across the street to the coffee shop to pick up road trip supplies. Her intentions were thwarted, however, when she found the sofa empty and the room devoid of any signs of life.

"Perfect timing," Nick said, coming back into the room carrying coffees and breakfast pastries.

"Hey," she said, combing her fingers through her damp hair. "I was going to do that. You messed up my plan. You didn't sneak a peek at the car, did you? I want to see your face when you see it for the first time."

"I didn't know there was a plan," Nick said, handing her a cup. "I'll leave the coffee-fetching to you tomorrow. How's that? And, no I didn't. How could I? I don't know which one it is."

"Alright, then," Robbie said, before taking a sip of her coffee. "Extra cream and three sugars?"

"That's what you ordered yesterday, right?"

"Man, you're good." Robbie was in charge of making the morning coffees with Nathan. He was strictly cream, no sugar. Had he ever brought her a coffee? Did he even know how she took it? "I'm pretty much ready to go. So, whenever you're ready, we can hit the road."

"Three minutes," he said, heading toward the bathroom behind her. "Do you need anything in here?"

"No," she said, turning to face him, then quickly looking away with her jaw hanging open. She hadn't expected him to be shirtless already. He'd set his breakfast down somewhere and had one hand on his belt buckle. "I'm good," Robbie squeaked, moving to the opposite corner of the room, pretending to search for something until she heard the bathroom door close, convincing herself the heat in her cheeks was from the steam from her coffee.

Opening the curtains, she gazed down at the town square. The mornings were getting brighter earlier now as the days stretched longer. Robbie liked this time of year best with the smell of spring and possibility in the air and the slow setting sun. She pulled her damp hair back into a braid, then finished packing her overnight bag. When Nick opened the bathroom door again three minutes later, Robbie was sitting by the window, bag zippered up, ready to go.

She kept her eyes diverted, just in case, until he stepped beside her, fully clothed. "Ready?"

"More than you know."

He reached for her overnight bag, and she let him. Grabbing her purse, and the bag of food he'd left on a chair next to the bathroom, she held the door for him as he carried the luggage.

"I can take my bag," she said half a flight down, reaching for the handle. It didn't seem right for him to keep toting her luggage across the country.

Nick stopped dead in his tracks, and Robbie stumbled to keep from running into him and tumbling them both down the rest of the flight. "I don't want to have this conversation every day," he said with an arched eyebrow. "Just let me carry the bag. It makes me feel good about myself."

Robbie smirked. "Well, if it helps your self-esteem."

"It does," he said, starting to walk again. "It really does."

Robbie sipped her coffee and studied the back of his head. "Not that you need any help in that area from what I can tell."

"What are you implying? That I'm full of myself?"

"Not at all. It's just that anybody who has supermodels hanging on his arm every week doesn't seem like the type who needs help with self-esteem issues."

"Robbie Chin, did you Google me?"

"I may have," Robbie said, joining Nick at the front desk. "You have quite the impressive circle of friends these days. A far cry from Scottie Lawson and that nose-picker Joey Something."

Nick chuckled. "Ah, well, Scottie, I still talk to, but we dropped the nose-picker years ago."

"Good decision-making." She paused and cleared her throat. "So, these supermodels. . ."

"Good morning," the innkeeper boomed, stepping out from a doorway behind the desk in the lobby. It was barely past six in the morning, but he was already in a full suit and tie. "Ready to check out?"

"Yes, thank you. How much for the night?"

The innkeeper's fingers danced in the air as though he were typing on an invisible keyboard. "One hundred fifty."

"Okay. One second," Robbie asked, digging in her purse for her wallet.

"No haggling?" he asked somewhat surprised.

Robbie looked from the innkeeper to a shrugging Nick. "Am I supposed to haggle?"

"Well, we haven't had much clientele like your people," he said as Nick stepped forward. "But the ones that I have had, they've always haggled. I've been practicing."

"You—" Nick started, but Robbie placed her hand on his arm and pressed her lips straight, knitting her brows together. Nick stopped talking but kept his fist clenched. Robbie gave him the car keys and motioned to the bags.

Finding her wallet, she quickly counted how much cash she had on her. "I thought your original price was fair for such a nice, large room for two," she said, slowly and deliberately counting out the bills. "But since you expected a negotiation, I'll give you one. Here is your payment. Seventy-five. Flat."

"That's not how a haggle works," the innkeeper argued. "The other Asians—"

"See, that's where you're mistaken," Robbie said, shoving the cash across the desk at him. "You're dealing with the Sicilian side now. My people don't negotiate. We tell you how it's going to be. End of story."

Robbie walked away from the discount-suited proprietor and met Nick out front on the sidewalk. With a tilt of her head, she led Nick to their new ride, now in too sour of a mood to enjoy his reaction.

"You got a lime green Ford Pinto?" Nick asked, shock emanating from every word. "And a wagon, no less?"

"It's one of the only cars I could pay for outright with the money they gave me that would hold my boxes. I didn't want to dip into my savings. I'm going to need it. This should get me through a year, I hope, while I save some more money and get back to someplace with a decent selection."

Nick placed their overnight bags into the backseat. "What year is it? 75?"

"It's 1974," Robbie said, banging on the hood of the car with her fist. "You should see the engine, though. Clean as a whistle."

"Pop it," Nick said, hopping from one foot to the other. "I want to see!"

Robbie shook her head but reached inside the car and pulled the lever anyway. He never was any good at hiding his enthusiasm. Nick whistled and ran his hand along the motor. "You're right. Looks brand new. It's like they put a Corvette's engine in here. Hand over the keys. Let's give this baby a whirl."

Although Nick's antics had lifted her mood some, Robbie felt him stealing glances at her until he found the entrance ramp to the highway. "You okay?" he finally asked as he merged into the traffic.

Robbie sank back in her seat and nodded. It had been a long while since she'd been that forceful with someone in public. Nathan would have laughed the guy off, made some joke and paid the full price, and she would have been thankful she didn't have to deal with it.

"Can I say something?" Nick asked. When Robbie nodded again, he said, "That. Was. Amazing. It was like watching you with those football players all over again."

"He was a jerk. He didn't deserve the one-fifty."

"Agreed."

Robbie stared out the window at the world passing by and waited for feelings of regret or shame to wash over her. "Just smile and ignore them," her mother would have told her. Mrs. Chin was the master of the old "smile and ignore" trick, at least while out in public. Behind closed doors was a different story. When no one but Robbie and her father were around to hear her, Mrs. Chin spent days lamenting about the store clerk who mistook her for Robbie's nanny. Robbie's father had asked Mrs. Chin once why she hadn't said anything, and Mrs. Chin had replied, "It's not worth it to make a scene."

Whenever her mother had heard of Robbie lashing out, she'd always tsk'd and hung her head as though Robbie had embarrassed her somehow. She remembered the look of relief on Mrs. Chin's face the first time she'd heard Nathan had handled a situation instead of Robbie. Not just relief, but pride.

"Ever been to Chicago?" Nick asked, pointing out her window hours later.

"Nope," Robbie said, watching the city's skyline roll by. "It's on my bucket list, though."

"If you thought Junior Bear's pizza was good, you gotta try authentic Chicago style," he said. "I'd take you for some now, but I'm afraid if we head into the city, we'll get stuck there."

"Bad traffic?"

"That, and you won't want to leave right away. The city sucks people in."

"We wouldn't want that," Robbie said with a grin. She definitely did not want that. She had a schedule to keep if she was going to find Nathan and win him back before arriving in San Francisco. "Next time," she said, then clamped her mouth shut. Why had she said that? It wasn't as though these cross-country road trips were going to be a regular occurrence between the two of them. When would there ever be a next time?

"Next time it is," he said with a glance to the Second City. "I'm gonna hold you to it."

"Sure. Just let me know when you have time between your jet-setting and your model escorting."

Nick swung the car onto an exit lane and cast her a curious glance. "This model thing really bothers you, doesn't it?"

"What?" Yes. "No." It shouldn't, but it did. Robbie chalked it up to latent feelings of protectiveness of the little boy she'd watched grow up, like he was that kid climbing too high on the monkey bars, and it was her job to make sure he didn't slip and fall. At least, that was what she told herself.

"If it makes you feel better, I wasn't escorting them. I was hired to take their picture, and someone snapped a behind-the-scenes photo with their phone and posted it. Those women wouldn't even remember me."

"They wouldn't remember the photographer that keeps them famous?"

"Okay," he conceded. "They'd remember me, but for nothing more than the person behind the camera." Nick pulled into the parking lot for a restaurant boasting the Best Burgers in Illinois. "It's not pizza, but this will do for now."

Seated across from Nick in the booth with cracked leather seats and a checkerboard tablecloth, Robbie watched his eyes roam over the menu, oblivious to her deception. She still hadn't confessed her reasons for being so obliging about the Vegas addition to the trip. Here he was, chatting away about the hundred different burger toppings, grateful to her for being so understanding about his work, when she had been planning on trying to manipulate him for her own gain the whole time.

"Nick," she blurted. She had to get it out before the waitress came to take their order. "I have to tell you something."

"What's up?" he asked.

"The reason I agreed to stop in Vegas was because Nathan will be there. He's going to a medical conference this weekend." Robbie held her breath and glued her eyes to the menu.

"How did you find this out?"

"I forwarded him the email invitation, and he messaged me back, and we chatted," she said, keeping her eyes on the laminated page.

"What's your plan, exactly?"

Robbie didn't know why she'd expected him to be mad at her. He still got what he wanted—a trip to Vegas. And, honestly, what did he care what she did with her personal life? Yet, when his voice sounded more curious than irked, she couldn't help but feel a little annoyed herself.

"Find him. Talk to him. Get some answers." Robbie leaned back in her seat and crossed her arms. The waitress arrived and took their orders—burgers for both. Robbie ordered hers with mushrooms and avocado so she could at least tell herself later she'd had some vegetables. "It all happened so fast," Robbie continued when the waitress walked away. "I never really said anything when it happened."

"So, it's closure you want?"

No. Maybe? "Yes. Closure."

Nick fiddled with the edge of the tablecloth. "Want to know what happened on the beach?"

That was it? No more questions? "Okay," Robbie said, relieved she wouldn't have to explain herself further, mainly because she didn't have any rational thoughts to share. She'd been impulsive and desperate. She knew that and was embarrassed about it. Having to detail her shame for him was too much to deal with.

"We walked about a hundred yards down the beach," he said. "And there was this cool rock outcropping I wanted to take a picture of. So, I went over to it and was testing the light, and adjusting the composition, and . . ."

Robbie raised an eyebrow.

"Too much. Alright," he said. "So, I was busy getting ready to take some pictures."

"Better."

"Next thing I know, one of the girls is screaming. And I mean, screeching her head off screaming. I stop what I'm doing and run around to where the rest of the girls are standing another thirty yards or so away. And they're watching this one scream like someone's chopping off her leg."

Robbie leaned forward, eager to hear what had caused all the dramatics. Shark attack in a lake? Piranhas? A giant snake maybe? "And?" The waitress arrived with the burgers and placed them on the table with a thud.

"And nothing," Nick said, throwing his hands in the air when she left. "She was literally standing there screaming. And when I asked if something was wrong, you know what her reply was?"

"What?"

"She said, 'I just wanted to see you running to my side.'"

Robbie curled her lip and crinkled her nose. "That's it? She just wanted attention?"

"That's it," he said. "By the time everyone calmed down, and I went back to the rocks, the light was all off, and I missed my chance at getting a phenomenal photo."

"That sucks."

"Yes, it did. But, now I needed to get that picture because I wasn't going to walk all that way listening to their incessant chatter about Zac Efron, or whoever, and not get my picture. So, I had to sit and wait for the sun to move out of its direct overhead position, which was why it took so long to get back to you."

Robbie laughed. "I don't understand why you couldn't tell me that yesterday."

Nick shrugged, a slight blush creeping up his neck and into his cheeks. "Didn't want you to think I was full of myself."

"I'm not blind. I see how women react to you," Robbie said.

"And how do they react?" As if he didn't already know.

"They want your approval." Robbie glanced over her shoulder to where their waitress stood chatting with the other servers, stealing bashful looks at her lunch partner. "See? Even the waitresses can't stop hoping you'll smile at them. I could hardly blame them for trying."

"You can't?" he asked, smirking behind his plastic cup of soda. "Are you saying you think I'm attractive?"

Robbie felt the heat creep up her face again, probably turning it redder than the bottled barbecue sauce sitting on the table. Robbie may not get sunburned, but she held the Olympic record for reddest face when flushed. "That's not what I meant."

"So you think I'm ugly?"

"I didn't say that, either." Tiny beads of sweat formed on the back of her neck. Why did he have to read into things so much?

His eyebrows shot halfway up his forehead, his eyes twinkling with mischief. "Which one is it? Or are you calling me fat?"

Robbie narrowed her eyes at him, then tossed her balled-up napkin at his head. "Alright, cut it out, *Ernie*."

"You make it way too easy, you know?"

"So I've been told." That seemed to be the theme lately. Nathan didn't want things that easy. He wanted a little drama, some push back. If he wished for confrontation, he'd get it in Vegas.

"Nathan, again?" Nick asked, motioning for the bill.

"Just something he said last night about how I made things too easy for him."

Nick visibly squirmed in his seat and fumbled with his wallet, almost dropping it in what was left of his home-cut fries. He was acting weird again. "What's going on with you?" Robbie asked.

The waitress dropped the bill on the table, lingering long enough to catch Nick's eye. Robbie gave him a pointed look as he flashed her his pearly whites, sending her away with a wide, satisfied smile.

Nick emptied the contents of his pocket—a wad of cash, a pack of gum, and his phone—on the table. As he sorted through the bills, his phone lit up. Again. He glanced at the caller ID, furrowed his brow, and returned to his money.

"You gonna get that?" Robbie asked, pointing to his phone. Three days with him, and she'd only seen him on the phone once, despite the persistent ringing. She was half a breath away from snatching it up and answering it herself to get it to stop taunting her.

"It's not important," he said, shoving the phone back in his pocket. Nick slid out from the booth without looking at her. "Lunch is on me, ready?"

"You paid for breakfast." She found it doubtful that someone as successful as he seemed to be would have gotten that way by ignoring phone calls. Which had to mean—those weren't business calls he ignored.

"You got the gas," he said moving toward the register. "And the car. And the room."

Robbie gathered her belongings and hurried to catch up. The subject of Nathan Tang wasn't the only thing Nick Wolfe got weird about. If Nick liked the old Robbie, the won't-go-down-without-a-fight girl, he was going to love what came next.

NINETEEN

Nick Wolfe—the slippery little devil—successfully evaded the topic of
Dr. Nathan Tang and the mysterious phone calls for the next hour. First
with a stop at the gas station, and then with the fortuitous timing of a
phone call from his sister, who after their conversation, sent a text to
Robbie asking why her little brother had become so talkative all of a
sudden.

"He's avoiding things," Robbie replied to Ivy, shifting in her seat to
face him .

"Enough stalling," she said. "Why are you so weird about Nathan?"

"I'm not."

"Yes, you are," Robbie said, jabbing her finger in his shoulder.
"Every time I mention him, you get all clumsy and awkward. I teach
teenagers. I know what guilt looks like."

Nick sighed, snatched the baseball cap from his head, and tossed it
into the backseat. "Promise you won't get mad."

Warning bells sounded in her head. Nothing good came after a
preemptive no anger promise. He might as well have asked her if she

wanted the good news or bad news first. "I can't promise that. What?"

He scrunched up his nose and tightened his grip on the wheel. "I may have done something when I borrowed your computer."

"And what is that?" Her fingernails dug into her palms as she braced herself for the worst. Though, what that could be, she couldn't begin to imagine.

"When you went to the bathroom, a message popped up from Nathan. He asked what you were doing and if you wanted to talk."

Robbie's stomach twisted. Nathan had contacted her. He'd reached out first, before the email, all on his own. "What did you do?" she asked. Nick kept his eyes forward and his hands at ten and two, but his jaw twitched. He had done something. He didn't just ignore the message and not tell her. He *did* something. "Tell me, Wolfe. What did you do?"

"I sent him a picture of you from the party. You were talking with a group of Holly's friends, and you were laughing and having a good time. It's a good picture."

Okay. Maybe it wasn't as bad as Robbie had thought. She had sort of wished Nathan could have seen her that night, and now he had. Nick's jaw twitched again, and she knew he wasn't done. "And?"

"I may have captioned it 'me without you.'"

Robbie wondered how to tell if she was having a heart attack. She should look that up, sooner rather than later, because whatever was going on in her chest was not healthy. "You did what?"

"I—"

"Yeah, yeah, yeah. I heard you." She clutched the door handle and pressed a hand to her sternum. "Why would you do that? You knew I was waiting to hear from him. Not only did you not tell me, but you replied in my name like *that?*"

"It may not be as bad as you think."

"How can it not be?" Good news. Bad news.

"He messaged you last night, didn't he? If anything, I think I helped."

Whatever newfangled dictionary Nick used to define the word *help* needed to be burned. "How do you figure?"

"Don't hit me," Nick said, glancing at her.

Robbie hadn't realized she had a fist raised in the air ready to strike until he pointed at it. She lowered her hand and took a steadying breath. "Go ahead."

"It's like the girl on the beach. You don't want to appear desperate. And didn't he say you made things too easy? If anything, my reply made him stop and think."

Robbie crossed her arms and faced the window. Her right leg bounced with pent-up aggravation. He was right about Nathan, but what he'd done was wrong, regardless of whether it worked to her advantage. She wasn't about to let him off the hook on a mere technicality—a *lucky* technicality. He'd had no way of knowing the repercussions of his actions at the time. He'd taken a gamble, and it had worked out in his favor, but he didn't need to know that now.

"Robbie," he said, his voice tentative.

She didn't look away from the window. "Not now. I'm not ready."

"Fair enough," he said, and then fell silent.

Robbie leaned her head against the window and watched the world buzz by. After stewing for a while, she decided she needed a second opinion. She picked up her phone and texted Ivy. "Am I too easy on Nathan?"

Not even a full twenty seconds passed before Ivy responded. "Yes."

Robbie groaned.

"What's wrong?" Nick asked, the first words he'd spoken in almost two hours.

"Nothing." Returning her gaze to the window, she chewed on her bottom lip, contemplating and mapping out the last six years of her life. Where had she changed? Nick insisted that the real Robbie fought for herself, but Nathan claimed she hadn't fought enough. Somewhere on the roadmap of her life, she'd veered off one path and started down another. Had it been before Nathan? During? But the bigger question than that was—did she want to go back? Could she even find her way if she wanted to?

Before she'd met Nathan, and after the fiasco of a boyfriend, Josh, there'd been Andrew Dillon. She'd met Andrew the first week of her freshman year at college. He was a year older and wiser, and Robbie had thought she'd struck gold. Andrew had that type of open personality that naturally drew people in. He was magnetic. She'd always thought that Andrew could walk into a room of fifty strangers and leave with fifty new best friends.

When she'd brought Andrew home to meet her parents one weekend, Mrs. Chin had smiled knowingly at Robbie, and at the first chance she'd gotten, she'd pulled her daughter aside and whispered, "Don't blow this. He's a good one." Robbie still remembered the expression on her mother's face, shocked and disappointed, when she'd walked in on a disagreement Robbie and Andrew had been having. Later that night, her mother had advised her to "not be so emotional. It's what he expects from a good Chinese girl."

"And the Italian in me, Mom?" Robbie had asked. "Maybe he expects that part of me."

Her mother had scoffed. "No one expects that from you. You look like your father."

Robbie marveled over the way her mother could turn on and off her prejudices with a snap of her fingers. If anyone else had told Robbie to "be more Chinese," Mrs. Chin would have shaken her fist at the cruelty of a world that would dare to pigeon-hole her daughter. But, put a prospective husband on the line, and she did everything short of wrapping Robbie in an embroidered cheongsam and preparing a tea ceremony.

Things with Andrew hadn't lasted long after that weekend. Every time Robbie had looked at him, all she'd been able to think of was her mother's words of wisdom, which had had the opposite desired effect. Robbie had found herself growing more hostile toward any suggestion or idea Andrew had voiced. She'd searched for any little reason to start a fight. Nothing the poor guy had done had been right. After a few weeks, he'd given up and ended things with Robbie. The week after, she'd seen him at a party with a new girl on his arm—one who had fawned over him and went along with anything he'd said.

Robbie supposed that had been the first turn. When Nathan had come along, his near perfection had enthralled her—his attractiveness, confidence, his fierce intelligence—so that she'd been scared to lose him. She hadn't wanted to give him a chance to see the bad in her. The messed-up lost girl who'd never known where she'd belonged. She hadn't wanted to fight anymore. Not with people giving her the side-eye. Not with him.

The sun had set while Robbie had been mapping out her failed relationships, and her stomach ached from lack of dinner. She swore she heard Nick's grumble, as well, but he wasn't going to break first. She'd asked to be left alone, and that was what he was doing.

"Why don't we stop for dinner?" Robbie said, her voice squeaking from hours of misuse. "Before these roadside stops get too sketchy. I know we've got a couple more hours before we hit Lexington, Nebraska, but we should fuel up for the last push."

"Best thing I've heard all day," Nick said. "Keep an eye on the signs. Let me know when you find something that sounds good."

They drove a few more miles as Robbie scanned the exit signs for something other than the typical fast food chains.

"There," Nick announced, easing the car off the highway.

"Where are you going? I didn't see anything."

"Trust me," he said. "You can't come to Nebraska without trying the Rocky Mountain Oysters."

They pulled up to what looked like an old miner's cabin. The weathered gray plank siding looked like it would blow away with a strong enough gust. The roof had lost a few shingles, and the shutters were chipped and warped. But the smell of the food wafting from the open front door had Robbie salivating before her foot hit the first splintered step leading up to the porch.

As neglected as the outside appeared to be, Robbie was pleasantly surprised to find the interior of the restaurant clean and updated, leading her to believe the exterior was all part of their marketing ploy. And it was well done. If Nick hadn't been with her, she would have dismissed the place as a rundown antique.

They were seated by the window, and Robbie settled herself without glancing at Nick once. She was hungry. She wasn't ready to give in yet.

Nick ordered for them both, two house specials, which turned out to be a large platter of the oysters to split between them, a side of coleslaw, and a couple biscuits. Robbie either stared out the window or played with her fingernails while Nick scrolled through his phone until the food arrived.

Scrunching her nose, she eyed the misshapen breaded patties in front of her. Nick helped himself and dug in while Robbie poked at one with her fork.

"Go ahead," Nick said. "Give it a try."

Furrowing her brow, she placed one oyster on her plate and cut into it. "What kind of oysters are these?" She'd never seen them this size and shape before.

"They're really good," he said, motioning to the red cocktail sauce for dipping.

Robbie took out her phone and opened the web browser. The glint in Nick's eye was an indication he was withholding information from her again. She didn't appreciate the first round of his nondisclosure, and she didn't trust this one now.

"What are you doing?" he asked.

"Looking for some information," she said, scanning an article on Rocky Mountain Oyster preparation. "Eew. Are you serious? You want me to eat that? I'll pass." She raised her hand in the air to get the waitress's attention. "They're all yours."

"You're not even going to try them?"

The waitress joined them with a sour expression on her face. "What can I do for you?"

"I was wondering if I could order a garden salad. Ranch dressing," Robbie said with as pleasant a smile as she could muster after seeing some graphic pictures accompanying the article.

The waitress eyed the uneaten patty on her plate. "Is there something wrong with the oysters?"

"Wrong? No. They're just not my cup of tea."

Nick slid two more on his plate with a grin. "More for me."

The waitress snorted and turned to walk away. "And you people eat dogs."

Nick's fork clattered against his plate as Robbie swung her gaze to meet his. It was as though someone had turned on a hose, dousing her with six years' worth of indignation. All the fights she hadn't fought. All the confrontations she'd walked away from. All the ignorance she'd let Nathan handle with a joke and a smile came rushing back, flooding her with anger and righteousness.

"Tell me how you want to handle this," Nick said, wiping his hands.

The annoyance she'd held for Nick melted away. Even after freezing him out all day, he sat here, ready to take her side. Not to be her hero. Not to be her shield. But to be whatever it was she needed at the moment. She just had to say the word.

"We're leaving," Robbie said, rising from her seat and stretching her petite frame as tall as she could. She marched to the front of the restaurant where the servers clustered, waiting for their orders. "Who runs this place?" she demanded of the group.

The uniformed servers dispersed, each woman breaking away, suddenly finding something much more interesting and urgent to do, leaving Robbie to face her sneering waitress. "Your *salad* isn't ready yet," the waitress said.

"I won't be needing it," Robbie said, squaring her shoulders. "I would like to speak to whoever is in charge here."

"About?"

"About the quality of service." Robbie raised the volume of her voice a notch after noticing the number of heads swiveling in their direction. Might as well make it easier for her audience. Good thing Mrs. Chin was a whole four states away. Although, with as loud as Robbie was willing to go, her mother might hear her all the way in San Francisco. "Manager? Owner?"

A woman in her fifties wearing jeans and a plaid flannel shirt stepped out from the kitchen. "My name's Annie. I own this place," she said, twirling her finger in the air to indicate the entire expanse of the miner's cabin. "How can I help you?"

Robbie thrust her hand out to Annie. "Pleased to meet you. My name is Beatrice Messina. I work for *Nebraska Life Magazine*. As I'm sure you are aware, the magazine adheres to a strict zero-tolerance policy regarding racism. You can hardly blame us in today's social climate. And because of that, I'm sorry to have to inform we won't be including your establishment in an upcoming piece featuring the must-stop places to eat when traveling in Nebraska."

Annie blinked several times, her mouth hanging open, looking from Robbie to Nick, then to their waitress, who had gone pale during Robbie's little speech. "I'm afraid I don't understand," Annie said, turning to her waitress for an explanation. "People love it here."

Robbie took a small step forward and dipped her chin, giving the illusion she lowered her voice when in reality, she kept it the same. "One of your waitresses, a representative of your brand, made a grotesque racial slur while serving our table. I'd lose my job if my boss found out I overlooked it and included this place in the magazine. Imagine the complaints and bad press that would follow, especially if anyone else came forward making claims."

"I'm so sorry," Annie stuttered. "Your meal is on the house, of course. What else can I do to rectify this situation?"

Robbie shook her head. "What's done is done. I would recommend, however, that you send that one," Robbie said, pointing to the offender, "to a sensitivity seminar as soon as possible."

With that, Robbie turned and found Nick standing with one hand already on the door, his lips pressed together and his brow knitted tightly. If she hadn't known him, she would have thought he was angry. But she recognized that expression. It was the same one he'd worn as a kid when he'd tried not to laugh while Ivy got in trouble for something.

One arch of an eyebrow on his part almost had Robbie breaking her character, as well. "We're done here," she said to Nick as she hurried out the door and to the car. She bent and picked up a piece of gravel near the tire. It wouldn't be the prettiest in her collection, but it would be one of the sweetest. They managed to hold it together long enough to lock themselves in the car. Then Robbie sank back in her seat and let out a howl of laughter, clutching the jagged rock to her chest. "That felt so good."

"I bet it did, Beatrice," Nick said, laughing right along with her as he drove away from the scene of the crime. "Why Beatrice Messina?"

"Beatrice is from Shakespeare's *Much Ado About Nothing*. And Messina is the writer of the article I read inside," Robbie said, leaning her head back and turning to face him. "I'm sorry you didn't get a chance to finish your dinner."

"Don't worry about it," he said. "You eat one bull testicle, you've eaten them all."

Robbie shuddered. "I will never eat those."

"Pizza in Chicago, yes. Testicles in Nebraska, no. Got it. Our next trip is coming along nicely."

Robbie smiled. It was nice being on good terms with him again. It was even nicer they didn't have to rehash it. She didn't need any more apologies, and he didn't need her to explain her anger. She watched him from the corner of her eye, the way his hands relaxed on the wheel, and his shoulders eased out of the bunched-up mess they'd been in for the last few hours. She knew he wouldn't bring up the incident with her computer again. She'd forgiven him, he knew it. The end.

TWENTY

Twenty years ago . . .

Robbie had been looking forward to this day for weeks, ever since the first hint of spring air had wafted from the bay and through the city. This was the day the swim club the Chins belonged to opened for the summer season with an all-member patio barbecue party. This was also the first year both she and Ivy would be allowed to swim in the deep pool without their parents next to them. Ivy had earned her "safe swimmer" badge the summer before, but Mrs. Chin had thought Robbie had needed another year of practice, being on the smaller side, before testing for the honor.

After eight weeks of winter swim lessons at the high school, Robbie had taken her water safety test and passed. Now her swimsuit sported the same green circular patch her best friend's did, and Ivy wouldn't be forced to stick to the junior pool to play with Robbie.

Robbie rode in the back of the family car, her legs unable to remain still during the ten-minute ride. She stared out the window, imagining all the possibilities a green patch would bring to her summer. A summer when, finally, she didn't have to be under her parents' constant supervision.

"Robbie, stop kicking the back of the seat," her father said, glancing at her in the rearview mirror. Robbie met his gaze in the reflection. Though his tone had been stern, his eyes crinkled in the corners the way they did when he smiled, and Robbie knew she wasn't really in trouble. Not yet. As long as she kept her legs still, she'd be fine. Except that she didn't think she'd be able to make it to the pool, so she tucked her legs under her in her seat.

"Looking forward to the summer, Robbie?" her father asked. There was still two weeks left in the school year, but to Robbie and her friends, opening day at the pool was the unofficial start to summer vacation.

"So much," Robbie said, throwing her hands in the air for emphasis. "Can I go to the pool every day?"

"Maybe not every day," Mrs. Chin said, flashing a smile at Robbie from over her shoulder. "A lot of days, though. You can come with me on the days I'm on duty."

Mrs. Chin was a board member for the swim club. Robbie wasn't sure what that meant, except that once a week, Mrs. Chin had to sit in a small office in the pool house while Robbie got to spend the whole day at the pool.

When Robbie saw the Wolfe's minivan already in the parking lot, she almost sprang from the backseat before the car stopped. "Robbie," Mrs. Chin called. "Help me carry this in."

Robbie jerked around as though an invisible rope tied around her waist had yanked her back to the car. "Come on. Let's hurry up," Robbie said, holding her hands out for the bundle Mrs. Chin placed in it. Mrs. Chin was in charge of the dessert table. She was always in charge of something, it seemed to Robbie. The book fair at school. The block party. The Christmas pageant. Robbie couldn't understand why. Her mother always complained about the work and how nobody did what they were supposed to. But every time something fun came along, there was Mrs. Chin. In charge. Bossing everyone around, including Robbie.

"When you get inside, put these on the dessert table. It's the one with the blue tablecloth. Can you do that?" Mrs. Chin asked as she pulled another box out of the car and handed it to Mr. Chin.

"Ye-es," Robbie whined. "Can we go now?"

Mrs. Chin bobbed her head, and Robbie took off to the clubhouse, dodging and weaving around the other members as they took their time to get out to the patio, where all the action was. Robbie found the blue table, dumped her armload, then raced—without running, running was prohibited on the deck—to find Ivy.

Ivy found her first and wrapped her in a bear hug from behind. "You're here! Drop your towel and let's go swimming." Robbie left her towel and cover-up with the Wolfes and proudly displayed her green badge. "You got it!" Ivy squealed, grabbing her hand. "Come on. Mom, we're going in the big pool."

"I want to go, too," Ernie said, struggling to get free from his mother and her bottle of sunscreen.

"You can't," Ivy said. "You have to stay with Mom. You don't have a badge."

"Not fair," Ernie said, looking to his mother for help.

Mrs. Wolfe shook her head. "Sorry, bud. You have to stay in the junior pool until either your father or I can take you in the big one. I'm going to help Robbie's mom set up first. Okay?"

Ernie jutted out his lower lip but held it together. Robbie's heart squeezed. She knew what it felt like to be left behind. It was just last year that she'd been restricted, too. Except she'd had Ivy to stay with her.

Robbie looked around the pool for Ernie's friends but couldn't find any of them. The pool had just opened, maybe they'd be there later.

"Come on, Robbie," Ivy called, dipping her toes in the water.

"Ivy," Robbie said. "Let's go with Ernie first." Ivy scrunched up her nose. "None of his friends are here yet. I feel bad for him."

Ivy grunted, but gave in, and followed Robbie and a beaming Ernie to the junior pool. Robbie's father stood on the perimeter of the lunch area watching. Robbie smiled and waved when she saw him, earning herself a thumbs-up. She loved her father's thumbs-ups.

Because he worked all day, Robbie sometimes worried her father only ever heard the bad stuff, like on the nightly news. One evening the year before, Robbie had been allowed to stay up later than usual and had sat curled in her father's lap reading a new book when he and Mrs. Chin turned on the news program. After a few minutes of listening to words like *fire, gang violence, theft, injuries*, Robbie had asked her father what he was watching. He'd told her it was the recap of things that happened that day.

When he'd arrived home from work the next evening, he'd kissed Mrs. Chin and asked how her day had been. Then he'd asked about Robbie's day. Robbie had stilled in the next room, straining to hear Mrs. Chin's recap of things that had happened in Robbie's day, worried it would sound a lot like the nightly news program—only the bad stuff.

Robbie always knew what kind of report he'd received by his reaction the moment he saw her after talking to Mrs. Chin. A thumbs-up meant she'd earned a good report. A shake of his head said Robbie was moments away from seeing her face on the news. She tallied the thumbs-ups in her head. Her total, including this poolside one, was at a respectable four hundred and ninety-two.

An hour later, the pool was filled to capacity, with almost every member of the club showing up for opening day. It was the kick-off to the summer social season, and no one wanted to be left out. Robbie and Ivy had left Ernie in the junior pool and had joined the rest of their friends in the deep pool, without their parents.

Robbie had just emerged from successfully completing a full underwater somersault when she heard her mother's voice booming from the speakers. "Lunch is served in the picnic area. Please help yourselves, and remember to keep the food in the designated areas."

One of the girls from Robbie's class giggled and pointed to the speakers. "Is that your mom?"

"Yeah, so?" Robbie said, unsure of where this was going.

"You don't look like your mom," the girl said.

Robbie sputtered and wiped the water dripping into her eyes. What kind of comment was that? It wasn't a question, though it sounded like it could be. It was more like an accusation. But she hadn't done anything wrong. Robbie bit her lip as her throat seemed to swell shut. Focusing on the way her hands appeared distorted under the wavy surface of the water, she tried to think of a response. Was she supposed to argue? Say thank you? The girl was still staring at her, waiting, and the more she stared, the more Robbie wished she could sprout a tail and swim out into the bay.

"Robbie, let's get some lunch," her mother said, appearing at the side of the pool like she was magic.

"Hi, Mrs. Chin," the girl said, all sweetness and light.

"Hi, Amy," Robbie's mother said, "your mom wants you for lunch, too."

"Okay, thanks," Amy said, making a dive for the ladder before Robbie could get there. Robbie watched as Amy climbed out and smiled like an angel at Mrs. Chin before hurrying off to her mother—a woman who looked like a bigger version of the girl.

"You, too, Ivy. Your mom's waiting with your dad and Ernie," Mrs. Chin said. The girls climbed out of the pool, grabbed their towels and flip-flops, and followed Mrs. Chin to the picnic area. "Your mom has your food already, Ivy. She's over there. I didn't know what you wanted, Robbie, so you come with me."

Robbie did as she was told and stood in the buffet line with her mother as it inched forward, still thinking about what Amy had said in the pool. Not really what she'd said—Robbie knew she didn't look like her mother—but the *way* Amy had said it, as though it confused her and she wanted an explanation.

"Mrs. Chin, how are you?"

Robbie glanced over her shoulder to find Amy and her mom directly behind them. Without saying anything, she turned her back on Amy's expectant gaze and focused on the row of hot dogs coming into view.

"Joanne, hello. I can't believe it's summer already. This year flew by didn't it?" Mrs. Chin said. Robbie covered her mouth with the corner of her towel to hide her frown.

"Tell me about it. And these girls keep getting bigger, don't they? Seems like yesterday Amy was a tiny little thing in a bassinet, now she's jumping off the diving boards."

Mrs. Chin nodded knowingly. "Blink again, and they'll be graduating college."

"Now, how long have you and Tom been married? Did you know Robbie when she was a baby?" Joanne asked.

Robbie stiffened and pulled her towel tighter around her shoulders. She glanced at her mother beside her, who stood with her hands clasped, smiling at the woman who'd just asked if she was Robbie's mother with the same tone her daughter had used in the pool. Robbie wanted to pull the towel over head and run back to the pool and dive in. She wanted to find her father in the crowd of partiers and squeeze into his side until he put his arm around her shoulder and held her close. She wanted her mother to deny the accusation in a way that Robbie couldn't.

Mrs. Chin placed a hand on Robbie's shoulder and gently pressed her forward in line as it moved along. "Tom and I will be celebrating our tenth anniversary next week," she said. Another gentle shove and Robbie found herself staring at a platter of hot dogs, but she'd lost her appetite. Mrs. Chin hadn't noticed and handed her a plate. Robbie sensed this was not the time to argue, so she took the plate and loaded it with a hot dog and fruit salad. "Have a fun day, Joanne."

When they found their seats, Robbie poked at a strawberry with her plastic fork. "I'm not that hungry, Mom."

Mrs. Chin brushed the hair off Robbie's forehead. "Me neither. But you've got to have something. Just eat the fruit, okay? And drink some water. You've got to stay hydrated on hot days like this."

Robbie furrowed her brow. She didn't want to talk about water. "Mom?"

"You better hurry up and eat. It looks like Ivy is almost done over there," Mrs. Chin said. "Where is your father? There he is. I'll be right back."

By the time the Chins returned to the table, Ivy had come to collect Robbie for round two of their swim day. To her surprise, her mother didn't say a word about her half-eaten lunch, and instead, waved Robbie off.

Later that night, when Robbie should have been sleeping, she sneaked out of her room and sat at the top of the stairs, listening to her parents talk in the living room below. The sound of her mother's raised voice had woken her, and Robbie wanted to make sure everything was okay, and the house hadn't caught fire or something.

"Can you believe that woman?" her mother was saying. "Standing there all smug, asking me how long I've known my own daughter? I never liked that woman, and now I'll have to deal with her for the Fourth of July party."

"You don't have to do the party," Robbie's father said in a much quieter tone. "You don't need to deal with that stress or that woman."

"Are you kidding me? Of course I have to, especially now."

"Why didn't you say something?"

"You know why," Mrs. Chin said. "I just hope Robbie doesn't want to be friends with her kid."

No worries there, Robbie thought as she crept back to bed.

TWENTY-ONE

Three hours after Beatrice Messina abandoned a platter of Rocky Mountain Oysters, Robbie and Nick arrived at a Holiday Inn, tired and hungry.

"We only have a queen room available. One bed sleeps two," the concierge said.

"That's fine," Robbie said, smothering a yawn and casting Nick a furtive glance. Any bed was better than another ten minutes in the car. They'd figure it out once they were upstairs. "You don't mind, do you?"

"I'm just happy to be done driving for the day," Nick said, picking up Robbie's bag as she took the key from the concierge.

"Elevator's on the left, by the vending machines." The concierge pointed over his shoulder. "If you're hungry, there's a twenty-four-hour pizza place that delivers nearby. Menu is in the room."

They nodded their thanks and trudged to the elevators. Robbie opened the door to their room, allowing Nick to dump the bags on the floor and immediately place an order.

"Hey," he said, covering the phone's mouthpiece, "do you still dip your pizza in ranch dressing?"

Robbie nodded, then smiled when she heard Nick order a large side of ranch.

"I will never understand that," Nick said as he hung up. "Why would you dip pizza in ranch dressing?"

"You were stuffing fried bull balls into your mouth a few hours ago, and you're questioning my choice of pizza condiments?" Robbie pulled her worn tee and running shorts from her bag and headed for the bathroom while stretching her arms over her head. What she wouldn't give for her yoga mat right about now. Who knew sitting still could cause so much back pain?

Nick was camped out on the bed when she returned. He had kicked off his shoes and tossed his hat on his bag. His laptop sat open on his lap. Robbie padded around the foot of the bed, trying not to think about the fact that there was no sofa in this room. Though, by the way her heart couldn't decide on a rhythm, and her palms were growing increasingly slick with sweat, not thinking about sharing a bed with Nick was a near impossible feat.

"Working again?" Robbie asked, straining to keep the shaky nerves from her voice. She hadn't shared a bed with any man besides Nathan in eight years.

"The client I'm meeting in Vegas?" Nick said, looking at her over the laptop screen. "He sent me headshots of potential models he wants to use for a shoot. He asked my opinion."

"So, nothing fun, then?"

"Want to see?"

She did. Forgetting her doubts, she jumped on the bed, nearly toppling the computer to the ground with the unexpected force. "Sorry," she said quickly, afraid he'd be annoyed at her childishness. Nathan had always warned her about her clumsiness when she got over-excited.

"Is that a hard no on seeing the pictures?" Nick chuckled, balancing the laptop again. "Here, take a look." He angled the monitor to give Robbie full view of the series of rectangular boxes lined up like mug shots. "You gotta get closer," he said, sliding his arm around her waist and pulling her almost on top of him.

Normally, Robbie would have pulled back and made sure to leave room for the Holy Spirit, as her junior prom chaperone had said, but she was so engrossed in the flawless beauties in front of her, she hardly noticed.

"Are these real women?" she asked. Next to each photo was a list of stats. Height, weight, hair color, eye color. Almost all of them were over six feet tall.

Nick shrugged. "Sort of."

Robbie swung her head around, not realizing how close they were, and almost bumped his nose. "What do you mean?" she asked, then gasped and turned back to the computer screen. "Are some of these dudes?"

When Nick laughed, both Robbie and the laptop shook, and she had to place one hand on the computer and one hand on the bed to keep either from falling. "Sorry," he choked out. "No, they're not dudes. But these aren't what they normally look like either. This is after all the airbrushing and editing."

Of course, Robbie knew that was how the photography industry worked. She'd seen all the exposés on the entertainment channels and in the supermarket checkout tabloids. Professional makeup, lighting, and technology. The holy trinity of celebrity. But there had to be something there to work with, didn't there?

"How different can they really be, though?" she asked.

A knock on the door announced dinner. "Hold that thought," Nick said, setting the computer to the side. Robbie opened her mouth to offer her share, but Nick gave her a pointed look while counting out the bills before opening the door.

Once each settled back on the bed, pizza in hand, ranch on the side table for Robbie, Nick returned to the subject of the models. "I've worked with some of these women before," he said. "Here, I'll show you."

A few clicks later, Robbie was staring at a picture of a brunette standing in front of a fountain. She looked like she could have been anyone. Granted, a more than average-looking anyone, but just another person lounging on the fountain's edge wearing sky-high stilettos and a couture gown. "Okay," Robbie said. "And?"

Nick toggled back to the model mugshots. "It's her," he said, pointing to the goddess in the third row.

"No way," Robbie said, putting her pizza down and toggling between the two photos. "This can't be the same girl." She focused on one feature at a time, finding similarities in the jawline. The fountain girl's eyes were too close-set, and her hair was thinner, though, Robbie supposed, that was nothing a few extensions couldn't fix. But fountain girl's nose was larger and rounder at the tip.

"It is," Nick said. "Pre-touch up."

Robbie sat back and scrutinized her pizza. "I feel bad for these models."

Nick choked down his mouthful. "You might be the first person in history to ever say that."

Dunking the edge of her pizza in the dressing, Robbie was a little surprised at her admission, as well. The models she saw in magazines had never been anything more than breathing mannequins to her. Robbie, along with most of the world, she suspected, didn't consider the fact that they could have feelings. They got paid to wear pretty clothes and get their picture taken. They got paid to be beautiful.

"Well, look," Robbie said, pointing to the picture at the fountain. "Obviously, she's a gorgeous woman. Right?"

Nick shrugged.

"Come on. You can admit she's hotter than the average woman walking down the street."

"She's okay."

"Whatever," Robbie said, rolling her eyes. "The point is, even as beautiful as she is, someone decided she's still not good enough, and her appearance still needs to be altered. I mean, that's got to take a toll on the psyche sooner or later, don't you think? And with all the editing, why even bother using live models at all? Just take a picture of the clothes and draw in whoever you want to wear them."

"I'd have a lot more free time, that's for sure," Nick said, reaching for another slice of pizza. Then, noticing Robbie staring at her slice without eating, he added, "Anything wrong with the pizza? That's regular Italian sausage on it. No Rocky Mountain Oysters, I swear."

"Ha-ha. No, it's not that. I was just wondering—is that what men expect? I guess, not expect. That might not be the right word, especially in today's day and age. There have been enough articles and social media posts comparing a real woman to the fantasy stereotype that any man who honestly expects this perfect woman to exist had to have just crawled out from under a rock," Robbie said, her head spinning too fast for the words to come out. "What I mean is, are men always searching for this—the unattainable level of perfection?"

"I don't speak for all men. But, for me, personally, I like real women, not the fantasy."

Robbie arched an eyebrow. She found that hard to swallow coming from someone who'd built his career creating the fantasy.

"Really. It's like you said. This perfection is fake. Anyone can look like the pictures in the magazines."

"Anyone?"

"Anyone," Nick said, pulling the computer back in his lap. "Watch this." His fingers flew over the keyboard, and the next thing she knew, she was staring at a picture of herself at Brolly's engagement party. His hand kept moving, and she watched as she seemed to grow a full six inches on the screen. Her hair thickened and added loose curls. Her willowy frame blossomed as though she'd hit a second wave of puberty, giving her an hourglass figure where she'd only been shaped as clock hands before.

Robbie gasped and leaned closer to the screen. "I'm gorgeous," she breathed. It was the version of Robbie Chin she'd always wanted to be. Tall, voluptuous, graceful. "This is my favorite picture of me by far."

"It's not real," Nick whispered in her ear. The screen changed, and she found herself staring at an image of her from the morning Holly had hijacked their road trip. Plain, cotton tank top, denim shorts, muddy coffee in hand, and her head leaning back against the car. She looked tired. "This is my favorite picture of you so far. This is real."

"You're crazy," Robbie said, shoving back from the screen. "I'm not even wearing makeup."

"Exactly. It's just you. You didn't give a damn who saw you or what they thought. Those have always been my favorite Robbie Chin pictures." His mouth still hovered near her ear. Every syllable sent a shiver down her spine, though she suspected it had less to do with his tickling breath and more to do with the words that came with it.

Robbie pushed off the bed and tossed her pizza crust in the trash, while Nick pulled back the covers and dusted any remaining crumbs from the bed. It was one in the morning, and they had a lot of driving to do the next day. She slid into bed, her pulse humming in her veins, and pulled the covers up to her chin. Rolling on her side and keeping her back to Nick, she lay as close to the edge of the bed as she could without falling off. The bed dipped and shook slightly as Nick climbed in on his side, rustling the blankets, sending a matching ripple of—anticipation?—through her.

Nathan was the one who was supposed to give her the shivers. And even though she was well aware of the fact that they were, for the time being, not a couple, she still felt as though she were cheating on him. But this was Nick. Childhood friend, Nick. Ivy's brother, Nick. Harmless, hangs out with models, Nick.

She'd never had that male best friend that seemed to be all the rage among her high school students. It had always been her and Ivy, the dynamic duo. She'd considered Nathan a sort-of best friend, more by default. But she'd never had a male friend for the sake of having a male friend until she'd picked up Nick from the forest.

This was new territory for her.

Nick turned out the lights. "Hey, Robbie," he said, just an arm's length away. "I know it's none of my business, but if this Nathan guy makes you feel like he's looking for something better, then he's not the right guy. You deserve someone who makes you feel like there is no better. You're it, baby, flaws and all, and he wouldn't have it any other way. My dad always says, 'You'll know you found the one when even while you can't stand them, you can't stand walking away from them.'" He let out one of his lion roar yawns. "But, what do I know? I haven't had a relationship worth mentioning since college."

Robbie squeezed her eyes tighter. He waited for a response; only she didn't have one to give. Was it Nathan who made her feel like he was searching for something else, or had she put that pressure on herself? Always trying to be perfect. Never wanting to rock the boat. Never criticizing or arguing. Never making a scene.

"Robbie?" Nick whispered in the dark.

Robbie puffed out a sigh that could have passed for a snore and remained quiet. She wasn't ready to face this new level of questions. She just had to get through the night. On her side of the bed. Alone.

Falling asleep hadn't been a problem. The problem occurred in the morning when Robbie woke entwined in Nick's arms without any recollection of how she got there. She had never been a cuddly sleeper by any means. Robbie had her side of the bed, Nathan had his. Yet, here she was, her head on Nick's shoulder, his arms looped around her waist, holding her close. One of her legs lay curled on top of his, and his stubble tickled the top of her head.

And she'd never slept more soundly.

This wasn't good. But it was. And she had to get out of there.

Sliding out from under Nick's arms, Robbie was careful not to disturb him. This had all been a mistake, and it would be best for everyone involved if she pretended it never happened. Not like anything had happened. They'd slept. That was all. Never mind the fact that those few short hours were the best sleep of her life. It was still just sleep. Neither of them had known what they were doing. Unless he did.

Robbie's breath hitched in her chest as Nick stirred under the sheets. Did he know? Had he woken at some point to find her cuddling up next to him? Had he pulled her close on purpose? Or just tolerated her sleep-snuggles?

This was why it was best to ignore the whole thing. If Robbie pretended it didn't happen, she wouldn't be forced to look for answers. Once Robbie was sure Nick wasn't waking up, she slipped out from under the covers and threw on her sandals. Shuffling down to the hotel lobby where they served complimentary breakfast, she arrived just as the first pot of coffee finished brewing. Stocking up on breakfast essentials and extra cups of coffee for both of them—three sugars and extra cream for her, two sugars and two creams for Nick—she carried her tray back to their room just as Nick stretched his way out of bed.

"You weren't kidding about being on breakfast duty today," Nick said, eying his choice of pastries, fruit, and cereal.

"Wait, there's more," Robbie said, ripping the cover off a plate piled high with pancakes, bacon, and scrambled eggs. "I didn't know what you'd be in the mood for, so I got a bit of everything."

Nick popped a piece of bacon in his mouth. "I might eat a bit of everything. Flip you for the bathroom?"

"Go ahead," Robbie said, relieved he didn't seem to know about their sleeping arrangements. Now they could get on with their day as planned without feeling weird. "I need to get some caffeine in me first."

Nick smiled and disappeared into the bathroom. Robbie busied herself with straightening up their midnight pizza party and getting her bags ready to leave.

"Hey, Robbie?" Nick called from behind the bathroom door.

"Yeah," she called back, digging into the bowl of fruit.

"How'd you sleep?"

Robbie froze and stared at the bathroom door. She pictured his eyes lighting up with his teasing smirk on the other side. The jerk knew. "I slept okay." Liar. Better than okay.

"Best sleep I've had in years," he said before she heard the shower running.

Robbie waited a few seconds to see if there was more. Hoping for more. But there wasn't. He seemed to need his "tease Robbie" time like she needed a cup of coffee, and like her coffee, she was learning to crave it as well.

Shaking her head free of thoughts about Nick in the morning, she pulled out her phone and opened her search browser. Typing "Las Vegas medical conventions," she held her breath and waited for the results to pop up. As she'd thought, it wouldn't be difficult at all to find Nathan. Two results appeared on the screen. One was for pharmaceutical reps, and the other was for physicians.

Robbie grunted, not doubting for one minute that it hadn't been a coincidence the two conventions happened to be taking place at the same time. Physicians and pharmaceutical representatives. Could it be any more cliché? She clicked on the physician convention link and saw that it was being held at the Aria Resort and Casino.

"Swanky," Robbie muttered, checking out the different rooms and the too exorbitant for her teacher's salary rates.

"What's swanky?" Nick asked, towel drying his hair from the bathroom doorway.

Robbie jumped in her seat. So engrossed in her sleuthing, she'd forgotten Nick was a ready-in-three-minutes-flat guy. She thought about lying, but he already knew what she had planned. And she didn't like the idea of keeping secrets from him, no matter how borderline stalker-ish they seemed.

"The hotel where Nathan's convention is."

Nick joined her, peering over her shoulder at the small phone screen. "The Aria," he said appreciatively. "Cool place. I've done some work for them."

He stood too close to her. She smelled his shampoo mingling with the fresh deodorant he'd applied. Were they those friends? The friends who appreciated the smell of the other's toiletries? They were share a hotel room friends—financial convenience, she'd told herself—but she was pretty sure this was crossing a line somewhere that someone had drawn in the sand. She turned off the phone's screen and rose from her seat. She didn't want to smell like another man when she found Nathan.

"Are you done with the bathroom?" she asked, gathering her change of clothes.

"All yours," he said, surveying the tray of breakfast. "Take your time."

A shower would do her good—and would wash Nick's scent off her. But the whole bathroom smelled like him. She couldn't help thinking the shower water helped his aroma absorb deeper into her skin. How was she going to convince Nathan they belonged together when Nick had seeped into her pores?

Robbie lathered on the hotel lotion, hoping to mask the smell, and resolved to drive with the windows open. That should do it. Nick scrunched his nose in the air like a dog picking up a scent when she opened the bathroom door. He must have smelled himself on her, too.

Color crept up the back of his neck as he turned his back to her. "I packed up what I could to take with us," he said.

"Ready when you are," she said. Her chest fluttered thinking about what lay ahead of them. By this time the next day, they'd be getting dressed in Vegas. Where in Vegas, she didn't have a clue yet, but she'd be there, within the city limits, just like Nathan.

"So, I hope you don't mind," Nick said as he deftly loaded their overnight bags in the Pinto wagon. "But I called my contact at the Aria and got us a room."

Robbie froze. In her mind's eye, she saw her bank account draining faster than the hotel bathtub.

"No charge," Nick said with a wink.

A smile spread across Robbie's face. She'd never been one of those people who knew people. She rather liked this having connections deal. "Don't mind it at all." Things were going to go her way. She felt it in the air. This was Robbie Chin's day.

TWENTY-TWO

Las Vegas. In all of Robbie's twenty-eight years on the earth, she had never seen anything as bright as the Las Vegas Strip. Even Times Square in New York dimmed in comparison. Robbie pressed her nose against the window as her Ford Pinto inched its way down the congested downtown streets.

So hypnotized, Nick had to lead Robbie through the hotel doors and into the resort lobby, where her breath escaped from her lips in a long puff. She'd always heard the Las Vegas hotels were over the top, but what stood before her was nothing like she'd imagined. The lobby, an easy three stories high, contained enough polished stone and glass that every surface twinkled, even in the middle of the night. Glass windows comprised three of the four walls, and she couldn't wait to see what the lobby looked like when the sunlight streamed through them in the morning. Giant, brightly colored glass butterflies hung from the ceiling, and large potted trees adorned the area, creating the illusion that Robbie had shrunk down to the size of an ant and had stepped into a butterfly garden.

"What do you think?" Nick asked, beaming down at her.

"If this is the lobby, what's the room like?" She gripped his arm in excitement. "Let's check in."

Nick chuckled and left her to marvel at her surroundings while he spoke to someone about the room promised to him. Then, she remembered what she was wearing. She'd dressed for fifteen hours in a car without even thinking what she would look like walking into a resort of this caliber. Nick appeared at her side and nudged her with his elbow. They walked past the casino entrance, where Robbie saw people dressed in their best designer or designer knock-offs. Women in sky-high heels and cocktail dresses. Men in suits and polished shoes. And here she was, nylon shorts and flip-flops.

The elevator door dinged. "That's us," Nick said.

Robbie rushed inside before any of the glittering patrons noticed her. As she rode the elevator in silence, she mentally cataloged the contents of her travel bag. She hadn't thought this through. The whole point of coming here was to impress Nathan with her bold and adventurous side. He'd seen all her clothes and clearly wasn't impressed with her shorts and T-shirt combinations. She had the dress from the engagement party, but Nick had sent him a picture of that, too.

"I have to go shopping tomorrow," Robbie said as the elevator doors slid open with a subdued chime. She stepped into the hall and realized only one door stood before them. Had they taken the elevator to the roof? "Where are we?"

Nick smiled and swiped the key card in front of the sensor. He waited for the tiny green light, then pushed the door open and held it for her. "Welcome to your home for the next two nights."

Robbie gaped at him as she walked into their accommodations. When Nick had said he'd gotten them a room, he'd failed to mention it was the penthouse suite at a five-star resort. Her breath caught in her throat as she turned questioning eyes on him.

Nick tossed the two key cards on the living room table—their hotel room had a living room!—and shrugged. "It was all they had with the convention here. You okay?"

Maybe it was the stress from this cross-country trip. Maybe it was the exhaustion. Maybe it was the sheer giddiness of being surrounded by so much sleek luxury. Whatever it was, the mere question as to whether or not staying in a palace was okay sent her into a fit of giggles. Her legs gave out beneath her, and she sunk to the floor, clutching her sides. Nick tried to hold out, but soon he was laughing, too.

They pulled themselves together when their luggage arrived, and Nick let the bellhop in. Robbie wandered around the suite, which could have fit two of her apartments, and wondered how rich someone would have to be to consider this a standard hotel room. Could a run of the mill celebrity afford to stay a week in a place like this? Or were they talking Bill Gates or Warren Buffet rich?

"Did you pick a room yet?" Nick asked as Robbie perused the selection of snacks and beverages left in the kitchen area for their enjoyment. "If not, I suggest you take the one facing the strip since this is your first Vegas experience. Next time, we'll switch off."

Robbie grinned like a kid in the candy store. This game of the planning out their next trip had grown on her after years of having been nowhere. It was fun thinking she could be this adventurous again, for no other reason than fun. "Interesting point," she said, forcing her features to take on a more serious expression. "But I'm afraid I can't commit to that course of action until I have thoroughly examined the options."

"By all means," Nick said with a slight bow. "Please examine."

Robbie ran past Nick, grabbing his hand and pulling him with her, as she dashed into the closest of the two bedrooms and jumped on the bed. Nick joined her, and the two of them were instantly six years old again. After a minute of jumping, Robbie suddenly stopped and shouted, "Next!"

She leaped off the bed and sprinted across the suite to the second bedroom on the other side. Nick hadn't missed a step and was hot on her heels, almost crashing into her as they treated the second mattress as a trampoline. Exhausting themselves, they collapsed on the bed, breathless and flushed.

"This one," Robbie said, panting. "I'll take this one."

"Because it bounces better?"

"No." Robbie shook her head. "Because I'm too tired to make it all the way to the other one again."

Nick propped himself up on his elbows and looked down at her, his hair falling into his eyes, and his chin covered in two-day-old stubble. If he wasn't Ernie Wolfe, and if she wasn't Robbie Chin, his sister's oldest friend, she could have sworn he wanted to kiss her.

"Are you ready for this?" he asked, his voice hoarse from their laughter as he leaned closer.

"Yes," she said without hesitation, realizing she had only guessed at his meaning, but her answer would have remained the same regardless. With Nick, it seemed she was ready for anything. She'd taken more risks in the few days on the road with him than she had in the last six years with Nathan. But, what kind of life was that? Didn't she need stability? Didn't she need structure? Didn't she need him to stop looking at her like that?

"Good," he said, with a gleam in his eye, right before his phone, which was pressed between his hip and her mattress, buzzed, sending ripples of vibrations up her spine. His eyes darkened as he reached across her and grabbed a pillow to throw on top of her. He bounced off the bed and smoothed back his hair. "Better get some sleep, Robbie Chin. Big day tomorrow."

With one last flash of a smile, he was gone, closing the door behind him. Saved by the buzz. Robbie laid in bed clutching the pillow to her chest. "Ernie," she grunted and rolled over. "Always a pain in the ass."

Robbie woke the next day fully clothed and still clutching the pillow to her chest. She found her bag waiting for her outside her bedroom door. Nick must have left it for her last night. After taking a longer than necessary shower in the largest bathroom she'd ever seen, she emerged from her bedroom ready to face the day.

The aroma of fresh waffles and coffee greeted her, and since, according to the conference website, check-in for the event didn't start until four, she had plenty of time to enjoy her breakfast. No grab and go this morning. She'd dedicated the entire day to taking her time. That way when she did see Nathan, she'd appear carefree and whimsical, not a frazzled, psychotic mess.

"There you are," Nick said, setting the morning paper down on the dining table as Robbie walked in. It was a scene so domestic, Robbie momentarily forgot they were in a hotel. "My turn to get breakfast, right?"

"Well done," she said, taking a seat across from him at the table meant for eight. "So, what's on your agenda today?" The question felt distant and cold on her tongue after spending the last five days together sharing one agenda. She poured herself a steaming cup of coffee to cover the taste the words left in her mouth.

"I'm glad you asked," Nick said, pushing a tray of flavored syrups in her direction. "My meeting is after lunch. So first, I thought I would lay around the pool and get a nice base layer tan going. Then, I booked us some appointments at the spa to help make us all pretty for our respective appointments. How does that sound? Unless, that is, you've made other plans."

Robbie arched an eyebrow as she watched the blueberry syrup pour like silk from the carafe and fill all the tiny squares of her waffle. "You know I didn't. Conference check-in isn't until four, so I've got all day."

Nick nodded. "Four. Got it. By then, we should have you all tanned and pampered. You'll be looking and feeling like a million bucks, which is about how much the spa package costs."

Robbie's silver fork clattered on the porcelain plate.

"Don't worry," Nick said, getting up from the table. "Part of the suite package. You think I'd let you blow a whole year's salary on a manicure?" He headed for his bedroom. "Will you be pool-ready in fifteen?"

Robbie swirled a piece of waffle in the little syrup lake she'd created on her plate. "Sure." Then, after washing it down with more coffee that must have been brewed with cocaine—it was that addictive—she called, "How much is the spa package?"

"You don't want to know," he said, before closing the bedroom door.

If he didn't want to tell her, the price tag must have been obscene. Something she would never in her lifetime dream of spending on something that wasn't completely necessary, like a kidney transplant. Friends with connections was the only way to travel, she decided.

The pool was already crowded, but they managed to find two empty chaise lounges together close enough to the bar to make up for the sight of too many Speedos.

"Why does anyone think that looks good?" Robbie muttered as they set their towels down and kicked off their sandals.

"Nathan doesn't own one, I take it?" Nick asked, reclining on the chaise.

"He wouldn't be caught dead in one. Why? Do you have one?"

"I did live in Europe for a while where they're all the rage," Nick said. "And you know what the say—when in Rome."

Robbie narrowed her eyes and settled back in her seat. "I don't believe you," she said. "I call bullshit. You're going to have to prove it."

"How?"

"You're a photographer. You must have a picture somewhere of you on a European beach."

"I think you're misunderstanding the basic premise of my job," he said, waving over a cocktail waitress. "Let me explain to you how it works. I *take* the pictures. I'm not in them."

"Are you telling me, in all your travels, you've never stopped to take a selfie?"

"I don't need a selfie," he said, then turning to the waitress, "Two Bloody Mary's please." Then, back to Robbie, "I know what I look like pretty much at any given point in a day. Why would I want a picture of my big head blocking the view of what could be a fantastic picture? I don't want to remember me. I want to remember what's around me."

Robbie thought of the picture on her phone of her and Nathan on vacation. At the time, it had seemed so imperative to record that moment for all posterity. Had she missed an opportunity to see something better? The waitress returned and set two glasses down on the cocktail table between them. Nick signed a slip of paper and flashed her his trademarked grin.

"If I grabbed your phone right now, there wouldn't be one selfie on there? What about a picture of you someone else took?" Robbie asked.

"Nope. Not one."

"Let me see," she said, holding her hand out to him. He did as she asked, dropping his phone in her waiting hand. Robbie scrolled through the photo album and was shocked. He was telling the truth. There wasn't one picture there of him in the hundreds of images he had saved. "You're a selfie virgin. This isn't right. Come here." She tugged on his arm until he leaned over, meeting her halfway between their two chairs. "Smile like you mean it."

"How do you feel?" Nick asked as she studied the resulting image.

"I've had better," she said with a smirk. "You have to keep the picture forever now so you can always remember your first time. If I find out you deleted it, I'll be very heartbroken."

"Don't worry, you won't find out," Nick said, waggling his eyebrows.

His phone buzzed in Robbie's hand, giving her full view of the caller ID. M.G.—the same caller that blew up his phone the day she'd picked him up. "You're getting a call," Robbie said, keeping her tone cool and casual. "An M.G.?"

Nick barely contained his grimace as he reached for his phone. "It's not important." He glanced at the screen, then set the phone face down on the table.

"What if it's a client?" Robbie asked.

"It's not."

"Girlfriend?" The word almost stuck in her throat.

"Not exactly."

M.G. "Megan? The ex?"

Nick sucked in a sharp breath in response. He didn't need to say anything else. Not yet, anyway.

"How long has it been?" Robbie asked before taking a sip of her Bloody Mary, not giving a second thought to how, in moments, she would match its color.

"Three years," he said, rubbing his chin. "I haven't returned any of her calls if you're wondering."

"I'm not wondering," Robbie said. She was totally wondering but had no right to. She had no claim on him. And she was here for another man. If anything, she didn't want to see him hurt again. "But aren't you? I mean, why is she calling you now? And all the time? Has she left messages?"

"One."

"And?"

"And . . . nothing. Megan said something about wanting to meet up. She's supposed to be in San Francisco next week for work," Nick said. He shifted uncomfortably in his seat.

Robbie's heart thudded against her chest. Why would his ex want to meet three years after breaking up? Because she found out how successful he was, that was why. The money grubber was looking to reconcile her way into his bank account. The pit in Robbie's gut burned, sending heat rippling through her limbs. Who did this woman think she was?

"Are you going to?" Robbie asked through a clenched jaw. He'd better not. Not that it mattered to her. She planned on being back with Nathan by then, didn't she? Well? Didn't she?

"I don't know. Maybe," Nick said.

Robbie pressed a hand to her cheek as though she'd been slapped. He couldn't be serious. He considered getting together with the woman who'd cheated on him? Who had broken his heart? "Don't be stupid," she said, then slapped a hand over her mouth. She blamed the vodka.

Nick turned to face her, his face made of stone. "What does it matter to you, anyway? You're here to get back with your ex. No one else is allowed to talk to theirs and consider starting over?"

"That's not what I meant."

"Well, what did you mean?"

It was a fair question. If only Robbie had a fair answer. The two situations were completely different, though. She hadn't been cheated on. At least, not that she as aware of. And her breakup had just happened. Like three days ago, not three years ago. Wasn't there a statute of limitations on how long to consider getting back together with an ex? Surely, an amendment could be added to the custody agreements for friends addressing this issue.

"It's just—well—the timing is weird; that's all." Robbie watched him from the corner of her eye. His stone features melted into a scowl. Robbie's heart continued pounding, moving into her ears. She was messing this up, saying the wrong things, but she couldn't help herself. "I mean, she cheated on you three years ago because you were traveling for work and couldn't handle the distance. Now, all of a sudden when you're successful and sought-after, getting penthouses comped in five-star resorts, now she wants to catch up and, what, say hi?" Robbie gulped down lungfuls of air as though she'd been drowning. "I don't want to see you get hurt again. That's all," she said, quieter and with her head down.

His phone buzzed again, and Robbie had to clasp her hands in her lap to keep from snatching the phone first and telling this Megan to crawl back in the hole where she came from.

"Text from Ivy," Nick said. "She wants to know how we're doing." He jabbed at the phone a few times, then set it in his lap. "I sent her my very first selfie."

Robbie nodded, sipping her cocktail. "See how handy they are?"

Nick cleared his throat, then without looking at her, said, "I didn't mean to snap at you like I did."

"I know. I deserved it, though. It's none of my business."

Nick dipped his head to his chest, his hair falling in his eyes. "I haven't decided what to do yet." Nick waved over the waitress. "I think we need something a little stronger and less tomato-y."

"What did you have in mind?" Robbie asked.

"Two Champagne cocktails, please?" Nick asked the waitress, whose ruby-red lips were pursed into a seductive pout that was more at home in a nightclub than poolside before noon. "Maybe the bubbles will make everything clearer."

After another hour, they'd decided the bubbles did nothing to clear up any situation, but at least things were much more amusing. Robbie didn't even care if her face was beet red. Everything was lighter and airier as they walked through the massive lobby to the bank of elevators to get ready for their spa appointments.

Nick furrowed his brow again as the elevator doors closed, sealing them off from the rest of the world. He stared straight ahead while Robbie studied his reflection in the sliding doors. She wasn't going to ask what was wrong. Partly because she already knew, and it was none of her business. But, if that was true, why did the other part of her struggle to keep from wrapping her arms around him until his brow smoothed out again?

When Nick had told her she was getting "the works," he'd meant it. Three hours later, there wasn't one part of her that hadn't been buffed, polished, and powdered by expert hands in the lush day spa. Check-in for the conference hadn't started yet, though the hotel had set up tables in the lobby for it, complete with balloons and laminated name tags. And since Robbie and Nick had agreed to meet back at the suite, unless

Robbie had luck finding Nathan earlier and plans changed, she cruised by the setup, casually taking her time glancing at the names staring back up at her. Her stomach clenched when she saw DR. NATHAN TANG printed beneath his picture attached to a lanyard.

Ducking into the nearest resort's ten boutiques, she was determined to find something that didn't look too complacent or predictable. Something like the dress back in Poppy Grove, but better. Robbie perused the racks, dismissing one item of clothing after another. Nothing seemed right. It was all too frilly, too plain, or too expensive. Growing more frustrated with every dress she refused to try on, she began questioning this whole plan of hers. If it was this hard to find something to wear to talk to Nathan, what would the rest of their relationship look like?

"There you are." Breathless and borderline frantic, Nick hurried into the shop. She hadn't seen him since they'd parted ways at the spa, and his clean-shaven jaw and new haircut momentarily stunned her. "I need your help."

Robbie smirked. "Don't tell me you've gotten yourself into trouble with a pit boss already. I'm a teacher. I don't make the kind of money to bail you out."

"Then as plan B, how about you join me at dinner with my client tonight?" he asked with a pleading lopsided grin. "I kind of let it slip that I wasn't alone, and he mistook you for my girlfriend. And before I knew it, he called his wife and made dinner plans for the four of us."

Robbie glanced at the rack of dresses in front of her and arched an eyebrow, considering. It wasn't like she had solid plans with Nathan. She hadn't even found him yet. What were a few more hours? Besides, it might be better to stumble upon him later, coming back from dinner and a few drinks. Fun Robbie.

"What time?" she asked.

"Seven," Nick said, then planted a kiss on her temple. "You're the best." He paused and surveyed the dresses in front of Robbie. "I don't have anything to wear that's comparable, and I have a few more meetings. Can you do me another favor?"

"Size?" Robbie asked.

"Forty-two chest." He kissed her cheek this time. "I owe you. Put it on the room. I've got to run. I'll meet you upstairs?"

He rushed out without waiting for an answer, but he didn't need one. Robbie had said she'd be ready, and she would. He had no reason to doubt her. Her phone beeped with an incoming message. Robbie snatched it from her bag and read her mother's text message asking for her time of arrival. Robbie pressed her eyes closed and took a deep breath. Then slid the phone back in her purse.

TWENTY-THREE

One year ago . . .

"Don't forget, we're having dinner with the chief of surgery tonight," Nathan said as they both readied for their days.

Robbie brushed her hair smooth, then tucked a piece behind her ear. "I'll meet you there on time."

Nathan's hands stilled in the middle of tying a Windsor knot. Robbie didn't know why he bothered—he changed into scrubs as soon as he got to the hospital, but Nathan said he liked the impression it gave as he walked into the hospital. "What do you mean, meeting me there?"

"I have parent-teacher conferences after school today. Remember?"

"Oh, yeah," he said, diverting his eyes. He had no idea what Robbie was talking about. "Are you sure you'll make it on time?"

"I promised you I'd be there. I'll make it on time." A knot formed in her stomach every time they had this conversation. If things didn't go precisely as Nathan planned, he had a meltdown. Constantly reassuring him that everything will be fine when she knew she had it all under control was tiring and caused more stress for both of them than either one of them needed. She'd never let him down yet.

Nathan slowly resumed his tie tying and lowered his eyes to her cardigan and slacks. "Are you wearing that for dinner?"

Robbie dropped her brush on the dresser and turned away from Nathan before he saw her frown. "Here," she said, holding up a garment bag she had laying on the bed. "I have a more appropriate outfit for dinner right here. I'm bringing it with me."

"What dress—"

"Nathan," she said, almost snapping at him until Mrs. Chin's voice chided her in her head. *Don't use that tone. He saves lives, after all.* "I've got it covered. You don't need to worry about anything. Have a good day at work, and I'll see you at dinner."

He dropped his hands to his side and joined her at the foot of the bed. "I'm sorry. It's just a really important dinner. It has me all jittery." He placed a kiss on her forehead. "It won't happen again."

Robbie wished she could believe him this time.

TWENTY-FOUR

Nick knocked on the bedroom door. "You ready?"

Robbie stared at her reflection. She'd done good. Way in the back of the shop, she'd found a copper sequined, sleeveless wrap dress. The last one. And her size. With her newly acquired tan from that morning and a diamond necklace—the last anniversary present she'd received from Nathan—she practically shone. She smiled at herself. Vegas Robbie was fun. Vegas Robbie was daring. Vegas Robbie was going to be late if she didn't stop staring at herself.

She slipped on a pair of nude heels and opened the door. Nick let out a low whistle. "Remember what I said the other day about my favorite Robbie?" She nodded. "This might be my new favorite. You look incredible."

Robbie bit her lip to keep from grinning like an idiot. "You're not going to take my picture, are you?"

"I might have to," he said. "But, later. Are you ready to go? I can't thank you enough. I thought telling him I wasn't alone would get me out of dinner. I didn't count on him expanding the party."

"It's fine," Robbie said, checking her hair one last time on the way out, smoothing any wayward strands. "A girl's got to eat. Where are we going anyway?"

"You like sushi, right?"

Robbie's mouth watered just saying it. She loved sushi, but Nathan did not. Over the years, it had become a rare treat for her to enjoy either when Nathan worked the overnight shifts or when she visited home alone. "How is the sushi in the desert?"

"It will be the best you ever had."

Nick hadn't exaggerated about the sushi. Nor had he exaggerated when he'd told her his client—who owned four Las Vegas resorts, and a few more in the Caribbean—would be the most colorful person she'd ever met. Literally.

Lyle Goldman sat across from her festooned in a bright purple blazer and lime green pants. Robbie could only imagine he got his wardrobe by rifling through leftover costumes from one of the hundreds of stage shows in the city. His wife, Bernie, was no more demure in her neon orange ensemble with the feathered—real feathers—skirt. She reminded Robbie of a bird Alice might come across in Wonderland. Robbie had thought she'd been daring with her dress choice but now felt shabby and bland compared to these two.

Despite their obvious flair for fashion, which only Vegas could truly appreciate, Lyle and Bernie were two of the most down to earth and fascinating people. Robbie sat in awe, hypnotized by their colors, and their obvious respect and regard for each other. They weren't just husband and wife; they were best friends and partners in every sense of the word. And that outshone anything they wore.

"What is it that you do, Robbie?" Bernie asked over a shared platter of sashimi.

"I teach high school literature," Robbie said.

"We adore teachers," Lyle said, squeezing his wife's hand. "And I can tell you're an excellent one."

Robbie rocked in her seat, rubbing her forearm where her hair had stood up at attention. "And how can you tell that?"

"It's your eyes," Lyle said. "You have the soulful eyes of a natural caregiver. People with eyes like yours are always excellent teachers."

"Or just mentors in general," Bernie added. "We have a couple of schools in Africa. If you ever want to travel and have an adventure, you can teach at one of our places. Just say the word."

Robbie chuckled as Nick raised his eyebrows at her. "Thank you for the offer, but I'm not much of a traveler or an adventurer."

"You could be," Nick said, pointing his chopsticks in her direction. "Nothing is holding you back."

"Listen, honey," Bernie said. "I didn't care for travel much either. Not until I met Lyle." She reached over and brushed an imaginary crumb from her husband's shoulder. Robbie suspected it was just an excuse for her to touch him again. They'd gone a full forty seconds without contact, and the strain must have been weighing on her. "You just need the right travel companion," Bernie said with a wink for Nick.

"Well, I mean . . . maybe—" Robbie stammered, stealing glances at her dinner partner, who looked too amused to step in and help her out of this situation.

"Don't embarrass the poor girl," Lyle said. He smiled lovingly at his wife to make sure Bernie knew he wasn't really displeased. "We don't know anything about Robbie and her relationship with our Nick."

Robbie turned to a smirking Nick and mouthed "our Nick" while Lyle continued.

"They might not be at that point in their relationship where they think of anything beyond breakfast the next morning."

"Now who's embarrassing them?" Bernie giggled. "You're always so bad. Besides, you know our Nick isn't one of those love them or leave them types." She leaned over the table and beckoned Robbie to join her. "Whenever he comes to Vegas, Lyle always tries to set him up with one of our showgirls, but Nick here always declines. There was a time when we thought he wanted to be a priest."

It was gratifying to see Nick squirm for once. All the teasing he'd dished out to her during this trip came back full circle at dinner, and Robbie sat back and enjoyed the ride. Lyle and Bernie regaled Robbie with stories about their world travels, some that even involved Nick, usually at one of their resorts abroad, and the thing that struck her the most was the ease they had with each other. One picked up where the other left off, sparing no detail or shrewd observation, one story more sensational than the last. It was a choreographed and well-rehearsed production, one that happened only after a successful run for decades.

Robbie tried to imagine her parents at a glittering dinner party entertaining their companions with their witty anecdotes and tales of their life but knew the *Chins: Live and Unplugged* would never make it, even far off-Broadway. Their production would resemble something closer to a local college theater department's rendering of *Our Town*, the empty set version. Though, Robbie had to admit there was something poetic in her parents' simplicity.

Her parents didn't jet-set around the world, or grope each other under the dining table, which clearly Lyle and Bernie were doing—both Robbie and Nick lowered their gaze to their dinner plates until the Goldmans composed themselves—but they had their own rhythm. Quiet but steady. Like a heartbeat that had lasted thirty years.

Robbie had never really thought about her parents in terms of a couple. They were Mom and Dad. Their existence in the world had been tied to Robbie—Robbie's needs, Robbie's care, raising Robbie. And like most kids growing up, she hadn't wanted to think of them as anything other than accessories to her life. *Her* means to *her* end. But there had been a Mr. and Mrs. Chin before there had been a Robbie. There had been a Tom and Cara.

Suddenly, her mother's anxiety over the party didn't seem so petty and annoying any longer. Maybe, just this once, Mrs. Chin wasn't picking on Robbie for picking's sake, but because this celebration meant something so much more to her. Robbie curled one hand into a fist in her lap and chewed her lower lip, thinking about Mrs. Chin's unanswered text message.

"Are you okay?" Nick whispered in her ear.

Robbie nodded. "Just thinking."

"They're great, aren't they?" Nick asked, tilting his head toward the Goldmans, who were still so caught up with each other, they didn't notice Nick and Robbie talking about them.

"They really are," Robbie said, watching the way Bernie gazed at Lyle like it was the first time she'd ever seen him. "What's the job they want done?"

"A Christmas shoot of all their properties, even the Caribbean ones. Though, they'll probably be photographed in August." Nick shifted in his seat and removed his phone from his pocket.

"How are you going to pull off Christmas in August?"

"Doesn't matter in the desert or the islands. They'll throw up some lights and Santas and be good to go. He told me earlier when you and Bernie went to the washroom to be sure to bring you with for the photoshoots. Bernie wants a gal pal to hang out with while the men work, he says."

"No problem," Robbie said with a wave of her hand. "I'll add it to our itinerary for our next trip. We needed a stop west of the Mississippi, anyway."

"Right," Nick said, then, with a wink, "since we can't stop for Rocky Mountain Oysters anymore."

Walking through the polished hotel lobby after dinner was a wholly different experience in her copper dress than it had been in crumpled running shorts. Robbie slowed her stride, taking her time, as though someone would catch sight of her glittering under the lights and spread the word of the bronze goddess among them. Word that, of course, Nathan would hear, spurring him to run from wherever he was to see this beauty, only to find it was the one he'd let slip away. "Here? But, how?" he would ask himself. She would see him from across the throng of her admirers, lift the corners of her mouth in a secretive smile, then disappear again.

"So, what now?" Nick asked, pausing in the center of the lobby, people swirling around them headed to the casino or one of the restaurants or clubs. He pointed to the conference registration table where a few straggling name tags remained. "Should we check?"

Robbie followed his lead to the table and perused the unclaimed tags, none of which read Dr. Nathan Tang. "He must have checked-in," Robbie said under her breath.

"Your call, Robbie Chin," Nick said with the same tone of voice he'd used in the Nebraskan restaurant. He was letting her take the lead again, and whatever course of action she decided, he would go along with.

Robbie's eyes flitted over the crowds of people. Nathan could be anywhere in the resort. Anywhere in the city. But she knew one thing for certain—Nathan was not in her hotel room. "Wanna play?" she asked, motioning to the casino floor entrance. It was still relatively early, and she'd never been to a casino before. An hour or two wouldn't hurt anyone.

"Really? Nick asked, his eyebrows shooting halfway up his forehead.

"Why not? We're here and dressed. And it's a waste of time trying to track Nathan down for an accidental meeting. Why not let fate take its course?" she said, questioning for the first time which way she wanted fate to go.

Mount Greenwich Academy hosted an annual fundraising casino night. The parents' association hired an entertainment company who decked out the gymnasium to look like a casino. Tables were scattered throughout, offering a chance to win at any number of games. Mini-skirted cocktail waitresses offered a selection of drinks. And vested dealers stood at the ready with unopened card decks waiting to be played. Robbie had always attended, sometimes with Nathan, usually on her own, and had tried her hand at a few of the games, all in the name of raising money for the school.

The Aria Resort casino, however, was nothing like the Mount Greenwich Academy gymnasium, making her wonder if any of the entertainment company's employees had ever visited Las Vegas. Not even the movies had adequately captured the atmosphere Robbie beheld as she crossed the threshold from lobby to casino. She'd always heard that to appreciate Las Vegas fully, one had to witness it firsthand. Never was she more a believer of that statement than she was at that moment.

Still sleek and modern, the casino lost the three-story windows from the lobby, but the number of lights from overhead, in addition to the gaming machines, gave the illusion of constant midday sun. Robbie marveled at the quiet. Several hundred people, at least, played various games, yet, she didn't have to strain her voice to be heard above the din of the crowd, nor could she immediately pick out the conversation of the people next to them. It felt as though they'd stepped inside a little bubble, just the two of them, that dulled all other noises.

"Pick your poison," she said to Nick, whose eyes zeroed in on the bank of blackjack tables. A trill of excitement rippled up her spine. Blackjack was the one game she halfway understood and wouldn't look like a complete fool playing. "A little twenty-one?"

"If you insist," Nick said with a smile, extending his arm.

She placed her hand on his forearm and let him escort her to the five-dollar table. They didn't need to get crazy about it. He pulled out a stool for her, then took the seat next to her. She shifted in her seat to cross her legs on an angle, the way she'd seen the movie femme fatales do, only her legs weren't long enough to reach the floor in an elegant manner, so she balanced her heel on the bar, stabilizing the stool legs.

Watching the other players at the table from the corner of her eye, she waited her turn to trade in her money for chips. Nick changed out several hundred dollars and began to slide her a stack. Robbie placed a staying hand on his. "What are you doing?" she whispered.

"Giving you some chips to play," he said with a confused expression. "I thought you were going to play, too."

"I am," Robbie said, reaching into her purse and pulling out a wadded up hundred-dollar bill. She always kept one stashed in the corner of her bag for emergencies, and while this didn't exactly qualify, she wasn't about to hand over the eight dollars and loose change in her wallet.

Setting her money on the table, she nodded to the dealer, who, with a smirk and arched eyebrow, took her cash and slid her a small pile of colored chips. Afraid at first that she would be expected to know what each color meant, she blew out a sigh of relief when she noticed the denomination printed on each. Following the other players' lead, she placed her opening ante on the table in front of her and waited for the cards to be dealt.

When the dealer placed a ten of hearts in front of her, Robbie's chest squeezed. She turned and watched as the dealer placed a four of diamonds next to Nick's seven of spades.

"What do you think?" he asked, leaning toward her. "Should I double down?"

Robbie counted the chips he already had on the table. Fifty dollars, at a five-dollar minimum table. Was he looking to lose money? But . . . he *was* the risk taker.

"Go for it," she said, letting Vegas Robbie take over.

Nick shoved a second pile of chips next to the first and tapped the table in front of him.

"Twenty-one," the dealer announced as she placed a queen of clubs on top of his first two cards. A couple at the end of the table nodded their congratulations, as a man stumbled up on the other side of Robbie, smelling of cheap cologne and expensive whiskey.

The dealer slid Robbie a second card. Ten of diamonds.

"What would you like to do?" the dealer asked. "Stay at twenty, or split."

Robbie looked to Nick, who appeared to be waiting on her answer, as well. "Are you going to stick?" he asked.

That was the big question, wasn't it? Regular Robbie would play it safe. She wouldn't risk more than she had to. She had a comfortable twenty. Why push her luck? But, was she Regular Robbie, or Vegas Robbie?

She wore the glittery dress. She'd been pampered at one of the finest spas, eaten at one of the top restaurants, and would fall asleep in the penthouse suite. Not one of those things described Regular Robbie, and she was having the time of her life.

"I'll split it," she announced, sliding a stack of chips to the center of the table.

"Good luck," the dealer said, before placing an ace of clubs down. The table erupted into applause. "Blackjack," the dealer announced and then placed a matching stack of chips next to Robbie's.

Robbie's head spun, and her palm grew slick with sweat. She understood why people liked Vegas so much. Besides the otherworldly accommodations and five-star food, winning was exhilarating. She pressed her palms together and held her breath, waiting for the dealer to give her her next card.

Five of hearts.

Robbie blew out a breath. Fifteen.

"What do you want to do?" the dealer asked.

"You gotta hit on fifteen, honey," the drunk man next to her said.

Robbie scrunched up her nose at the smell wafting off him. Leaning closer to Nick, she whispered, "Well?"

"He's right," Nick said, leaning back and slinging his arm across the back of Robbie's chair, glowering at her neighbor. Robbie leaned closer to Nick. Carrying her bags was good for his ego, but feeling Nick's protective urges come out to play was good for hers.

"Do it, girl," the woman on the other end of the table said, while her husband nodded his agreement. "It's your night."

Robbie looked up at the dealer, whose stone face revealed nothing. She knew it wouldn't. These dealers had been through extensive training. And it wasn't as though the dealer knew what the next card was anyway.

She tapped her fingers on the felt table the way she'd seen Nick do it. Six of diamonds. Twenty-one.

The table cheered again, and in a blink of an eye, Robbie had tripled her money. She squealed and gathered her winnings, then placed another small stack of chips down for her next hand.

"You sure?" Nick asked, squeezing her shoulder.

Robbie waved over a cocktail waitress, dropped a few chips on the girl's tray, and ordered two glasses of champagne.

"It's my night."

TWENTY-FIVE

Robbie dropped her now heavier purse on the suite's living room table and flopped on the sofa with a wide grin. "I can't believe it's after two in the morning," she said, pulling her hair back into a ponytail. She kicked off her heels and propped her feet on the table next to her bag holding her night's winnings.

"Time flies when you're busy winning," Nick said, leaning a shoulder against the wall separating the sitting room from the dining area. "Are you hungry at all?"

Robbie shook her head. "Just tired. I think the adrenaline rush has finally worn off." She rubbed her eyes, then groaned when she noticed the black smudges on her hand. Wearing what she called "fancy makeup" was not in her normal routine, and she'd forgotten she'd gone all out and had even used the eyeliner she reserved for black tie events. "Great. Now I look like a raccoon."

There was a click then a flash. When the floating circles left her vision, Nick was standing there holding his camera as though he'd conjured it from thin air.

"Now?" she asked. "Now you take my picture?" She hurled a designer throw pillow at his head, missing by a foot. "You couldn't have done that earlier before I ruined my makeup?"

Nick checked the image on his camera, then set it down. "That wasn't the Robbie I wanted to remember."

"This is?" Robbie asked, waving her hand over her crumpled dress, her sore feet, and her ruined hair and makeup. "Why would you ever want to remember this?"

"Because," Nick said, taking a hesitant step forward. "This is my Robbie. The one no one else gets to see." Maybe it was the champagne haze, but somehow the room folded in on itself, leaving Nick standing directly in front of Robbie instead of across the room. "Don't get me wrong," he said, and then Robbie was magically standing, too. "You were absolutely stunning tonight. But, right here, right now . . . this is the part of the night I look forward to. When you're you again, and no one gets to see it but me."

"You're Ivy's brother," Robbie whispered.

"And you're her best friend," he whispered back, tilting his head forward until his lips were just an inch away from hers. Kissing distance. All she had to was close the space.

Her eyes drifted closed. She felt the heat coming from his body. His hand grazed her arm, her skin tingling under his fingertips. Champagne or not, she wanted this. She wanted his hands to pull her to him. She wanted to feel his lips on hers. She'd wanted it for a while, but she'd held herself back because—well, because. But what happened in Vegas stayed in Vegas, right? Ivy didn't need to know. And it wasn't like she was cheating on—

"Nathan," she blurted out, instantly regretting it. Nick's eyes widened, and his head jerked back, and Robbie couldn't help feeling like she'd just dumped a whole Aria pool full of ice water over him. She didn't know why she'd said Nathan's name. She hadn't wished Nick had been him at that moment. Wanting to be with Nathan had been the farthest thing from her wishes.

"Right," he said, stepping back. "Sorry you didn't get a chance to find him tonight."

"That's not what—"

"It's late," he said, shoving his tingle-making hands in his pockets. "I've got a few small things to take care of tomorrow morning with Lyle, but then I can leave whenever you want."

He backed away from her, and Robbie's head screamed to stop him, grab him, make him stay, but her damn arms wouldn't move. Her mouth stayed pressed shut. Her head may have been Vegas Robbie, but her arms and mouth remained Regular Robbie.

He paused, and his eyes bore into her, pleading for a response. *Ask him to stay*, her head said. *Tell him you don't want Nathan anymore.* But even as she thought it, her gut clenched. It had been the first time she'd admitted that to herself, and it knocked her off balance. Was that true? It was easy to say she didn't want Nathan a moment ago when Nick was there in front of her, his warmth seeping into her, his hand on her arm. But, did she really not want Nathan at all? Ever? When had she thrown away almost a decade of her life? When had she closed that part of her heart?

She needed to think about this more. No, she needed to talk to her best friend about it and sort this out properly. But, how could she talk to Ivy about feelings she was having for her brother after spending hours just days ago crying over Nathan? Robbie's heart ached as she realized that if she couldn't talk to Ivy, the next person she wanted to talk to was Nick. And she couldn't do that either. She was on her own for this one, and she had no idea where to begin.

"Have a good night," she squeaked out, then walked away, each step driving the wedge between her and Nick deeper. She went to her bedroom and closed the door behind her without turning around. Pressing her back against the door, she waited until she heard the click of Nick's door closing before she sunk to the ground and put her head to her knees.

Nick had left the suite before Robbie emerged from her room the next morning. She'd hoped that would be the case, and had purposely waited locked in her room longer than necessary to give him the time and space. They each had some business to take care of before they dealt with each other.

She'd done some sleuthing while she'd been hiding out, and she'd been able to uncover the medical conference itinerary. Feeling confident she'd be able to pick out which sessions appealed to Nathan the most after years of listening to him drone on and on about work—funny, just a week ago, she sat in rapt attention and now she didn't know how she'd endured it—she had a reasonably detailed map of his day.

Robbie planned to find Nathan as he exited one of the sessions, march right up to him, and kiss him. Right then, right there. In front of all his colleagues and every other Aria Resort patron. Let the bellboys and cocktail waitresses watch. Let the doctors and dealers gawk. This was the definitive way, once and for all, to determine if she had any feelings left for Dr. Nathan Tang. If kissing Nathan made Robbie feel like she had the night before with Nick, then maybe there was something worth fighting for.

Abandoning her fancy dresses for the simple cotton sundress she'd fished from the bottom of her duffel bag, she brushed her hair and slipped on a pair of flip-flops. Anything more than that at ten in the morning screamed desperation. Though, what did showing up at his medical conference uninvited say? She grunted to herself and snatched her purse from the table where she'd left it the night before after cashing in her chips and returning to the suite with Nick. She was over-thinking again. What was it Dostoyevsky had said? *To think too much is a disease.*

One step at a time. That was the answer. Step one: leave the hotel suite. Step two: take the elevator to the lobby.

She checked the conference itinerary notes she'd taken on her phone. It was almost ten. The panel discussing pulmonary catastrophes was almost over, which meant Nathan would be walking out of the Bristlecone Ballroom Meeting Room Five in a matter of minutes. It would take about that much time, if not longer, to get to the convention center wing of the resort from her suite.

She knew she wouldn't be allowed in the actual conference without the proper security badge, but the hotel couldn't stop her from loitering outside the ballroom. She hoped her gut was right about Nathan needing to stretch his legs after sitting for so long in one place. As an emergency room doctor, he was always on his feet, and whenever he sat still for too long, his legs got twitchy. It was one of the reasons she hated going to the movies with him.

Keeping her stride hurried, but not to the point of jogging, she arrived at the Bristlecone Ballroom as the first wave of attendees filtered out of the conference doors. Robbie stepped behind one of the massive potted plants in the hallway separating the Bristlecone and another ballroom. She scanned the entries and realized she'd miscalculated the ease of her plan. There were at least a dozen different doors he could exit from, and while she'd assumed he'd be in room five, she had no way of knowing where in the massive space room five was, or if she'd been right about his itinerary.

Panic set in as small droplets of sweat ran down her back. It had all been so clear in her head the night before. Robbie would see him from across the room. She'd march through the crowd of people, past their curious stares and their whispered conjectures. Nathan would catch sight of her approaching. He'd furrow his brows, confused at first as to why she was there, but then his features would soften into something like pleasant surprise. With hair shining in the desert sunlight streaming through the wall of windows—which Robbie now knew was only on the casino side, not the convention side—Robbie wouldn't say a word. She would just reach an arm around his neck and pull his mouth to hers. There might even be clapping or cheering from the onlookers.

But there were too many people. Hundreds, maybe thousands, of doctors swarmed the convention hall floor. So many, Robbie wondered who was manning the hospitals. This was not a good day to need medical attention.

She checked the time and strained to see around the clusters of people who'd stopped in the middle of the hallway to talk. Still no sign of Nathan. She should have looked for him the night before instead of playing the night away with Nick. A lump formed in her throat. The truth was, she hadn't even thought about looking for Nathan while she'd been with Nick. Not until she'd been standing inches away from Nick, with his hand on her arm, and her aching to close the distance.

This was stupid. Robbie had other things to do with her time, like help her mother prepare for her anniversary party—a party Nathan had neglected to tell her he wouldn't be attending with her for weeks after he'd made other plans, she reminded herself. Plus, Nick had secured them their room as a favor. She couldn't be rude and occupy the most expensive suite at the resort any longer than she had. It was time to call it. She'd indulged this little fantasy of a reunion with Nathan long enough.

She'd already hurt Nick, and for what?

Stepping out from her hiding spot, she kept her head down and hurried along the corridor back toward the casino side of the resort. She'd almost made it until she caught sight of the back of his head. She should have guessed. Nathan had made a beeline straight to the gourmet coffee stand outside the ballroom.

This was her chance. He was still fourth in line, and he hadn't ordered yet. She could get in and get out with the information she needed with barely a hiccup in line. She veered in his direction, straightening her back, and hoping the fluorescent lights still made her hair shine.

But someone beat her to it.

A woman Robbie had never seen before stepped beside Nathan and snaked her arm around his waist while he draped his over her shoulders. Robbie watched as he bent his head to the mystery woman's and placed a small kiss on her temple.

Robbie stood behind them with doctors and medical professionals swirling around her, yet not one of them noticed the woman who had gone catatonic in the middle of the hall. No one stopped to ask her why she'd gone so pale, or if she was going to pass out. No one rushed to get her a drink of water or find her a seat like they did in the movies. They all just kept moving and going about their days. And Nathan and the woman kept standing there with their arms around each other as though he hadn't been in a long-term relationship days ago. As though the last eight years with Robbie hadn't been anything more than a hobby to be put aside after growing out of it.

Robbie backed away and hurried from the convention wing before Nathan could turn around and find her. With each step she took away from Nathan, warmth returned to her face and hands. Her phone buzzed with an incoming text from her father, of all people. "Your mother wants to know when to expect you."

Robbie froze in her tracks, her chest squeezing her breath out of her lungs. She couldn't put it off any longer. Dialing her father's number, she ducked into the coffee shop and covered one ear while pressing the phone to the other.

"Dad?" she said when she heard him pick up.

"Robbie, is that you?" her father asked. "It's loud on your end."

"Dad, I've had a change of plans," she said, raising her voice. "I'm on my way, but I drove instead of flying. I'll be home a few days earlier than planned. Can you tell Mom?"

There was a pause on the other end, and she imagined her father telepathically conveying her message to Mrs. Chin, partly because she couldn't think of one time—ever—when she had seen her father deliver a message of any sort to her mother. Yet, somehow, they'd remained in sync all these years, so the messages had to get through somehow, didn't they? Telepathy was the only sensible answer.

"Is everything okay?" her father finally asked. "Is Nathan with you?"

Robbie braced herself. "No, Dad. Nathan's not with me. We broke up. I'm moving back to San Francisco, but I'll be staying with Ivy."

Her father never raised his voice. That was reserved for Mrs. Chin, the feisty Italian, he called her behind her back. Her father's mode of admonishment was equally as effective but with a quieter tone. His voice would first go flat, robotic, devoid of any emotion. Then, calmly, he would explain how her actions had upset him. It wasn't the text, but the subtext, that gutted Robbie each time. Somehow, with very few words, her father could make her feel that she had ripped his heart out with her bare hands.

"That's probably for the best. Drive safely," Robbie's father said at last. "We'll see you when you get here."

Robbie shook her head at her blank phone screen and continued her trek to her suite. She'd overstayed her welcome in Vegas.

By the time she returned to the suite, a sweat had broken out across her forehead. Nick looked up from his computer, his eyes bright and wide, and his bag packed and standing by the door ready to go. "You okay?" he asked with no trace of awkwardness from the night before, as though they hadn't been moments away from tumbling into bed together, probably ruining her friendship with Ivy forever, and sealing her fate with Nathan before she'd known it had already been sealed.

Robbie clutched the diamond pendant she still wore from the night before and pressed her lips together. Why did none of the men in her life grieve the loss of her companionship? Whether it was the better part of a decade, or a drunken moment in time, or her own father—for once, it would be nice if someone missed her.

She'd been up all night worrying about how Nick would feel in the morning. Was he hurt? Embarrassed? Had it been a mistake on his end and he hoped Robbie hadn't read too much into it? And if for a moment her mind slipped away from Nick, it landed on Nathan. What had he been doing since they broke up? Did he regret ending things? At all?

But it was painfully clear that neither one of them had given her a second thought. Nathan had moved on before she'd even reached San Francisco. And Nick? The night before might as well have never happened with the way he was acting.

"I'm ready to go," she said, charging into her room and lugging her bags out. Nick stood and reached for her duffel, but she pulled away, holding the bag closer to her chest to hide the trembling in her arms. They didn't need her. Fine. She didn't need them, either.

TWENTY-SIX

Nine hours in a confined space was a long time to ignore someone. Robbie had only managed two of those hours before the pent-up pressure in her head forced her to do something to release it.

"Did you square everything away with Lyle?" she asked, keeping her head turned from Nick. This was her peace offering. It wasn't much, but it was the best she could do at the moment.

"I did," Nick said. "Both he and Bernie said to say goodbye, and they hope your parents' party goes well."

"That was nice of them." Robbie cringed, hating the way their voices sounded, completely disconnected from each other. As though they were strangers bumping into each other on the street. *Excuse me. Please, you go first.* She reached for her phone, needing something to focus on other than the way her heart ached to talk to him in the way they had before last night. "Dammit."

"What's wrong?"

"I forgot to charge my phone last night, and it's almost dead. Seven percent." Robbie groaned. "And my charger is in my bag in the back."

Nick shifted in his seat and reached into his pocket. "Here," he said, handing her a coiled cord. "Since when do you let your phone go that low?"

"Since last night," she mumbled. "This cord won't work in here. They didn't have USB ports in 1974. I don't suppose you have an adapter for the cigarette lighter in that pocket of yours?"

"Sorry," he said with a sympathetic shrug. "We'll pick one up at the next gas stop."

Robbie hadn't spoken to Ivy since they'd arrived in Vegas and she was going to bust if she didn't tell someone about what she'd seen at the Aria Convention Center. She darted a glance in Nick's direction. No doubt about it—he was the wrong choice for that particular conversation.

Robbie swallowed the lump in her throat as flashes from the night before came to mind. If it hadn't been for Robbie's stupid outburst about Nathan, her adventures as Vegas Robbie would have ended in a very different manner. But she had to be careful not to tell Ivy any of that.

"Hey," she texted Ivy, dipping her toes into the water.

"How'd it go?" Ivy fired back as though she'd been waiting for Robbie's text. She probably had been.

"I saw him. He was with another woman."

"With with?"

"Arm around her. Kiss on temple."

"Could be anything. Old acquaintance?"

Bless Ivy and her need to make Robbie feel better. Ivy said these things for Robbie's benefit, not because she believed them. Ivy wouldn't say it, but she wanted Nathan gone. It must have been hard for Ivy, considering she was probably mid-cartwheel while she typed out her messages.

"You don't have to pretend. I'm fine." Robbie stared at her screen waiting for Ivy's next response. Tears formed in the corner of her eye. She blinked them back, holding them in. Tears were for later when she was locked away from the world with Ivy and a glass of wine. Not now. Not with Nick sitting next to her.

The truth was—she wasn't fine. Not really. How could she be? Eight years she'd been with Nathan. Almost her entire adult life had involved him in a significant way. All the plans she'd made for her future featured Nathan front and center. Then, with no warning, all of that changed.

She didn't just lose a boyfriend; she'd lost everything. Her comfort and security. Her home. Her job—oh, God, her job, who wanted an answer by the end of the day regarding her employment. She would have to remember to email them later whenever they stopped. Robbie supposed she could go back to New York and stay at Mount Greenwich Academy. But what was New York without Nathan? Every friend she had made there was connected to him. Every memory, every special place. There was nothing in New York that wasn't attached to Nathan, and if she was no longer going to be part of the Nathan and Robbie equation, then what was there to stay for?

"Stop!" Robbie cried out, the tears streaming down her face. She dropped her phone on the center console and covered her face with her hands.

"What's wrong? Are you sick?" Nick asked, panic seeping into his tone.

"Please, just pull over," she sobbed. She couldn't stop crying. If this was going to happen, she had to do it somewhere else. *Don't make a scene. Don't let anyone see you cry.*

Nick threw a worried glance in her direction and exited the highway at the next ramp. Robbie swung the door open before he pulled to a complete stop and jumped out of the moving car, walking as far away from the car as she could. Nick shouted for her to wait, but there was no more waiting for her.

She'd waited for Nathan—to finish medical school, to complete his residency, to start his career—and where did that get her? On the side of the road in a 1974 Ford Pinto pea green station wagon. Her beautiful Jeep, the one she'd taken care of like the way she thought she'd taken care of her relationship, had refused to part with her life in New York and left Robbie to drive off to her future in a rusted piece of junk. If that wasn't some symbolism to throw at her third-year American Lit students, she didn't know what was.

Laughter bubbled out of her as she wiped the tears from her face. As much as she couldn't have stopped crying, she couldn't control the laughter now. She gripped the side of her waist and doubled over, her cheeks aching. Nick, who remained standing outside her stupid life metaphor, tilted his head and watched her drag herself back to where he watched her with curiosity.

"What's going on?" he asked, a grin tugging at the corners of his mouth. Robbie saw he wanted to laugh, too, but didn't know if he should.

"I hate this stupid car," Robbie said, kicking its front tire. "It's ugly, and it smells."

Nick looked over his shoulder at the pile of junk and shrugged. "Or, it's unique with an interesting back story."

"You're a very glass-half-full type of guy, aren't you?" Robbie asked, grinning though she felt the tears trying to build up again. She'd had her outburst. This time, she'd hold them in.

His smile broke free this time, lighting up his features for the first time that day. "Only when I think it will make you feel better."

"And if it didn't?"

"Well, then," he said, stepping closer to her and dropping his voice like they were conspiring against the demon car, "I guess I would have to find a way to fill the glass and end the debate."

Robbie wanted to throw her arms around him. Not because of the night before. Not because she wanted anything other than for him to hold her. But because he was her friend, and he understood her, and she knew, without a doubt, if she told him about Nathan and her reason for running from the car, he would understand that, too. He would find the right thing to say, despite everything else. And he would always try to fill her glass.

Robbie blew out a heavy breath and bit her lower lip. "I need a hug."

Just like she thought, and with no questions asked, he pulled her to him and held her against his chest. He stroked her hair and placed a small kiss on the top of her head without saying a word. He didn't ask for explanations or apologies. He didn't offer advice. He just held her and kept her from crumbling while she closed her eyes and put herself together again.

When Robbie buckled herself back in the car, she checked her phone to find Ivy's response. "You will be more than fine."

They arrived in San Francisco after nine. Robbie rolled down her window and breathed in the sea air. The sun hadn't fully set yet, and the sky lit with hues of blue and purple stretching out over the water. Robbie hadn't realized how much she'd missed watching the sun disappear behind the ocean, and made a note to watch as many sunsets as possible from now on.

"Should I take you to your parents?" Nick asked as he navigated through the city streets they'd grown up on.

Robbie shook her head. "I sent them a message a while ago. I told them I'd be home in the morning. I need to get my head straight first." He didn't ask anything more, knowing what Robbie needed the most now was his sister.

Parking the car in Ivy's narrow driveway, Nick waited for Robbie to make the first move. Robbie sat and stared at Ivy's house, where she'd spent almost as much time growing up as her own. Ivy had had it painted since she'd taken over the ownership. Gone were the bright rainbow colors that had been favored when they were young. Muted grays and blues were the style choices now. And while Robbie preferred the more subdued modern look, a part of her missed the cheery yellow siding that had always greeted her when their days were simpler.

"Ready?" Nick asked. Robbie nodded. "Go on in. I'll get the bags."

"You're here!" Ivy squealed, wrapping her arms around Robbie and squeezing so hard Robbie struggled to take a breath. "Mrs. Chin?"

"I'll deal with her tomorrow," Robbie said, hugging her friend tight. Dorothy had it right; there really was no place like home.

"Good. You're mine tonight." Ivy led Robbie into the living room, where she had not one, but three bottles of wine chilling, and an assortment of goodies laid out to eat. "I've made preparations."

"I don't want to interrupt," Nick said from the doorway. "I just wanted to let Robbie know I put her bags in the guest room."

"Thank you," Robbie said. She'd meant "thank you for everything." The company, the talks, the compassion and patience. But she was afraid saying anything more would open another flood gate. But, if he were still the Nick he'd been from the road, he'd hear it all in the two words she managed to squeeze out.

In response, he dipped his chin to his chest before turning to his sister. "You need anything else?"

"Yeah, a hug from my brother who I haven't seen in a few months." Ivy held her arms out to him, and he dutifully returned her greeting. "Catch up later?"

"You can make me lunch tomorrow." He saluted his sister, winked at Robbie, then turned and disappeared.

"He's not staying here?" Robbie asked, watching Nick retrieve his bag from the Pinto and start walking away.

Ivy shook her head. "He has a place three blocks down. He hasn't lived here since mom and dad moved. Look, I love the dork, but we'd kill each other under the same roof for more than a day. It's very convenient for me to water his plants when he travels."

Robbie smiled, keeping her eyes on the back of his head. "He has plants?" The idea of him taking care of something besides himself warmed her.

"Some," Ivy said. "If it's a long trip, I get the mail and kind of watch the place, too. Light dusting. Empty his fridge."

"You're a good sister," Robbie said, finally turning away from Nick's retreating back. "He's lucky to have you."

"I know." Ivy patted the sofa beside her, then poured two glasses of wine and handed Robbie one. "Okay, time to spill. Everything and from the beginning."

So Robbie detailed for Ivy the events of that fateful day a week before. One week. That was all that it had been since her world turned upside down. One week ago, her life had been traveling down one path, and now—who knew where it headed. Robbie certainly didn't. What did she know? This Robbie, the version of herself that had arrived in San Francisco, was not the same as the version of herself who had left New York.

"Well, now," Ivy said when Robbie had finished her tale of woe. She took a long sip of her wine and eyed Robbie over the rim of her glass. "How do you feel now? Like, right now at this moment? If Nathan walked in that door, what's your first gut reaction?"

Robbie tried to imagine Nathan walking through the door, head hanging, an apology on his lips, but all she could picture was Nick leaving. She pressed her fist into her sternum to quiet the fluttering in her chest.

"I really can't picture him," Robbie said. "It's strange because all week all I could think about was Nathan coming to his senses and racing across the country to be here when I arrived, to sweep me off my feet with his regret and promises of never even thinking of breaking up again. And now that I'm here . . . nothing."

"What did you feel when you saw him with the other woman in Vegas?"

"Hurt. Betrayed," Robbie said, remembering the way Nathan so easily slipped his arm around someone else.

"And now when you think about it?"

Robbie took a deep breath and a steadying drink of wine. "After my freak out on the side of the road on the way here? Numb. Is that normal so soon? Is there something wrong with me?"

Ivy laughed and pulled her friend closer until Robbie rested her head on her shoulder. "There's nothing wrong with you. And if you think about it, you'd already been broken up a week when you saw him—a week of you living your life without him. Having adventures without him. Doing things you would have never thought to try if you were still with him."

"That's true," Robbie said. Ivy had a point. "Can I tell you something?"

"Always."

"When Nick and I were in Vegas and playing in the casino, I didn't think of Nathan once. It was like I had completely forgotten why I was there in the first place."

"Can I tell you something?" Ivy asked.

"Always."

"I think the reason you were able to forget him and were numb after your freak out is that you finally realized you didn't really love him."

Robbie bolted straight in her seat and opened her mouth to say something, but Ivy held up her hand to stop her.

"Hear me out," Ivy said. "I love you and will support you no matter what, but indulge me for a moment." She paused while Robbie collected herself, then gave Ivy a tentative nod to continue. "Close your eyes for a minute and picture your life with Nathan. Every day. What does that look like? Comfortable. Reliable. Steady. But are you smiling? Are you laughing? Are you playing?"

"When we started dating—"

"Forget about when you started dating," Ivy interrupted. "Everyone is starry-eyed and full of fluttery giggles in the beginning. I'm talking about after eight years together. Did you smile every day? Did you laugh? Did he make you feel special and loved? Or just . . . comfortable?"

Robbie squeezed her eyes tight and crinkled her nose. If she was honest with herself, truly honest, then Robbie had to recognize the fact that most days, while she wasn't unhappy, she wasn't happy either. More like going through the motions.

"Could this break-up be a blessing in disguise?" Ivy asked.

"You're just saying that because you want me to move back to San Francisco," Robbie said, nudging her friend with her elbow, then pouring herself more wine. "And you never liked Nathan."

"Not true," Ivy said. "Well, yes, I would love it if you stayed here. But I always fully supported your move." That was true. Ivy had been a pillar of support at that time when Robbie's nerves had been on hyperdrive. "And it's not that I didn't like Nathan. I just never thought he was the *one*. He was exactly who you needed in your life at the time. But that phase of your life ended."

"And the relationship should have ended then, too," Robbie mumbled. She covered her face with her hands and groaned. "Mrs. Chin is going to kill me. I ruined her happily ever after plan."

"She'll come around."

Robbie sat in silence for a few moments, contemplating everything Ivy had just said and measuring her breaths. She imagined her life moving forward without Nathan. What would she do now? Start over? Find another job. Move in with Ivy. Then what? She'd had it all planned, all mapped out, and now there was nothing ahead of her.

She switched her focus and tried to picture growing old with Nathan, but that image never came into view. What had been so clear and tangible the week before was nothing but a mirage, a trick of the light, better left in the desert.

"Just another adventure," she heard Nick's voice say in her head. This time, however, it didn't sound so scary.

TWENTY-SEVEN

A high-pitched bleating pierced through Robbie's wine-fueled dreams, dragging her reluctant conscious back from the depths of sleep. Dehydrated from both the drinking and the tears, Robbie thankfully gulped the bottle of water Ivy must have left for her on the bedside table before going to pass out in her own bed. God knew Robbie was in no condition to think of putting it there herself before passing out.

She threw her arm over her eyes, blocking the sun already streaming through the window. She had to get up. She had to get dressed. And she had to go to her parents' house. She couldn't put off the inevitable for too long. By this time, Robbie was sure her father had already informed Mrs. Chin of her relationship status, and Robbie was certain her mother would drag her home for an explanation if Robbie didn't go willingly. Forcing herself out of bed, Robbie showered and dressed with her eyes half closed. It wasn't until she was slipping on her shoes that she noticed she had a message, from Mrs. Chin.

"We know you're back in town," her mother's voice said way too loudly. "It's time you came home."

Robbie groaned and rubbed her temples. The jig was up. Her parents knew something was going on, they'd given her space, and now she had to face the firing squad.

"Heading out?" Ivy asked, padding into the hall still in her pajamas.

"I've been summoned," Robbie said, holding up her phone as evidence.

Ivy clucked her tongue and shook her head. "You knew you couldn't avoid it forever. What are you going to tell them?"

"The truth," Robbie said, running her hand through her hair. She was determined not to make a dramatic scene. Her parents didn't like emotional outbursts. Sobbing meant Robbie had something to be sorry for. It meant she'd been at fault somehow, like she hadn't done enough, tried enough, to keep the relationship going. If Robbie had given it her all and it still hadn't worked out, there was nothing to be sad about. Her mother had told her that the first time Robbie had cried over a boy.

Her parents loved Nathan, sometimes more than they loved Robbie, it seemed. But it was Robbie they were stuck with, and it was time they faced that fact, as well.

"Good luck," Ivy said with a quick hug.

"Thanks. I'll catch up with you later."

Robbie walked the one block to her parents' house, though it would have been fun to see her mother's reaction to her new car. One thing at a time, though. She wasn't sure how much Mrs. Chin could handle in one day. Robbie trudged up her childhood home's front stairs, each step a depressing thud. She had just reached the stoop when the front door swung open.

"Get in here," her mother said, her lips pressed into a thin line.

"What is this business about you driving all the way across the country and you don't even come to see your parents?"

"It's not like that, Mom," Robbie said, feeling younger and younger as the seconds ticked by. "It was late. I didn't want to wake you."

"You didn't want to talk to me, you mean." Her mother turned and walked to the back of the house toward the kitchen, where Robbie heard dishes clattering, expecting her to follow.

Robbie's father stood by the counter, piles of dishes stacked in front of him. "Hi, Robbie," he said, before setting a handful of salad plates down. "Good drive?"

"It was fine," Robbie said, her eyes scanning the empty cabinets. "What's going on? The party's not for another week. And doesn't the catering company provide the dishes?"

"Robinson Chin, start talking," Mrs. Chin said with an abrupt subject change.

Robbie sighed and set her bag on the few inches of clear space on the table. "Nathan and I broke up, Mom."

It was Mrs. Chin's turn to sigh, long and loud, the exasperated sound of her last thread of hope for her daughter fraying. "Your father told me that much," she said. Robbie knew she was making it difficult for her mother by not willingly providing the details the woman wanted, but twenty-eight had a way of feeling twelve in her parents' house, and she couldn't help herself. "Why?"

Because Nathan didn't love her, and after hours of discussion over wine and pizza rolls, Robbie had concluded, she hadn't loved him either. Or, she wasn't "in love" with him. She was still a little fuzzy on the distinction sometimes, but Ivy had it down cold and could explain it better. But the crux of it all was that neither one of them loved each other in a way that was meant to last. Nathan had figured it out first.

"We're not meant to be," Robbie said. "Not in the long run."

"Long run? What do you call eight years?"

"Six years too long?" Robbie said. Then, when her mother pinched the bridge of her nose and took a deep breath, Robbie switched to a different approach. "We're not right for each other. Not anymore. Neither of us would be truly happy if we stayed together. And isn't that what you want? For me to be happy?"

Mrs. Chin threw her hands in the air and looked to the ceiling for a translation she could understand. "Happy? She wants to be happy. Not everything in life has to make you happy. You weren't unhappy, were you?"

"Okay, then, don't you want *Nathan* to be happy? That's the real problem here, isn't it? That I blew it? I lost you your chance at a superstar son-in-law? Maybe you two could still be friends. And he'll be just fine, Mom. I have it on good authority he's already got a replacement lined up. You'd probably like her."

Robbie's heart pounded in her ears. Why was it always so difficult to have a conversation with her mother? Why couldn't she take Robbie's side for once? Be on Team Robbie. Hug her and tell her everything would be fine, and that she'd find someone perfect and more amazing when the time was right?

"Did you quit your job?" Mrs. Chin folded her arms over her chest and waited.

"Yes." Sort of. Not really. She'd let the deadline slip, but she planned on sending the principal official notice anyway.

"What are you going to do now?" Mrs. Chin fired back. "What about your future?"

"What about my future? I can get another job." The thought of calling Nick's friend for a favor turned her stomach, but she might have to choose the lesser evil to keep Mrs. Chin off her back. "And I have plenty in my savings until then. We're not in the 1800's, you know. You don't have to worry about marrying off your spinster daughter before she's homeless and on the streets."

Mrs. Chin wheeled back as though Robbie had struck her. In all Robbie's teen angst years, when the two of them had argued so often it felt like a daily routine, never had Robbie seen her mother look so wounded by something she'd said. She thought she would feel oddly victorious at the moment, but instead, Robbie stood in stunned silence as her mother worked through her mix of emotions, all of which were written across her face—shock, followed by hurt, before finishing off with disbelief.

"Why don't we all sit down and have a cup of coffee," her father said, stepping between them, his hands outstretched to each of them. "Robbie, your mother is just concerned about you."

"Concerned? That's what this is?" Robbie asked, feeling her insides coil, making ready for another attack. "People break up all the time. I've done it a few times already. Why all the concern now?"

Mrs. Chin squared her shoulders and lifted her jaw. "You won't understand until you're a mother."

Robbie threw her hands in the air. She couldn't stand there looking at this woman anymore. Every second standing under her mother's scowl caused her blood pressure to tick up a notch. She hadn't come to fight. It was Mrs. Chin's shock and disappointment talking, she told herself. Had she come home sooner, or given her mother a warning, maybe this conversation would have gone differently, though Robbie doubted it. It just would have given her mother more time to come up with reasons why Robbie had failed.

"Where are you going?" Mrs. Chin asked as Robbie scooped up her purse and headed for the door.

"Out," Robbie said without stopping.

"We're not done," her mother called after her.

"We are for today," Robbie called back over her shoulder.

Robbie pounded her feet like a pouting six-year-old straight through the house, out the door, down the steps, and onto the sidewalk. This reunion could not have gone any worse. In all the ways Robbie had imagined this conversation going, the actual event far surpassed her worst predictions. Disappointment she'd expected. The questions were a surety. What Robbie hadn't expected was her mother's conviction that without Nathan Robbie was lost in the world.

Robbie seethed as she walked. She hadn't planned on going anywhere particular, but when she paused outside Cover to Cover, the small bookstore she and Ivy had often visited in their younger days, Robbie knew she'd reached her safe place. A place that had always eased her problems in the past. A place where Robbie could get lost in other people's drama and forget her own. She warmed with satisfaction to see it still held its ground in the wake of the digital age. She'd always preferred the feel and smell of real books over the digital, but she also recognized the convenience of having a thousand titles at your fingertips with the simple download of an app.

She couldn't resist going in—to see, not to buy. Maybe only one, if they had something in stock Robbie had been wanting to read. The shop didn't have as large a selection as the national chains due to limited space, but the owner was more than willing to special order any requests.

"Robbie Chin, is that you?" Drea, the shop's owner, said skirting out from behind the register. "I haven't seen you in ages. Are you in town visiting?"

Robbie smiled wide and held her arms out as Drea grabbed her in a friendly embrace. "I moved back here, actually," Robbie said, catching her breath after Drea had squeezed it out of her. "I'm living with Ivy right now."

"Your mother must be thrilled to have you back," Drea said. Not having any children of her own, Drea had a way of romanticizing the parent-child relationship, her own parents having passed when she'd been a young woman.

Robbie simply smiled. *Thrilled* was not the word she would have chosen to describe her mother's feelings on the topic of her return, but she didn't want to be the one who ruined Drea's fantasy.

"How's everything with you?" Robbie asked, scanning the worn but full shelves. "Business still good?"

"It is," Drea beamed. "I'm telling you, those first years of the digital books nearly wiped me out. But we weathered the storm, and now there seems to be a renewed interest in print. Not to mention the university students who like to think they're somehow going to bankrupt the big-box stores by buying a book from me. But who am I to argue, right? You have to love their gusto."

Robbie chuckled. She'd missed talking to Drea on her habitual book browsing trips, something she planned on rekindling. They chatted a few more minutes about the neighborhood before a group of those silly university students strolled in, designer coffees in hand, and began combing through the new releases.

Drea nodded in their direction. "There's some of the new batch of regulars. They come in once or twice a week, always with a coffee, and always wanting to know when I expect new arrivals. I always tell them I'd be happy to order them anything they want, but they never seem to know what that is." Drea clucked her tongue disapprovingly. "They don't want any suggestions either. They'll know what they want when they see it, they say. I tell them you can't judge a book by its cover for a reason, but they don't want to hear that."

Robbie studied the group clustered together. First-years, she guessed, out in the world on their own for the first time. Upperclassmen preferred the bars. If they were highbrow or had something to prove— the wine lounges. They looked like the type of kids she could have taught this past year, which gave her an idea.

With a wink to Drea, Robbie strolled to the new release shelves and pretended to peruse the selection. The little group glanced her way but ignored her and continued their analysis of modern science fiction. Robbie cringed when she heard them reference George Lucas as the father of the genre.

"Excuse me. I couldn't help overhearing," Robbie said, finding the right lull in their conversation, "but if it's really outstanding science fiction you're looking for, you should try some of the classics that defined the genre. Mary Shelley. Jules Verne. H. G. Wells."

They all blinked at her in unison without saying a word for so long, Robbie wondered if she'd actually spoken English, or had her great-grandmother's wish come true and she had somehow learned to speak Chinese, after all.

"Do you work here?" one of the two girls in the group asked. She had a ring in her nose that must have been a new addition because she kept flaring her nostrils as though she was trying to get used to the feel of it.

"No," Robbie said. "I'm just a big reader. Maybe if you're bored with the current state of the genre, you should go back to the roots, back to when it was groundbreaking before there were tropes or expectations. When it was considered scandalous to write about some of these things."

They looked from one another with hesitation, playing some weird game of chicken. A tall, lanky boy in desperate need of a haircut lost and spoke up first. "Are those books here?"

Robbie smiled and pointed to the back corner. "If memory serves me correctly, they're on the top shelf with the classics."

They shuffled to the corner she had indicated, and Drea appeared at her elbow. "Well done," Drea said. "You'd make an excellent bookseller."

Robbie laughed and shook her head. "It's just one of those Jedi mind tricks you learn as a high school teacher. If you make something sound dangerous or rebellious, they'll go for it."

"Too bad," Drea said. "I'd like to retire one day, but I hate the idea of closing the store. Guess I'll just have to live forever."

Robbie watched Drea moved back to the register as the group of students made their way back to the front of the shop, each with a book in hand. Robbie smiled to herself as she recognized the covers for some of her favorite Mary Shelly and Jules Verne novels. They wouldn't be sorry.

"Now," Drea said, clapping her hands together. "Are you looking for anything specific?"

Answers about life. A job. A book about dealing with your stubborn and opinionated mother. "Not really. I just thought I'd look around for a bit."

Drea nodded thoughtfully. "I know that face."

"What face?" Robbie asked.

"That one you used to wear all the time when something bad happened and you wanted to take your mind off it. You thought I didn't notice because I didn't say anything, didn't you?"

Robbie nodded.

"I noticed. But I also understood the healing power of literature, like you did. You had your friend to confide in to soothe your heart. You came here to soothe your soul." Drea smiled, almost sadly. "I'm sorry for whatever happened. Take your time."

Drea puttered around the counter for a few more minutes before disappearing into the back room. Robbie didn't mind. She knew this store like the back of her hand. Like Robbie knew her childhood bedroom at home. Like she knew Ivy's. Drea wasn't wrong. Robbie had loved coming into this store after a bad day, and standing in the middle of it now, the same feelings of peace and security washed over her.

Running a hand along the book spines, Robbie wove through the shelves. It was a game she used to play when she wasn't looking for any specific title. She would walk up and down the aisles, brushing along the books, waiting for one of them to catch her attention. Sometimes a song would come on the speakers that would make her stop in her tracks. Whatever book her hand had landed on was the winner. Sometimes it was an impatient Ivy calling to her to hurry up, that forced her hand.

This time it was Drea holding out a cup of coffee. "Join me?"

Robbie smiled and accepted the mug. In all her hangover-fighting, she hadn't stopped for coffee or breakfast. She turned to the last book her hand had touched and pulled it from the shelf. It was an annotated *Alice's Adventures in Wonderland*. She didn't have that one yet. Maybe her day was starting to look up.

Robbie sat with Drea at one of the tables in the center of the store sipping their coffee and catching up. After the lively discussion on what they'd been reading and which new releases they looked forward to most, Drea, with all her mentor wisdom, steered the conversation back to Robbie.

"So, teaching. You like it, then?" Drea asked, rising from her seat as two women walked in dragging their toddlers behind them. "Hello, ladies.

Can I help you find something?"

"I think we'd just like to look around," one of them said with an apologetic smile as her young son pulled on her hand.

Drea bent down to the boy's eye level and exchanged looks with him and his little friend. "Do you boys like Legos?" They both grinned and clapped their hands in response. "Good. Back there in the corner, there's a table and a whole box of them just for you to play with while your mommies look around. Okay?"

The second woman appeared hesitant to release her child. "Are you sure?"

Drea waved off the children and pointed them in the direction of the play area. "That's why they're there. Plus, you'll notice, you can see that corner from anywhere in the store—just in case. It's just the four of us in here right now, so take your time."

Robbie laughed as the boys took off as fast as their legs could carry them to the box of building blocks and other assorted toys. Drea wasn't lying: she had made sure every aisle had been angled in the exact right way so parents can keep a watchful eye on their little ones. Also, so she could keep a watchful eye while perched at the counter. It was pretty genius.

"Where were we?" Drea asked, rejoining Robbie at the table. "Teaching. You like it?"

Robbie thought about her answer before delivering her canned response of, "I've always loved literature." It was true, but not the answer to Drea's question. "I'm good at it." Still not an answer, and Drea knew it.

"Being good at something and having a passion for it are two different things. I'm great at roasting vegetables, but I hate eating them."

Robbie chuckled. "Fair point." She shrugged. "I enjoyed it enough, but I wouldn't say it's my passion."

"Will you be looking for another teaching job now that you're back?"

Robbie groaned and rubbed her temples. "I suppose I should. Ivy's brother has a friend who can get me into San Fran University High."

Drea's eyebrows shot up. She was impressed. She should be. The school was the west coast version of Mount Greenwich Academy. "Let me guess. You're not too keen on the idea."

"The thought was nice. I just can't stand the idea of someone pulling strings for me. It's not right," Robbie said, crossing her arms over her chest.

It felt like when her high school counselor had advised her to mark the Asian box on all her college applications. He'd told her it had been the only way her top picks of schools would accept her application. There had been nothing else special about her. Not her stellar grades. Not her extracurriculars. Not her volunteer hours and letters of recommendations. Robbie never did check that damn box on any of the applications. And when her letters of acceptance rolled in, she'd made sure to leave copies of them with her counselor.

"I want to earn my career on my own, with my own merits, you know?" Robbie continued. "It's the only way I'll ever know if I was ever any good at something."

"I do know," Drea said, nodding. "Well, if not teaching, then what?"

Drea left her to ponder that question while she took care of the two women who had seemed to settle on a few titles for themselves and their little ones. The two boys reached for their new books as soon as Drea scanned them, their eyes lighting with excitement. *It must be nice to see that excitement every day*, Robbie thought.

TWENTY-EIGHT

Robbie swung the door to her pea-green Pinto Wagon closed, cringing as the screech from the hinges grated on her nerves. She trudged up the steps, returning from a job interview that would most likely lead to nowhere. This one was for a tutoring center. Not what she had been looking for, but in the same family, at least. And they'd been the only one of the dozen applications she'd sent out that had responded.

She missed her shiny, slick Jeep. The way the doors whispered past her and ended in a cushioned thud. The way the seat had molded to fit her slender frame. The shock system. That she probably missed the most, the feeling of driving on a cloud. Not like driving her current mode of transportation, which exaggerated every crack, pebble, or bump in the pavement.

But she was stuck with the green machine unless she found herself a job—which was taking longer than she'd like.

Resentment bubbled inside Robbie, something that had been happening more frequently as her days of unemployment limbo dragged on. Had Nathan pulled the plug when he'd booked his Vegas trip, she would have been ahead of the game, right in peak job-hunt season. Instead, she was scavenging for the last fruits of the harvest. And these schools knew anyone looking for a job now would take just about anything. The ball was in their court, and they were going to take their damn time weeding through the players.

And to top it all off, she hadn't heard from Nick in five days. When Robbie had finally returned from her battle with Mrs. Chin the day after their road trip had ended, Ivy had informed her that Nick had said goodbye, but he had to go to Los Angeles for an important meeting, and he'd be back in time for the party. Robbie had spent the last few days quietly fuming over his radio silence.

"It hasn't even been a full week yet. You have to give these things time. Do you want me to call Ernie's guy back?" Ivy offered while getting ready for a lunch date as Robbie moaned about her current situation.

"No, please don't," Robbie said, her chest squeezing at the thought of another favor, especially one from Nick, whom she hadn't seen or talked to since the night he'd dropped her off at his sister's. "I'm just being dramatic. You're right. It's only been five days. I have to get through the weekend and my parents' party, and then I'm hitting the pavement hard."

Ivy looked doubtful but agreed. "If you change your mind . . ."

"I'll let you know, but I'm sure I'll hear something from someone soon."

"What are you plans for today?" Ivy asked, dabbing on her lip gloss.

Robbie sighed. She'd promised Mrs. Chin she would stop by and help her clean out the storage space in their basement. Most of their communication since their blowup had been brief text messages, assuring each other they were still alive. Then Mrs. Chin had called and reminded Robbie how she'd promised to help them get ready for the party, and apparently, cleaning out a basement storage room, where Robbie could guarantee no one from the party would ever see, was a top priority. Robbie knew a Mrs. Chin ploy when she smelled one but figured it was time to start burying the ax before either one of them was tempted to take another few swings.

"I told my mother I'd help her clean the storage room today," Robbie said, pulling her hair back into a ponytail, shivering at the thought of getting caught in a cobweb. "I'll bring you back something pretty."

"Unless it's that light-up Lucite phone your parents had in the kitchen for years, I don't want it."

Robbie snapped her fingers. "Got it. Grab the phone. Have fun today."

Robbie walked to her parents. Driving the one block had seemed ridiculous at the time, but Mrs. Chin had other ideas. "How are you going to bring everything back with you without your car?"

"What everything, Mom?" Robbie asked. She'd thought she was coming to haul things to the trash out back, not go on a treasure hunt. Robbie had gone through most of her belongings six years ago when she'd moved to New York, and the few things she'd left—like her box of rocks—she'd already moved to Ivy's two days ago when Mrs. Chin had run errands. Robbie couldn't think of anything she'd left behind that she'd want now.

"You know," Mrs. Chin said, waving her toward the basement. "All your things. Now that you don't live here anymore, it doesn't seem right that we store everything. We can use the space."

Robbie followed her mother down to the back corner of the basement where there was one door in the house that Robbie had never wanted to open as a child—the storage room. The rest of the basement had been outfitted with overhead lights that turned on with a flip of a switch. Not the storage room. This room was lit only by the bare bulbs hanging from the ceiling on a chain that had to be turned on by individual cords. It was the setting of every horror movie she'd ever seen growing up. Windowless. Airless. Full of dust and webs. Robbie couldn't imagine the space as anything but a storage room. Maybe Mrs. Chin had other ideas for that ax.

"Mom," she said, brushing at her arms and hair. She felt the stringy webs reaching out to wrap their tendrils around her as she walked. "Is this where you plan on leaving my body?"

Her mother turned and pressed her lips into a thin line.

Apparently, they weren't ready to joke yet. "Sorry. It was only a joke," Robbie said.

"We need the space," her mother said.

"What do you need this space for all of a sudden? It's just the two of you. Are you telling me this isn't enough house for you and Dad? Plus, your party is in two days. Aren't there other things more pressing we should be doing? Unless . . . Mom, is this where you plan on leaving the bodies of all your guests? Because, I have to tell you, I don't think there's enough room. Unless you stack them. Then, maybe."

"Robinson Chin," Mrs. Chin snapped. "Are you done yet? We just need the space. And yes, this has to happen now. We won't have much time after the party."

Robbie surrendered. "Okay. You need the space. And what do you mean, there won't be enough time?"

Mrs. Chin pointed to a pile of boxes all labeled ROBBIE SCHOOL. "Why don't you start with those?" she said, then shook her head. "You really should have brought the car."

Robbie didn't remember seeing these boxes the last time she went through the great purge of her belongings.

"Take it or get rid of it," Mrs. Chin said.

Robbie peeled back the lid of the first box and pulled out a pile of construction paper. Handprint turkeys. Tissue paper ghosts. Cotton ball Santa beards. "Mom, why did you save all this?" Robbie asked.

Her mother shrugged while digging through a box of her old maternity clothes. "It seemed so important at the time. All the other mothers talked about finding places to store these things like they would one day be worth millions. They wouldn't dare throw anything away that had their child's handprint on it. What if their child found out and felt unloved?"

Robbie laughed. "Well, I'm perfectly fine with getting rid of this stuff. I'd always assumed they were thrown out anyway once they left the refrigerator door."

"Fair point," her mother said, then held up a pair of striped pants with an elastic waist. "Do you think you'd ever want these? You know, one day when you have a baby?" Robbie crinkled her nose. "Didn't think so." Mrs. Chin tossed the pants back in the box and closed it up. "Let's make a garbage pile over here," she said, dropping the maternity box outside the door.

For twenty minutes, Robbie watched her mother set one box after another on the garbage pile. Cleaning and organizing usually brightened her mother's mood, giving her a sense of order and control in her life. But no matter how many boxes her mother cleared out, her disposition remained unchanged.

"What's going on for real, Mom?" Robbie asked after she'd added all her school boxes to the garbage pile and several boxes of broken Christmas decorations. "Why the sudden need to get rid of everything? And right now?"

"You might as well know," Mrs. Chin sighed and her shoulders sunk. "We're selling the house."

Robbie's jaw worked up and down as she struggled to put words together. "What? When? Why?"

Her mother's legs melted beneath her, and she sat on the edge of a large plastic bin to keep from sinking to the floor. "Your father thought it would be best. He wants to retire in the next few years, and this seems like a logical first step. You're right. It's too much space for just the two of us. It's time to move on."

"Move on to where?" They were leaving? They'd bought this house right after getting married and had lived in this one place Robbie's whole life. This was the epicenter of their world. Where would they go? It had never occurred to Robbie that her father would retire one day. Other fathers did. Mr. Wolfe had. But her father had always said he'd planned on working until the day he died. He'd said retirement looked boring and he wouldn't know what to do with his time.

"A condo," her mother said. "In the suburbs." Mrs. Chin covered her face with her hands and sobbed.

Robbie had never seen her mother cry before. Ever. Not when they'd fought. Not when her parents argued. Not through anything. She hadn't even realized her mother could cry. Yet, there she was, perched on a bin of memories, tears streaming down her face.

"Is Dad okay? He's not sick or anything, is he? He always said the only way he'd retire was if . . ." Robbie's palms grew slick with sweat and the room around her tilted. She reached for the wall for support.

"What?" Mrs. Chin gasped. Then seeing how pale Robbie must have gotten, quickly added, "He's fine. Healthy as a horse. All that talk about never retiring was just that. A bunch of talk."

Robbie pressed her fingers to her temples and waited for the swirling in her head to stop. "Don't scare me like that," she said, moving to her mother's side and testing the support of the plastic bin. "Mom. It will be okay. Think of how much easier it will be to maintain. No more yard work. No more trash hauls. I bet they even have an on-call handyman to take care of any minor issues."

Mrs. Chin wiped her cheeks. "I know. It all sounds so much easier. It's just . . ."

"Just what?"

"I always had it in my head that one day you would come here with your children. And we would turn your old bedroom into the grandkids' room so they would always have a place to spend the night. We'd have Christmas mornings here. Birthdays. Then your father springs this on me. I don't have a plan for grandchildren visiting a condo." Fresh tears sprang forth, and her shoulders shook with her sobs.

Robbie took a deep breath. After all these years, she and her mother finally had something in common.

"Mom," she said, putting her arm around the older woman's shoulders. "First of all, that whole grandchild thing is still a long way off. You have plenty of time to figure out where to stash them in a condo."

Her mother chuckled, then hiccupped, as she tried to bring her sobs under control.

"Second, I know a thing or two about having to make changes to plans," Robbie said, giving her mother a gentle squeeze. "I'll walk you through it. But can I ask what the hurry before the party is?"

Mrs. Chin wiped her eyes on a tissue she'd had stashed away somewhere Robbie hadn't seen. "Your father already has people lined up to see the house on Sunday."

"The day after your party? Already?"

Mrs. Chin nodded, and Robbie blew out a heavy sigh.

"Well," Robbie said, "I guess we'd better get to work."

Rather than returning home after leaving her parents' house, Robbie continued walking straight to Cover to Cover to visit Drea. With nothing better to do with her days, passing a few hours with good company, talking about good books—an activity that rarely cost more than a cup of coffee—seemed like the right antidote to her all-too-literal lazy days of summer this past week. She helped Drea take inventory, reorganize the shelves, and order new stock from more current authors the younger set were drawn to that Drea hadn't yet heard of.

"I wish I could hire you," Drea said as they shelved copies of a new vampire series. "But, right now, the shop doesn't make enough to support more than two part-time employees—"

"I wouldn't dream of it," Robbie said, a half-truth. "Being around all these books relaxes me. This is my mental health time."

That much was true. But Robbie would be lying to herself if she didn't admit she'd fantasized about not just working in, but owning the shop ever since Drea had mentioned it during her first return visit. She hadn't taken Drea's comments seriously then. Robbie had been looking at Drea through the eyes of a teenage Robbie, back when things like retirement and old age were a distant concept. But Robbie had begun noticing the way Drea rubbed her lower back every time she bent to reach a low shelf. And how it took her longer to get up from her seat, and even how often Drea sat these days. When Robbie had been in high school, she'd never even seen a chair behind Drea's counter. The one Drea perched on now in between tasks looked well-used.

Drea brushed the book dust off her hands and smoothed her blouse. "There's something I want to talk to you about. I've been doing some thinking."

A sense of deja vu swept over Robbie. It was Robbie's mother telling her about selling her childhood home all over again.

"My sister in Scottsdale wants me to come stay with her," Drea continued. "She's getting on in age and could use some help getting around. Her son doesn't like the idea of her living alone, either. He lives in Dallas, and my stubborn sister refuses to move."

"People can be set in their ways," Robbie mumbled.

"It is lovely there," Drea said, wringing her hands.

"Are you telling me you're moving?" Robbie asked, her pulse slowing to a sluggish thud in her chest. In one afternoon, Robbie had managed to lose not one, but two, pillars of her life. All she needed now was for Ivy to kick her out and the trifecta would be complete. "What are you going to do with the store?"

"If I can't find someone to buy it, then I'll have to contact a broker," Drea said. "My nephew says there are quite a few who specialize in selling businesses like this. Otherwise, I guess I'd close up shop. I'm sorry."

Robbie couldn't lose the bookstore. There was so much potential in these four walls Drea hadn't even begun to tap into. Author events. An actual website. There was room in the back for a small coffee stand or a playing area for local musicians. The neighborhood needed a place like Drea's. Robbie couldn't imagine how different her life would have been growing up without the bookstore.

How had it come to this? Coming home was supposed to be easy. It was supposed to be safe and familiar. Everyone was supposed to remain exactly as she'd left them six years earlier. And though Robbie felt just as shaky as she had then, everyone else seemed to have aged without her.

Ivy was in a serious relationship. Robbie's parents were talking about retirement and moving. Drea was closing up shop. Even little Ernie had grown into Nick. And Robbie was back where she'd started— without a job and living off the people around her. But she couldn't be mad. Not really. It was her own damn fault for not seeing her relationship with Nathan clearer before. She couldn't expect everyone else to put a hold on their lives until she caught up.

Later, Robbie contemplated this strange, twisty path her life was taking. Nick would call it an adventure if he'd been around. Robbie didn't know what she'd been expecting, but she'd thought they'd have some communication going forward. Their road trip might be over, but she hadn't predicted that to be the end of their friendship, too. Her glass was empty and could use some filling up right about then.

Instead, she had to be satisfied with the bits of vague information she got from Ivy. Robbie couldn't help wondering who exactly this meeting was with. Megan, maybe? She knew Nick purposely didn't provide Ivy with all the details regarding his relationship with his ex, and telling his sister about some random meeting was just the sort of cover story he would use.

Robbie sighed and pushed him from her mind while ignoring the gnawing feeling in her chest. She'd had to do that a lot lately. The last Robbie had spoken to Nick about Megan's invitation, he hadn't known what he wanted to do. But the longer she went without hearing from him, the more she convinced herself Nick had finally made up his mind. If she learned anything from Nathan, it was that no communication didn't lead to happy endings and emotional reconciliations. That was one thing all the books got wrong.

TWENTY-NINE

Robbie woke early and crabby the next morning after spending the whole night pretending she didn't miss Nick, and that she wasn't upset over her parents' impending move, and that what she'd said to Drea about not wanting to take over the bookstore had been the truth.

She checked the time. It was early, but DeLucca's Bakery would be open in twenty minutes. DeLucca's apple pie and coffee was just the thing Robbie needed. If she left soon, she could beat the morning commuter rush and avoid having to stand in line for too long.

Sneaking out of the house so she wouldn't wake Ivy, Robbie breathed in the fresh morning air still heavy with springtime dew. She didn't care what anyone said: there was a definite difference in the air between the two coasts. People had assured her that moving to New York wouldn't be too different from San Francisco, that she wouldn't miss the ocean since New York was coastal, as well, but they had been wrong. Robbie smelled the difference as soon as she'd arrived in New York. San Francisco smelled like home.

As she had planned, she'd arrived at DeLucca's soon after they'd unlocked the doors and there were only two people in line ahead of her. She ordered her coffee and apple pie, disregarding the questioning looks from the other patrons—she was a grown woman and could eat what she wanted for breakfast—and instead of taking it back to Ivy's, Robbie marched to the corner table and made herself comfortable.

She'd come prepared with her computer and notebook and set right to work. She had résumés to send out and applications to complete. But when the buttery pie crust and cinnamon apples first hit her tongue, her fingers danced over the keyboard, researching the bookstore business instead of teaching jobs.

Robbie spent the next hour reading one article after another regarding the pros and cons of going into the retail sector. The more she read, the more she couldn't contain her excitement. She could do this. She could really do this. Learning the business side—inventory, accounting, etc.—wouldn't be a problem. She'd already been helping Drea with all that the past week. With proper time allotted for training, Robbie knew she'd be able to pick up whatever else there was to learn. She had a list of ideas for marketing and promotions, including adding a website and social media presence that Cover to Cover currently lacked. Any physical changes to the store would come in time.

"Another coffee?" the young woman from the counter asked.

Robbie looked up from her research and noticed the humming crowd had died down some before the next wave of commuters descended on the place. The woman, who had the DeLucca nose, must have been the owner's granddaughter.

"Yes, please," Robbie said. "And another piece of pie, when you have time."

Robbie turned back to the list of pros and cons she'd made in her notebook while researching. None of the drawbacks seemed insurmountable. Hard work, sure. But, impossible? Not in the slightest. And there was only one pro that interested Robbie: she would love it.

The problem was, she had no idea what price Drea wanted for Cover to Cover. She still had the money she'd been saving for her future with Nathan. She hadn't used much of it on the trip home, even refusing to dip into the fund for a better car. Her stomach tightened. She'd been saving for so long the thought of depleting the account took a sudden and unexpected jab at her. If she used her savings, she would have nothing left to fall back on.

Except for her winnings from Vegas, which wasn't much, but a few thousand was better than nothing. Robbie twisted the diamond earrings she wore while she scribbled figures on a clean sheet of paper. Jewelry. She had jewelry. If need be, she could sell some, maybe all, of her pieces and use that money, as well.

She swallowed the second piece of pie in four bites between gulps of coffee. Everything seemed to hum around her. The world was moving at a frenzied pace, and Robbie did her best to match pace. She calculated sums, then adjusted formulas, and calculated again. She needed more information, but she couldn't stop herself from smiling as a new plan started to take shape.

It was still too early for Cover to Cover to be open to the public, but Robbie knew Drea like to arrive a few hours early and ready the store. She couldn't always count on downtime during the open hours to clean or restock, so Drea did it before. There had been more than a few times when she'd let Robbie in early to loiter among the shelves. Robbie hoped this would be one of those times.

But when Robbie arrived at the bookstore and peered through the window, she saw that Drea wasn't alone. She was standing in front of the counter with a suited man who looked too serious to rank as a favored customer. She was just about to turn around and sneak away before either of them noticed when Drea caught sight her of her and started waving her in. Out of politeness, Robbie shook her head and pantomimed coming back at a better time.

But Drea wouldn't have it and rushed to the door, swinging it open. "Come on in, Robbie. I want you to meet someone."

Robbie hesitated for just a second before her curiosity got the better of her and she followed Drea back into the store.

"Robbie Chin, this is Patrick Averman, that business broker I was telling you about," Drea said.

Robbie looked from Drea to this Patrick Averman. When Drea had mentioned finding someone to sell the business, she'd done so in an offhand, no-second-thought, sort of way. And she did not specify a broker in particular—definitely not Patrick Averman.

"Business broker?" Robbie said, taking Patrick Averman's outstretched hand. "That was fast. You only mentioned it yesterday."

"My nephew thought it would be best to get started since these things can take some time," Drea said.

"Hopefully not too long," Averman said with a slick salesman smile plastered on his face. He must be related to Sam, the auto shop owner in Poppy Grove, and his car salesman cousin. They all had the same hungry smile. Robbie wondered if Averman had some good news for her. "With an established business like this in a neighborhood who prides itself on its homegrown shops, if priced right, I don't see why this would take more than a couple weeks."

Robbie's hand fluttered to her neck where she checked for her pulse because she was pretty sure her heart had stopped. She was seriously standing here while this man, this Patrick Averman, talked about selling *her* bookstore in a matter of a couple of weeks. Robbie was still in the planning stage. She had come to Cover to Cover in the hopes of talking to Drea and getting more information regarding the feasibility of the plan. But now this suit was trying to sell it right out from under her.

"Did you hear that, Robbie?" Drea said. "A few weeks."

Robbie had heard it, all right. The figures and calculations she'd worked on over breakfast floated in her head. Robbie suppressed a groan as she struggled to recall how much was in her bank account. She clenched her fist at her side. She wasn't built for this—quick, on the spot decision-making. It had taken her two weeks to decide if she was going to move to New York with Nathan, and six years to realize she didn't love him.

She felt the weight of all the books in the shop pressing down on her. She could turn around and leave. Get her answers a different time, take a few days to talk to the bank, run more numbers, draw up a business plan of some sort. An outline at least. Something with more structure.

Or, as Nick's voice in her head reminded her, she could go on an adventure.

"How much?" Robbie asked.

Drea's eyes widened. "How m—"

"How much for the bookstore?" Robbie asked, taking a step forward and squaring her shoulders. "I want it. I have some money saved. How much?"

Averman cleared his throat. "I haven't done the final calculations yet, but—"

"Sold," Drea cut in. "Sold. Sold. Sold." She clapped her hands once before pulling Robbie into a suffocating embrace. "I don't care about any other offers. Let's sit down and chat."

"Mom, I'm here to help with the party," Robbie called as she walked into the Chin's house. For the last two hours, she'd been going over terms and details with Drea and her broker—all the while, Robbie was unable to verify when the man was happy with such a fast sale or disappointed he didn't get to push for a higher price.

Drea had been firm in her asking price—which, according to Robbie's research that morning, had been more than fair. Drea also insisted on self-financing the purchase. She wouldn't hear of Robbie going through a bank. Robbie agreed to a healthy down payment that used up almost her entire savings account, and the rest she would pay to Drea in monthly installments.

"Where are you?" Robbie asked, floating into the kitchen where she found her parents in quiet conversation. She was on such a high from her day already, she almost missed the way her parents' heads bent together in quiet conversation. "What's going on?"

"Robbie, we need to talk," Mrs. Chin said, pulling a kitchen chair out for her daughter to sit.

Robbie froze. Those were four words no one ever wanted to hear. "Are we breaking up?" she asked with a nervous twitter. "Because, I don't think you're allowed to do that, and I've had enough breaking up for now."

Mrs. Chin pressed her lips together. Robbie could never get the timing right to suit her mother's humor. "Sit, please."

"Ok-aaay," Robbie said, taking a seat at the kitchen table. "Now you're scaring me."

"We want to talk to you about your job situation," Robbie's father said, taking his traditional seat at the head of the table.

"Is that all? I've got it covered. There's nothing to worry about."

She should tell them. Robbie knew that. But it didn't feel right. Not yet. They weren't the first people she wanted to tell. Maybe because she knew Mrs. Chin would chastise her for making a rash decision without enough research or due diligence. *There's many a slip 'twixt the cup and the lip*, Mrs. Chin used to always say. Of course, she had used it about couples breaking up, but she would make it work in this situation, as well. The last thing Robbie wanted was someone to dampen her spirits.

If Robbie were honest, maybe she didn't want to tell them yet because the whole walk from Cover to Cover to the Chin house, she'd been planning on how she would tell Nick. Nick was the one she wanted to divulge her secret to first. Not Ivy. Not her parents. Nick. So engrossed in her little fantasy, Robbie had almost convinced herself she would find Nick waiting for her at Ivy's. But Nick wasn't there. He was probably snuggled up somewhere with Megan.

"Robbie, how long can your savings last you?" Mrs. Chin asked, shaking Robbie out of her moment of bitterness.

Not as long as one would think, anymore. "Mom, really, don't worry about it," Robbie said, getting up from her seat to study the to-do list her mother had left on the counter. After years of waking up to one of these lists taped to her bedroom door on Saturday mornings, Robbie could spot a task list a mile away. "Let's get some of this stuff done. The party is tomorrow, you know. Let's go. Chop-chop."

Robbie's parents had offered to feed her after their afternoon of cleaning and manual labor, but all Robbie wanted to do was be alone with her notebook and dreams of owning Cover to Cover. Ideas had been swirling in her head as she scrubbed floors and polished furniture. She tried to scribble down as many as she could on the sly, but Mrs. Chin in classic party prep form was everywhere all at once.

But now Robbie was free, and she was going to take advantage of it as soon as she found something to quiet her stomach. Italian. It was a beautiful evening to walk the eight blocks to Lupa's Italiano. The sun wouldn't set for a few more hours, so she had plenty of time to walk there, place her order, and walk home before it even got dark. Her mouth watered thinking about Lupa's mushroom fettuccine. The perfect way to celebrate.

As she walked, she took in the sights around her, like Robbie had been doing all week, wondering how she could have left this city behind so easily before. She loved San Francisco. She loved her neighborhood. This was home.

Aberbrooke, New York, had never felt like home. Even after six years, she'd still had the sense that it didn't belong to her. It had tolerated her presence but hadn't wanted her there. Like she was the vegetable side dish that had to be eaten before getting to the chocolate cake dessert.

But San Francisco, Noe Valley, in particular, this was her sweet spot. Every sight, smell, and sound was as familiar to her as the house she'd grown up in. This was her turf. The place where she'd learned to stand her ground. She felt stronger in San Francisco. And now she owned a piece of it. She would be a part of its pulse, its life, the way it was a part of hers.

By the time she arrived at Lupa's, she was ready for her pasta. She deserved it—and a glass of wine.

"Good evening," the hostess said when Robbie walked in. "Do you have a reservation?"

"No, I don't," Robbie said.

"Okay," the hostess said, scanning the laminated seating chart. "Dine in or carry out?"

Robbie surveyed the cozy dining room. Overhead speakers played soft music punctuated with the light clinking of silverware on porcelain.

Heavenly aromas wafted from the kitchen every time the door swung open. Her mouth watered, and her notebook of scribbled ideas under her arm pressed into her side, demanding attention.

"Dine in," Robbie said. "Table for one."

THIRTY

Robbie arrived at her parents' house promptly after breakfast, as had been requested, to help Mrs. Chin with any last-minute preparations. The caterers were already busy bees, unpacking boxes of platters and serving pieces. The backyard had been transformed into a paradise garden for the party. Small twinkling lights wrapped around every tree. Strings of bulbs hung overhead that would create a blanket of stars once the sun set. Tables dressed in a pale green stood along the edges of the yard, sentinels guarding the temporary dance floor in the middle.

"Mom," Robbie breathed, amazed how much had already been accomplished. Though with the army Mrs. Chin had employed for the event, it shouldn't have been too surprising. "It's gorgeous."

"The flowers aren't here yet," Mrs. Chin said, tapping her chin with a painted nail. "Those won't get here until after two. I hope the florist has enough time to get everything set up before the guests arrive. Three hours doesn't seem like enough time."

"They're professionals, Mom," Robbie said, trying to sound as soothing as possible. "I'm sure they'll get it done. Besides, you want the flowers as fresh as possible."

"I'm sure you're right," her mother murmured with a distinct lack of confidence. Then, straightening her back, she whirled around to face Robbie, planted her hands on her hips and narrowed her eyes. "Are you ever going to tell me what happened with Nathan?"

Robbie sighed. "Is now really the time for this conversation?"

"You've been avoiding it all week," Mrs. Chin fired back. "I just want to know."

Mrs. Chin wasn't wrong. Robbie had been avoiding it after their first attempt at discussing it. She had hoped, in vain, that Mrs. Chin would come to terms with Robbie's new Nathan-free status and let it lie. But Mrs. Chin wouldn't be Mrs. Chin without one last push to get her way.

"I didn't think there was anything left to say about it," Robbie said. "We're just not right for each other anymore. That's all. I'm fine with it. You should be, too."

"Fine? I don't understa—"

"Cara," Robbie's father called from the doorway. "Robbie said she's fine. She's an adult. Let her be."

Robbie widened her eyes as Mrs. Chin clamped her mouth tight. Never had she ever heard her father speak to her mother like that. Never mind her father's tone. Never had she ever known Mrs. Chin to *listen* to anyone else.

"We have a lot to do today," her father said with a wink. "Your lists aren't going to check off themselves."

Robbie lowered her head to keep from laughing at the way Mrs. Chin pouted at being scolded before she walked away without another word. Robbie's father turned to follow her, but not without flashing a smile at his daughter and giving her one of those longed-for thumbs-ups.

By a miracle, Robbie and her mother avoided direct contact with each other for the rest of the day while finishing the party preparations. Mrs. Chin had thoughtfully made a list of all the chores she wanted Robbie to take care of, including dusting every light bulb in the house, even the ones in the basement where Robbie was certain no one would be going. But she knew part of Mrs. Chin's normal neurotic behavior was due to potential buyers coming to inspect the house the next day.

When the florist arrived, Mrs. Chin assigned Robbie the task of ensuring every arrangement was placed in the exact spot she had marked on a hand-drawn schematic of the yard. And if that hadn't been enough, Mrs. Chin had placed sticky notes around the yard where vases should be placed with the name of each arrangement to be used. Heaven forbid the star lilies and the calla lilies sat on the incorrect tables. What would people think?

An hour before the party was to start, Robbie slipped out the front door and back to Ivy's house to pick up her things to get ready. Ivy had already left to pick up her boyfriend, who Robbie had yet to meet in the week she'd been home. Ivy said she hadn't wanted to make her feel bad, but Robbie suspected it was more that Ivy didn't want Robbie to see how serious she'd become with this guy. Ivy had always claimed she wouldn't even think of getting serious before the age of thirty-five. She was only seven years early.

After showering the day's work off her, Robbie stood staring at the dress she'd hauled across the country when she'd thought she'd be attending this soiree with Nathan. It suited Nathan. It suited Mrs. Chin. It was black and unembellished. Straight cut, no frills. It was a serious, quiet dress meant for a serious, quiet person. It was the sort of dress that blended in anywhere.

She went to her closet and retrieved a different dress waiting to be worn again. One that she'd had a fantastic night in. One that she'd felt beautiful in. One that suited her.

Robbie shoved the black dress back in the corner of the closet where it belonged. It wasn't the first time this past week she'd changed plans. She'd developed quite a talent for it.

A light tap on Robbie's childhood bedroom door announced Ivy's arrival at the party. Robbie stood at her window overlooking the backyard as her parents' guests filtered in, filling in the gaps between the tables and potted plants. She let out an audible gasp as her mother's tennis partner moved one of the three-foot-tall arrangements in the corner to have a place to set her gigantic handbag.

"What's wrong?" Ivy asked, rushing to her side and peering out the window with her.

Robbie pointed to Mrs. Lane's offensive handbag. "She moved Mom's plant."

Ivy shook her head and *tsk'd* as Mrs. Chin hurried over, greeted Mrs. Lane with a warm hug, and while keeping up the pretense of friendly banter, moved the bag and returned the plant to its proper place. "She's good," Ivy said with a touch of awe. "She should have been a high school teacher. Nobody in her class would get away with anything." She turned and smoothed a wayward hair away from Robbie's face. "Are you hiding?"

"I'm not hiding," Robbie said. Not exactly. "I'm just waiting until there are more people to divert her attention."

"Speaking of more people," Ivy said, tapping on the glass. "Look who made it back in time for the party."

Robbie looked where her friend indicated and let out an audible sigh. Nick. She caught sight of him near the edge of the dance floor with his head tilted up toward her window. When he met her gaze, he smiled, and Robbie couldn't help smiling back.

"Robbie, can I ask you something?" Ivy asked, stepping back from the window.

The grin melted off Robbie's face. She heard the question in Ivy's tone already. Robbie perched on the edge of her bed, folding her hands, and pressing them between her knees. "Go ahead."

"You and Ernie . . ."

"We're friends," Robbie said with a firmness that surprised both of them. She realized they'd both been expecting a different answer. "Good friends. At least, I hope he thinks so, too."

Ivy rubbed her forehead. "Oh, he does." She sat on the corner of the bed and stared at a spot on the floor. "His heart has been broken before, you know? He doesn't talk about it much, but it was bad."

Robbie nodded. She couldn't give too much away—she'd promised. But she knew all too well what he'd been through her. "He mentioned an ex-girlfriend. I think she called him while we were driving."

Ivy jerked her head back as though Robbie had elbowed her in the jaw. "What a bitch." She smoothed her skirt and played with the hem. "I never really liked her. It was like she was always looking for the next best thing. I didn't trust her." She shook her head and swatted away the bad memories. "Never mind. She doesn't matter. Can you promise me something? Can you promise me you won't break his heart? Because, honestly, I can't watch him go through that again. And selfishly, I don't want to have to choose between Team Ernie or Team Robbie."

"I don't think he thinks of me that way," Robbie said, her skin tingling. She tried not to react to Ivy's words, but her body wouldn't cooperate. She pressed her hands together to keep them from shaking.

Ivy arched an eyebrow. "Are you kidding me? He's had it bad for you ever since he was a kid. I haven't seen him this loopy over a girl since, well, ever. He wasn't even this crazy over the ex."

Robbie's hands went numb as she squeezed them together so tight her knuckles turned white. "What are you talking about?"

Ivy stood and went to the mirror to smooth her hair. "The way he's always asking about you. Are you okay? What are you doing? It's actually very annoying. Almost like he's trying to take my place or something."

Robbie leaped from her seat and pulled Ivy close, crushing her in a bear hug, messing up her friend's hair amid her squeals of protest. Her giddiness over the thought of having the power to break Nick's heart spilled over because, to break his heart, she'd have to hold it first.

Ivy broke free from Robbie's grasp and smoothed out her dress. "He tried to take my place, didn't he? That brat."

Robbie bobbed her head up and down. "He even wanted to start a No Ivy club. I told him unless the clubhouse came with a hot tub and gourmet kitchen, he was out of luck."

"You're a dork," Ivy said, sticking out her tongue.

Robbie stood and checked herself in her mirror. "Yeah, well, you're the dork who's stuck with me now."

"I'll take it," Ivy said. "Come on; let's go introduce you to Adam."

"Adam? He has a name?" Robbie said, moving back to the window for one last look at the crowd. Who was she kidding? She was hoping for another look at Nick. Nick, who apparently always had a crazy crush on her. Her heart skittered in her chest as she thought about him asking about her. She'd spent all week worried about him and Megan, and he'd spent all week asking about her.

Her cup was so full at the moment, she quieted the voice asking why he hadn't called her himself. For now, just knowing he had some feelings for her was enough. She would deal with the rest as it came. No plan needed.

Ivy bumped her hip against Robbie's. "New York made you funny. Good. San Francisco needs funny. You look fantastic, by the way. Let's go get a drink."

Robbie had to hand it to Mrs. Chin: the woman knew how to throw a party. What Robbie had dismissed as obsessive controlling when she was younger, she now appreciated as uncompromising attention to detail. There wasn't one inch of the backyard that hadn't been touched or transformed in some way to fit the ethereal aesthetic her mother had been striving for. Candles and lanterns—battery operated, of course— lined the fence bordering the yard. The twinkling lights on the trees and overhead offered the perfect amount of light as the sky darkened.

It seemed Mrs. Chin even commanded the weather. It was a beautiful evening, with a slight enough breeze to keep the air perfumed with a mix of floral scents wafting from the numerous bouquets but not enough to cause a chill. White-gloved servers passed silver trays of hors d'oeuvres and champagne around the growing crowd of guests and well- wishers without making a sound, and Robbie had found that a glass had magically found its way into her hand, as well.

Ivy floated away to find Adam while Robbie smiled to herself. Ivy might not know it yet, but Robbie did: this was it. Adam was the one. Robbie was sure of it the instant she saw the expression on Adam's face as Ivy approached him. It was about time someone made an honest woman out of her friend.

The skin on Robbie's arm prickled despite the warm evening, and she turned her head to find her mother staring at her from across the lawn. Not really her, though, Robbie noted, her dress. Robbie had chosen to wear the red dress from Poppy Grove instead of the more subdued black sheath she'd initially planned on wearing. Her mother furrowed her brow, deepening the creases on her forehead, then turned her attention back to the couple she'd been talking to.

Mrs. Chin didn't approve. She'd never approved of any dress that drew attention to Robbie, that made people turn their heads in her direction. It had never stopped people from looking anyway, so why the hell not? She had nothing to be ashamed of.

Robbie Chin was here, and if someone didn't like it, too damn bad. This was her family's home, after all, not theirs.

"You look lovely," her father said, sneaking up behind her. He brushed a kiss on her cheek.

"Happy anniversary, Dad," Robbie said. "How did you do it? Thirty years."

He shrugged and took another drink. "You love who you love. Some days, it's easy. And some days . . ." Her mother's laughter rang out across the yard, causing several people to turn their heads in her direction. "I haven't always made it easy for her, but we've always done the best we could." With that, he patted her shoulder and walked away.

Robbie watched her father walk away, confused by their exchange. She didn't have enough time to think about it, though, as she was soon joined by another man who never seemed to need to be told much.

"So, we meet again," Nick said, sidling up to her as though he were a spy in an old black-and-white film. "Nice gams," he said, waggling his eyebrows in an exaggerated way.

Robbie nudged him with her elbow as she felt the heat rising in her neck and face. "It's not like you haven't seen this dress before."

"I liked it then," he said, lowering his mouth to the top of her ear. "But I like it better now."

Her face and hands tingled, and not in the way they did when she drank too much. "Why is that?"

But he didn't get to answer as Ivy rushed over, a flushed Adam in tow. "Robbie, I want you to meet Adam," Ivy said, pushing her date forward. "Adam, this is my best friend and new roommate, Robbie Chin."

Adam shook her hand. Firm, but not constricting, dry palms. All a good sign. "Nice to finally meet you, Robbie," he said with genuine warmth. "Ivy's told me so much about you."

"It's nice to finally meet you, too," Robbie said, liking this guy already. "I hope you're enjoying yourself."

"I am. Thank you," Adam said, then turning to Nick, he extended his hand again. "Ernie, nice to see you again."

Nick shook his hand and clapped Adam on the shoulder. "Hope Ivy's not giving you a hard time."

Ivy punched her brother's shoulder in the way she had since they'd been kids, but smiled as Adam said, "I'll take anything Ivy wants to hand out as long as I get to be near her."

Ivy flushed a deeper red than Robbie's dress, and Robbie couldn't help stretching her mouth into a wide smile. Yep. He was definitely the one, and Ivy knew it, too, judging by the way she beamed up at him. Three months. Six, tops, before they were having a party to celebrate another couple. Robbie could already imagine what type of engagement party she would throw her friend. Maybe she would ask Mrs. Chin for help since she had a knack for these things. Then again, maybe not. Why borrow trouble?

Mrs. Chin lifted her eyebrows at Robbie from across the dance floor, a look that Robbie knew to mean she'd been playing with her friends too long and it was time she toured the lawn, greeting her parents' guests, none of which included her extended family, she noted. None of their parties ever included extended family, Robbie realized. Friends and family didn't mix. Not in the Chin house.

"I would love to stay and chat, believe me," Robbie said. "But I'm getting the eye."

Ivy nodded and looked over her shoulder at Mrs. Chin. "We'll find you in thirty."

Robbie mouthed "thank you" and moved away from her friends, but not before Nick leaned in and whispered, "Save me a dance later."

Robbie concentrated on keeping her stride even and purposeful when her legs wanted to bounce and skip, feeling lighter than she had in months, years maybe.

Robbie could deny it all she wanted, but the glaring truth was that Nick Wolfe was much more to her than just a good friend. She hadn't planned on that happening. Ever. It had never been on her radar, but here she was, grinning like a fool because he wanted to dance with her again. Her heart sped up at the thought of him holding her close, as he had in Poppy Grove. But first, she had a mission to complete.

Swallowing the hard lump in her throat as she approached a group of her mother's friends, Robbie steeled herself for the onslaught of questions regarding what she'd been doing these past six years, since the last time they'd gathered to celebrate her leaving. And what about that nice young doctor she'd left with? She plastered a smile across her face as the first cluster of chatty women opened up to swallow her whole.

THIRTY-ONE

Six years ago . . .

"So, tell us, Robbie," Mrs. Watkins, Mrs. Chin's Bunko club friend, said, "will there be other parties coming up? Maybe an engagement party?"

Robbie's face would have flushed at the bold question regarding her relationship with Nathan, had she not already grown numb after being asked no less than four times in twenty minutes if she had any plans to get married. She'd told her mother inviting all these nosy broads to her going-away party would result in nothing but one annoyance after another, but Mrs. Chin insisted it was the right thing to do. These women had known Robbie since she'd been a little girl. Of course, they would take an interest in her life.

Robbie found Nathan across her backyard huddled with a group of Mr. Nosy Broads, practicing their golf swings. Lucky. Robbie wouldn't mind taking a swing at a few things, too.

"Mrs. Watkins, I'm only twenty-two. I just graduated. I have plenty of time," Robbie said. It was the same rehearsed line she'd been using all night.

"Well, you never know," Mrs. Watkins said with a raised eyebrow.

But Robbie did know. She'd brought up the subject of their future to Nathan a few times since he'd asked her to move to New York with him. She'd wanted to know, like all the women in her yard did, if he saw their relationship progressing to something more than roommates. Was this the first step down the aisle? Or was he nervous about moving across the country by himself? Each time she'd mentioned plans for the future, Nathan had shut down the conversation, politely, but decisively.

"Robbie, we've got so much going on now with the move and trying to get our careers up and running. Do we need the added pressure right now? You just graduated. There's plenty of time to worry about the future," he'd said.

And she'd agreed with him, mostly. She wasn't ready to get married, despite what her mother thought. And Robbie had never lived with a boy before. Who knew? Maybe she'd come running home after a week when she'd realized living with Nathan was nothing like she'd anticipated.

"Don't worry," Robbie said, preparing to take her leave from Mrs. Watkins and her suggestive eyebrows. "You'll find out as soon as I do. I'll make sure Mom calls you first."

Robbie smirked as she walked away. Mrs. Chin was going to have a lot of phone calls to make if—when—the day came when Robbie announced an engagement. She'd made half a dozen promises of the first phone call already. She imagined chaos and catfights erupting when the news of the real pecking order emerged. Would there be grudges and vendettas sworn over something as simple as being the first to find out when Robbie Chin was getting married? She chuckled to herself at the image while pouring herself a glass of punch.

"What's so funny?"

"Ernie Wolfe," Robbie said, setting down her cup. "Where have you been?" She smelled the beer on his breath and noticed the way he leaned against the table, trying to appear casual, but just holding himself up. "Ivy was looking for you."

Ernie swung his head around and squinted his eyes. "What did she want?"

Robbie shrugged. "I don't know. I think your Mom wanted you." The color drained from his face. "Don't worry. I think she's inside."

"Worry? Why would I worry?" he asked.

Robbie pulled a bottle of water from the cooler at her feet. "Here. You look thirsty. It's hot out today."

He took the bottle, cracked it open, and guzzled half of it down. "Thanks." Once he got more of his bearing back, he stood a little straighter. "So, you're really leaving San Francisco?"

"Looks like it."

"With that guy?" he asked, pointing across the yard to Nathan, who was busy charming Mrs. Chin and her friends.

"Nathan. Yes."

"I don't get it," he said, shaking his head.

Robbie pinched her eyebrows together and strained her neck to look up at Ernie. When had he gotten so tall? "What's there to get? We're in a relationship. It's what you do. The next step, and all that."

Ernie swallowed the last half of the water bottle, then crushed it in his hand. "He's just not what I pictured for you."

"Who."

"What?"

"He's not *who* you pictured for me."

"Right. That's what I said."

"No. You said what."

"I said he's not who I pictured for you."

Robbie grunted. "I know that. I meant—"

Ernie let out a loud rumble of a laugh. "You're going to be a great lit teacher."

Robbie took a deep, steadying breath. Ever since the kid hit puberty and grew taller than her, he thought it gave him free rein to drive her crazy at every opportunity. "You'd better go hide. I see your mom coming this way."

Ernie clamped his mouth shut and backed away while scanning the crowd for a sign of his mother, or worse, his father. Mrs. Wolfe was always a sucker for her son's quirky smile, but Mr. Wolfe was no-joke strict about how a young man should conduct himself.

"Hey," she called after him, "aren't you going to say goodbye? This is a going-away party."

Ernie lifted one corner of his mouth in a sly grin. "Parting is such sweet sorrow," he said with a wink. "But, no, I'm not saying goodbye. Goodbye is too final like you're not coming back." The smile disappeared from his face as he pointed to the yard and all the festive decorations. "And that's not something I want to celebrate." His eyes darted to the side, he dipped his chin, then took off as fast as his long legs could carry him.

"Where is he going now?" Ivy asked, coming up behind Robbie.

"Anywhere you and your Mom are not," Robbie said, sliding an arm around her friend's waist. "I'm going to miss you."

"Hey," Ivy said, giving her a quick squeeze then pulling away. "It's not time for that yet. That's tomorrow when we spend all day together crying and hugging. Not now. Now, Mrs. Chin needs you by the patio. Her book club has just arrived, and you get to go answer a dozen more questions about your relationship status."

"You're enjoying this, aren't you?"

"You're the one who decided to move across the country and break up the dynamic duo. So, yeah, consider this your punishment."

"Don't leave me," Robbie said as Ivy pushed her closer to the lion's den. The four women standing with Mrs. Chin faced her with wide smiles exposing their teeth. They smelled fresh meat. "Ivy?"

"Play nice," Ivy whispered in her ear. "I'll come get you in thirty."

THIRTY-TWO

Robbie circulated the anniversary party the way her mother had taught her all those years ago when the adult's definition of politeness and courtesy trumped a child's fear. She shook hands, asked after families, complimented outfits, and when asked about her own life, steered the conversation in a different direction. She never spent longer than three minutes with any group, always excusing herself to see to some daughterly duty that was never taken care of because she would get stopped by the next group before she took four steps.

It was excruciating.

By the time she'd made the full loop around the yard, her face ached from the forced smiles. She had just started to scan the crowd for Ivy and Adam, who she was sure she'd seen huddled in the corner, when someone caught her arm and swung her out on the dance floor.

Robbie gasped then broke into a wide smile. "Can I help you?"

Nick grinned back and wrapped an arm around her waist. "Mrs. Chin told me I should dance with you."

"Oh, she did, did she?" Robbie said, spying her mother over Nick's shoulder, nodding in approval.

"At least once, she said. Preferably twice." He raised her arm and spun her in a circle before pulling her back to him. "It will take some of the focus off your newly single status."

Robbie shook her head. "I shouldn't be surprised, and yet . . ."

"She means well," Nick said. "Besides, I was already planning on taking you for a spin on the dance floor. Why not do it with Mrs. Chin's approval?"

"Miss me?" she asked. She had sure missed him and that twinkle in his eye.

The thought struck her hard and sharp, lodging itself in her sternum. She'd been with Nathan for eight years, and she'd never felt this pain when they'd been apart. Ever. Not even after she'd packed her belongings and left their shared home. She'd been disappointed, confused, in shock, even. But not whatever it was she felt now. Somehow Nick Wolfe had managed to earn a position in her life that warranted this heartache.

"Of course I did," Nick said, his eyes darkening, but not dimming. "I know we haven't talked in a while. My fault, I know," he said, pulling her closer. "I haven't been a very good friend lately. I want to make it up to you."

"What did you have in mind?" Robbie held his gaze steady as Ivy's warning played in her head. *Don't break his heart.* Right now, with the way he held her, Robbie thought the heart in danger might be hers.

"Have you been to Lupa's since being home?" he asked.

"Actually," Robbie said, lifting her chin in the air, "I have. A few times. By myself."

Nick's eyebrows shot straight up to his hairline. "You mean to pick up take-out?" Robbie shook her head and waggled her eyebrows. "To eat? Right there in the dining room?" Robbie nodded, and he let out a whistle. "That *is* something. I'd still like to take you. As an apology."

"I think we can arrange a time," Robbie said, giving his shoulder a gentle squeeze.

Nick spun her again and flashed a grin at Mrs. Chin, who was still watching them from the edge of the dance floor. "So, tell me, what's next for Robbie Chin? What great adventure is lurking around the corner?"

She still hadn't told anyone yet. Not her parents. And not Ivy— which was killing her. The official paperwork would be signed first thing Monday morning, as well as the money transfer, and then it would be legally binding. No turning back. Her parents could disapprove all they wanted then. And though she ached to tell Ivy—she'd never kept a secret from her, except the one Nick asked her to keep—it felt right that Nick would be the first person she told, but not like this. Not here in her parents' backyard. Not yet.

"Can I show you something later?" she asked. "Maybe we can slip out in a little bit and take a walk?"

"You're not just trying to get me alone because you have a crazy crush on me, are you?" he asked with a wink.

"Like the one you have on me?"

Nick's footing on the dance floor faltered for the first time. Blushing an adorable shade of pink, Nick stammered, "Where . . . who told you that?"

"Ivy," Robbie said. "She told me you've always had a crazy crush on me." He avoided her gaze and cleared his throat. "It's very flattering if it's true. A girl can do a lot worse than Ernie Wolfe."

"And what about the woman?" he asked, his voice dropping lower as he held her closer to his chest. "Is it still flattering if I told you that I never grew out of that crazy crush? That any time I ever met a woman, my first thought was always: *How does she compare to Robbie?* And that after Megan and I broke up and people asked me why I didn't fight for our relationship more, I thought to myself, *Maybe if she were Robbie*."

Robbie sucked in a breath, her hand involuntarily holding tighter to his. "A woman could do a lot worse than Nick Wolfe, too," she squeaked out. "You never said anything."

"I was a kid with a dream," he said, his mouth inches from hers. "Then you moved away while I was still a kid. It didn't mean I stopped dreaming, though."

"You're not a kid anymore," Robbie said. She wasn't sure who she was reassuring, him or herself.

He swung his head back and forth slowly. "No, I am definitely not. And you're here. In front of me. In my arms. And it feels right."

"What about Megan?"

Nick furrowed his brows. "What about her?"

Robbie arched an eyebrow and waited for him to catch up.

He threw back his head with an audible sigh. "I didn't see her," he said, returning his gaze to Robbie. "I called her back and told her there were no hard feelings and wished her well. That's it."

"Robbie?"

A chill spread over her despite the warm evening air. Robbie closed her eyes and pretended she didn't hear Nathan say her name. As long as the music played, and Nick kept her wrapped in his arms, it didn't happen. All she had to do was face forward, and the ghost would disappear.

"Can I cut in?" Nathan asked.

Nick stilled, and Robbie knew it was over. There was no ignoring it now. Nick's eyes flitted across her features, his mouth set in a firm line, but he hadn't released her. She somehow knew he wouldn't without her permission. He wasn't that guy. Even without knowing what she had seen in Vegas, Nick would never abandon her to someone with the potential to hurt her without her telling him to.

Mrs. Chin watched their exchange with curiosity from her corner of the yard, her hand clenching around her mini-tartlet so tight, it turned the poor thing to crumbs before it had its chance to fulfill its destiny. Robbie cringed at the hope she saw spring forward in her mother's eyes. She knew Mrs. Chin saw Nathan's unexpected arrival at their party as a sign that Robbie would get her mother's version of a happily-ever-after after all.

But worse than the hope was the downturn of the corners of her mother's mouth. The same grim expression Robbie had seen on an almost daily basis as a teenager. It was the look that said, "Don't make a scene."

Still not acknowledging Nathan, Robbie squeezed Nick's arm where her hand had been resting. "It's fine. I'll be okay," she whispered. "I have to take care of this."

Nick inclined his head toward her as though considering options other than leaving her side. Then, slowly, he released her and stepped away.

Nathan slid into Nick's spot, his arm winding around her back, and his other hand taking hers. She let him lead, as he always had, without saying anything. Anything she'd planned on saying to him she'd left behind in the lobby of the Aria Resort and Convention Center. He could probably find her words flying around with the giant butterflies.

"Are you surprised to see me?" Nathan asked.

"That's one way of putting it," Robbie said, carefully keeping her eyes from meeting his. "What are you doing here, Nathan?" The memory of his arms around another woman came to mind. Robbie squeezed her eyes shut, but the image didn't disappear. It burned brighter, sparking her resentment and anger.

"I came to talk to you," he said. "I didn't like the way our last conversation went."

It seemed so long ago when Robbie had been a solid seventy-two percent confident she'd end up with Nathan. "I didn't either, at first," Robbie said, controlling the level of her voice for her Mrs. Chin's sake. Then, using Nick as an example, "But I made my peace with it if that's what you're worried about. You were being honest. You have nothing to feel guilty about. I wish you well." Her mother's eyes locked on them, following every sway and movement. Robbie swore she could see her trying to read their lips. "Listen, I already told my parents we split. You shouldn't be here. It's just going to cause more confusion and gossip."

Nathan looked around the party as though seeing it for the first time. "I guess we are drawing quite a bit of attention. Is there somewhere else we can talk?"

Robbie sighed. Both Nick and Ivy had agreed that Robbie had never gotten her closure on the relationship. Nathan had caught her off guard with the break-up, rendering her incapable of saying anything in response. So while Nathan had the chance to unburden himself of all his reasons to end the relationship, Robbie had never had the opportunity. Time, distance, and the much-needed perspective from her best friend had given Robbie the confidence she needed to say, "Follow me."

Mrs. Chin and the ladies from her Wednesday night Bunco club had homed in on their location and were inching closer to eavesdropping range. Robbie dropped her hand from Nathan's shoulder and motioned to the open gate. "Out front."

Nathan glanced at Mrs. Chin and gave her a grin. When he looked back at Robbie, his smile—the Prince Charming one she'd fallen for so long ago—still in place, she found herself holding back an exasperated eye roll instead of melting into a puddle.

This had been what she'd wanted when she'd set out from New York, wasn't it? Nathan showing up unannounced, wanting to work things out. He hadn't exactly begged her to come back, but she figured that was what he was about to do. She was hours away from her plan coming to fruition. But she didn't want it anymore.

Robbie led him around to the front of the house where they could sit on the front stoop and talk in relative privacy.

"Not inside?" he asked.

She pointed to the windows all lit up. "There are people in there, too." She sat on the step and folded her hands in her lap while studying Nathan under the glow of the street lamps as he paced along the curb.

Here he was, the embodiment of everything Mrs. Chin expected of her and for her. Everything she'd been raised to believe she needed: a stable life, a steady husband. But if Nathan was who she was supposed to be with, why did her mind keep going back to Nick? That was all the answer she needed.

"About last week," Nathan finally said. Robbie blew out a heavy breath. "Things got a little out of control."

Robbie furrowed her brow and blinked hard. How did he think things got out of control? Nathan had come home from work, sat down to dinner, then halfway through the meal, he'd announced he was done with the relationship. Robbie hadn't even cried until after he'd left. She hadn't made a scene. She hadn't begged for him to change his mind. What break up was he referring to?

"I'm not sure I follow," she said. "I thought everything was rather civil. To the point."

"You were great," he said. Robbie fought to control her eye roll. It was nice to know she'd been great while he'd turned her life upside down. "It was me. I hadn't meant to take it as far as I did. All I wanted to do was bring up some issues I thought we were having. The next thing I know, I said . . . I hadn't planned it. It just came out."

Robbie straightened in her seat. "Are you telling me, you *accidentally* broke up with me? You made plans to go to Vegas weeks before. Without me. The weekend before you were supposed to attend my parents' party with me, knowing full well you can't take two weekends off work. And you want me to think the breakup wasn't premeditated? You even told me you waited for the school year to end."

Nathan grimaced and shifted his stance. Robbie had never seen him so uncomfortable. She rather liked having the power in their dynamic for once.

"I lied," Nathan said, dropping his chin to his chest in a show of contrition.

"Which part was the lie? Just now about not planning to breakup? Or when you told me you had planned it weeks ago?" Robbie asked.

"The part about planning it weeks ago."

He couldn't even look her in the eye. Was that a bead of sweat forming? Robbie's pulse quickened as she inhaled deeply, like a hunter with her prey in sight. She waited for Mrs. Chin's voice to ring in her head the way it had any time Robbie had wanted to fight with Nathan. But, this time, Mrs. Chin remained quiet.

He was a liar.

"So, when you booked your conference trip . . ."

"I'd forgotten about the party when I booked it. But then it was locked in. Nonrefundable. And I didn't know how to tell you."

"Right," Robbie said, slowly and deliberately. "The next logical thing to do was to break up with me instead of coming clean?"

He shifted again, looking uncomfortable in his own skin. "I already said it was a mistake."

"And the woman in Las Vegas? Was she a mistake, too?" Robbie asked for fun, a smile on her face. The truth was, she didn't care anymore. He'd bruised her ego but not broken her heart. And the ego healed much faster.

"How did you—" Nathan started, but then chose a different route. "She doesn't matter. None of this matters. I'm not even upset you were dancing the way you were with another man when I walked in."

"And how exactly was I dancing?" Scooting to the edge of her seat, she leaned forward and her breath caught in her chest. She'd been wondering if anyone else had noticed anything between her and Nick.

"You know how," he said with a confident glint in his eye as though he had won back the upper-hand. "Like you had plans for more than dancing. And that dress you're wearing. That's no Robbie Chin dress. But I understand. We've been through a lot these last few weeks, and you needed to let out some steam. But I'm here now, so we can go home and let things get back to normal. Make our plans for the future, just like you always wanted."

"Oh, I see. She made you work too hard for it, huh?" Robbie asked. "What happened? She didn't let you have your way, or call all the shots? She had a mind of her own? Wasn't everything you thought it would be, so why not go back to Robbie, who made everything easy for you?"

"Robbie—"

"Save it, Nathan," Robbie said, standing and brushing off the back of her skirt. "You're lazy. Always have been. Nothing you say now will change anything. You were right to call it off. We should have done it years ago. We're not the right fit. That Robbie you want back? She's not the real Robbie. I may have never been the real Robbie with you, and that's not fair to either one of us. I was miserable. I just didn't know it."

"You dance one time with someone else, and suddenly you were miserable for eight years?"

Robbie tilted her head and nodded. He had a point. She could give him that. "Maybe not the whole time, you're right. But, yes, toward the end I was. Thank you for ending things when you did. I may not have had the strength to do it myself otherwise. But I do now." She turned and headed for the back gate and Nick, dismissing Nathan for good. "And it wasn't just one dance."

THIRTY-THREE

Ivy appeared at Robbie's side the moment she stepped through the gate. "What do you need?"

Nick. But she couldn't see him anywhere. "The dessert table."

Ivy grabbed her hand and led her through the crowd to the farthest corner of the yard. Mrs. Chin had spared no expense for the catering, and the sweet table was covered with anything anyone could want. "What are we thinking?" Ivy asked, grabbing two plates. "Is this a bit of everything talk, or go straight to the chocolate?"

Robbie surveyed her choices. What she wanted was the one thing not on the table. Shrugging, she put a brownie and a shot glass filled with a pudding concoction on her plate. "This will be fine."

Ivy looked skeptical, but she didn't say anything. Instead, she snagged one of each of the five kinds of cookies, a piece of chocolate cake, and a mini cheesecake. "Just in case," Ivy said, grabbing some napkins, too. "Incoming," she whispered as they turned to walk away.

They'd been too slow.

"Was that Nathan?" Mrs. Chin asked, blocking them from leaving.

"Yes, Mom," Robbie said. "He couldn't stay. He says happy anniversary, though." He didn't, but she thought she'd throw the woman a bone. Maybe it would make her feel better to believe he thought enough about her to wish her well.

"Is he coming back?" her mother asked, stepping closer. Robbie saw the glint in her eye, and her stomach twisted at the thought of telling her the truth.

"No, Mom, he's not."

Mrs. Chin eyed her daughter up and down, then with a snort—Robbie could never tell if it was from approval or disapproval, they were so similar—she turned on her heel, raised her chin in the air, and sauntered off to find someone she hadn't spoken to yet.

"Brave move," Ivy whispered next to her. "Has Mrs. Chin ever given you the last word about anything?"

Robbie shrugged. "Trust me. She didn't this time either, but we already had it out once over Nathan. She's just biding her time."

"Come on." Ivy nudged her with her elbow. "Let's go find a seat so you can tell me everything."

"There's not that much to tell," Robbie said, her eyes scanning the crowd, sure she would find Nick in the corner somewhere behind his camera. "Where did your brother go?"

Ivy smirked. "Not much to tell there either, huh?"

"I don't know what you're talking about," Robbie said, turning away from Ivy's knowing stare. She could never lie to her best friend. Ivy always knew, and in some cases, long before Robbie did. "We're just friends, like I said."

"Sure," Ivy said with a sarcastic nod. "I think I saw him go inside."

Robbie smiled and placed a hand on her friend's arm. "I'm okay. Really okay. And a lot of that has to do with having you. Go have some fun. There's something I need to do."

Ivy stopped her as she started to walk away to find Nick. Their moment on the dance floor had been rudely interrupted, and not just by Nathan's ghost, but by the man himself, and Robbie needed to finish this conversation. She couldn't let this one slip away as it had in Vegas.

"Robs," Ivy said, "Don't break his heart."

Robbie squeezed Ivy's hand. "I'm not planning on it."

Robbie slipped through the sliding glass doors separating Mrs. Chin's fairyland party and the living room. People were scattered around the living room, either to take a break from the music and dancing or get first crack at the food as it came out of the kitchen. Robbie smiled and nodded politely as she moved quickly toward the front of the house.

"Robbie, we need to talk," Mrs. Chin said, materializing out of nowhere and taking hold of her elbow.

Robbie jumped and pressed a hand to her chest. "Mom, what are you doing? I was just—"

Mrs. Chin waved her hands in the air, swatting away her excuses like the nuisance they were to her. "Come with me," she said, leading Robbie toward the stairs. "This won't take long."

The two Chin women remained silent as Robbie followed her mother up the stairs and into the master bedroom. Mrs. Chin closed the door behind them with a soft click so not to alert anyone of their absence from the party.

"What is this about, Mom?" Robbie's eyes darted to the windows. She hoped Nick hadn't left yet. If he did, she didn't know when she would speak to him again. The last time he left without saying goodbye, he'd remained silent for a week. How long would he stay gone if he left this time? She knew it looked bad—her leaving his side to go to Nathan's. But it hadn't been like that. And he needed to know that.

Sooner rather than later.

"Nathan," Mrs. Chin said, her hands loose at her side, but her lips pressed tight. "Sit."

Robbie held back her groan as she took the seat her mother pointed to. "We're not getting back together," she said, crossing her arms over her chest like the pouty thirteen-year-old she felt like.

Mrs. Chin sighed and sat next to her on the foot of the bed. "Your father told me you asked how we made it thirty years," she said.

Robbie's jaw fell open. She hadn't expected that. She'd always assumed because her father didn't talk to anyone when it wasn't necessary, that it must have included her mother, as well. But that's ridiculous, now that she thought about it as an adult. That was a child's thinking, which was fine for when she saw her parents as a means to an end, the ones put on this Earth to cater to her needs.

She was an adult now and needed to start seeing her parents as an adult would: two people in a loving and committed relationship. Hadn't her father stepped to her mother's side when he'd sensed her anxiety during their fight? Hadn't he, for thirty years, always made sure to stock the kitchen with Mrs. Chin's favorite flavored organic coffee exclusively sold at the health store across the street from his office? And her mother, who hated curry chicken, but made it faithfully on days when her husband seemed quieter and grumpier than usual because it was his favorite?

"It must seem odd to you, our marriage," her mother continued. "I tried looking at it from your eyes. The subdued husband and father. The nagging wife and mother. You've probably asked yourself a million times how your father could put up with me."

Robbie didn't need to confirm her mother's suspicions; Mrs. Chin could read it in Robbie's eyes. But still, Robbie's guilt overwhelmed her, turning her stomach. When she saw the hurt written across her mother's features, she lowered her chin, wishing there was a way to rewind the past week and take all the pain and anger away. She shouldn't have fought with her mother. Or, if she had to, which some days it did feel like a necessity, she should at least learn to control her words instead of letting them loose on the world.

"I wasn't always like this. Your father wasn't always this way either. Believe it or not, we were fun." Mrs. Chin paused and fiddled with her sleeve. "Do you ever wonder why we don't see the extended family much?"

"Nobody lives near here. Your family is in Chicago. Dad's side is in Honolulu," Robbie said, sensing her reply was a child's answer that any five-year-old could give. It was too simple of an explanation. If it were as easy as distance, Mrs. Chin wouldn't bother asking.

"We could have lived anywhere," Mrs. Chin said. "We chose San Francisco for a reason. Robbie, nobody wanted your father and me to get married. Not my family. Not his."

"What?" Robbie gasped. "That can't be true." While it was true that distance made frequent family gatherings difficult over the years, there had been some visits. Before Robbie was in high school, they'd gone to Hawaii every summer for a week. They'd spent every other Thanksgiving in Chicago. Robbie couldn't remember why those trips had come to an end. Every summer turned into once every three years. Every other Thanksgiving stretched into every five years. Until, eventually, it all ended. Occasionally, they would receive a random visit from a family member, but nothing like the big gatherings of her youth.

There were no fights or feuds that Robbie remembered. Her parents never had anything bad to say about her extended family. They never had much to say about them in general. Though, as Robbie was realizing, there was a lot more said behind the scenes than there was in front of her.

"It was a different time, thirty years ago. Mixed marriages weren't something that happened every day. Less than one and a half percent of marriages, in fact. It wasn't too long before then that mixed marriages had been banned completely."

"But still," Robbie tried to argue, "I can't believe no one who supported you. Gram? Nona?"

Mrs. Chin nodded thoughtfully. "My brother and sister did. But they're younger and were still in school at the time. What could they do about it? And your father's family? Well, they had already picked out a nice young girl from China for him to marry, and they were livid when he refused."

"They still do that? Arrange marriages?" Robbie thought of her aunts and uncles on her father's side and wondered if any of them had been arranged, too. Later, after Mrs. Chin finished saying whatever it was she was trying to tell her, she would have to remember to ask.

"Not everyone, but they did. But it wasn't just the marriage they opposed. The biggest reason they didn't want us to get married was because of you—well, any children we would have. You should have heard the things they said." Mrs. Chin paused and wiped her brow like the memory was enough to cause her to break out in a cold sweat. "Both sides would go on forever about how our children would be outcasts, and would never be accepted by anyone, doomed to live a life of mockery and solitude."

"Harsh." Though, it hadn't been too far off base.

"That was them putting it nicely. Your father and I ignored them, obviously, and got married anyway. Love conquers all and all that. We thought living here, in San Francisco, marriages like ours would be more common, less of a novelty item to be discussed at cocktail parties. Let me tell you, the looks we got when we were in public together," Mrs. Chin shuddered, "well if this was the way people were here, we couldn't imagine it being better anywhere else.

"But we were okay. We were happy. We walked into our marriage with our eyes open and ready to take on the world. Then you came along.

"The first time someone asked me if I was your nanny and not your mother, I think I cried for three days. There was one time when your father and I took you for a walk around the park. This group of women came over to see the baby because you know no woman can resist a baby stroller, and I remember one of them looking at you, then your father, and in a hushed tone, asked him what happened to the baby's mother."

"Right in front of you?" Robbie asked. She'd never heard these stories before. Growing up, she'd been so wrapped up in her daily battles, it had never occurred to her that her mother might have been fighting a few of her own.

"Yep. Your father, he just put his arm around me and said, 'Are you okay, honey? Did something happen to you?'" Mrs. Chin chuckled and shook her head softly. "I could have married him again right then and there. But see, that's when I realized, *we* may have chosen to put up with those types of questions and comments, but *you* didn't. You were so little, so innocent, a sweet little angel of a girl, and complete strangers were giving you the side-eye and whispering about you behind your back. Just thinking about it makes me sick to my stomach still."

"So, growing up . . . all that stuff about only being American, not being too loud, or too showy—"

"I was trying to protect you." Mrs. Chin sighed. "If you blended in and didn't call too much attention to yourself, maybe you could skate by without drawing the talk and the questions."

Robbie barked out a laugh. "It was a nice try, Mom."

Mrs. Chin shifted in her seat. Never one to take criticism lightly, she gripped the edge of the bed as though hanging on for dear life. Robbie could see the determination in her mother's eyes it took for her not to get up and walk away.

"Sorry, Mom," Robbie said. "Go on."

"We did the best we could," Mrs. Chin said, releasing the bed to wring her hands in her lap. "Or at least, what we thought was the best. I guess over time your father withdrew more so he wouldn't stand out. And I . . . I guess you can say I overcompensated. If we were involved in everything, then no one could leave you out. If everything was perfect, then no one could criticize."

"So, that explains your refusal to take part in the World Culture Day at school," Robbie said, piecing together moments in her childhood when she'd wished her mother could be normal. It turned out that had been exactly what Mrs. Chin had been trying to do. "Or why you never wanted me to wear any of the things Gram sent from Hawaii in public. You always said they were too Asian-looking." Tears sprang to Robbie's eyes. She'd hated hearing her mother say that. It had never sounded like she'd been talking about the clothes. "I always thought you meant I was too Asian-looking, which upset you."

"Oh, Robbie, no," Mrs. Chin exclaimed, wrapping her arms around Robbie, pulling her close. "You are beautiful. And I'm sorry you ever thought that." She wiped the tears from Robbie's cheeks. "Now, about Nathan."

Robbie groaned and pulled away. "Mom, we were doing so good here—"

"Hold on," her mother said, "let me finish." She cleared her throat. "Nathan's a good man. He'd be a good provider. And I suppose I always thought that if you two were together, people would stop looking at you like an anomaly. You'd be with someone like you. But I never saw it until tonight—the look in your eyes when you're with him. He's not the one. I know that now. He doesn't make you happy, not really happy."

As Robbie shook her head, the weight of guilt and other people's expectations that had been piling on top of her fell away. "No, he doesn't. It took me a long time to realize that, too. I think I wanted it to work because it made you so happy. But no, he's not the one, Mom."

"Okay, then," Mrs. Chin said, rising from her seat. Back to business. "Then you do what you need to do."

"Not worried about people looking at me anymore?"

Mrs. Chin smiled. "They should look. You're marvelous. Now, go get him."

Robbie's eyes widened as she slowly rose from her seat.

"I'm not blind," Mrs. Chin said with a wink. "I saw other things on the dance floor, too."

Robbie released a long, cleansing breath. "Mom, I have to go. But tomorrow, can we talk? There are some things I would like to tell you, things about my career."

Mrs. Chin embraced Robbie and stroked her hair. "I would love that. I can't wait to hear what you've got planned."

THIRTY-FOUR

"Nick," Robbie called, hurrying as fast as she could in her heels. He'd almost made it to the corner by the time she caught up with him. "Nick, hold on."

He stopped at the sound of his name and pivoted to face her, his hands jammed in his pockets, and his mouth turned down slightly at the corners, and she knew she hadn't lost him yet. If he'd already written off their moment in each other's arms as another miscalculation, then he would have answered her with some smart quip, some teasing remark.

"Aren't you missing the party?" he asked. "Mrs. Chin will lose it when she notices you're missing."

She noticed he didn't meet her halfway, instead, planting his feet on the ground waiting for her to catch up. "She told me to go, if you can believe it," Robbie said, slowing to catch her breath. "You owe me another dance."

Nick tilted his head back and looked back in the direction of the party over her head. "What about—"

Robbie shook her head. "He's gone. I sent him away. He should never have come here to begin with." She took a step closer and took his lack of moving away as a good sign.

"But isn't that what you wanted? For him to beg for you to go home?"

"Plans change," Robbie said. "This is home."

Nick's shoulders relaxed as a cab pulled up to the curb. "Wanna come with me?" he asked.

"Where are you going?" she asked. Nick was supposed to be going with her—to the bookstore, so that she could share her news.

"To Market Street," he said, opening the back door for her.

"What's on Market Street?" When the only response she received was a devilish grin and a tilt of the head, she added, "Adventure, right?"

"Now you're getting it," he said, helping her into the backseat.

It wasn't a long ride to Market Street, but sitting inches from Nick, feeling the heat from his closeness, stretched the minutes into months. It was torture. She ached to tell him her news about the bookstore and see his reaction. He'd be happy for her, of that she was certain. Impressed by her risk-taking, even. He'd ask the right questions and get excited when she did. Any worries that surfaced, he would deftly reassure her of her capabilities and offer help where he could. He would do his best to fill her half-empty cup until it brimmed over with joy. But it still wasn't time. They had to be there, standing in front of the store and all the possibilities. She wanted to throw her hands in the air and make a grand pronouncement. He'd appreciate that sort of reveal.

But along with that ache, there was something else thrumming through her veins.

Robbie cast a glance from the corner of her eye to where Nick sat gazing out the window as they drove through the city. His hands rested in his lap, and she longed to reach out and take one. She warmed, remembering what could have been in Las Vegas. The heat intensified as the memory of his arms around her on the side of the road while she sobbed coursed through her. By the time she thought of the two of them dancing in her parents' backyard, a thin sheen of sweat had broken out on her forehead.

"Can you keep a secret?" Nick asked as the cab came to a stop.

"Of course," Robbie said, grateful to have something to think about other than his hand on her skin.

Nick paid the driver extra to wait for them and swung the door open. He held his hand out to help her from the car, but this time, when she placed her hand in his, he didn't let go. "Good. I haven't told anyone this yet. Not Ivy. Not my parents. No one." He led her to an empty storefront on a trendy section of South Market Street. "This is it."

Robbie looked from the darkened windows to Nick, then back. "This is what? What am I looking at?"

"This," he said, still not dropping her hand, but instead, drawing her closer to the building and pulling out a set of keys, "is my new gallery and photography studio."

Robbie's eyes stretched as wide as they could go. Had she heard that correctly? Was the wanderer putting down roots? In her city? Their city? "What do you mean, your studio?"

He unlocked the door and pushed it open, bringing her along with him. Only once they were inside did he let go of her hand long enough to find the light switch. Robbie gasped at the beauty of the space. Open and airy with high exposed ceilings, it was an artist's dream.

"This is what I was doing in Los Angeles—securing an investor. Signing a bunch of paperwork. Can you see it?" he asked, standing in the middle of what was to be his showroom. "There's enough space to display multiple collections at once. There will be seating scattered throughout. Maybe a wine bar over there," he said, pointing to a space in the corner that wasn't conducive to hanging artwork. "I can rent out the space for events and parties for extra income, too," he continued. Clearly, he had thought out this plan of his. "This is the best part over here."

Nick walked toward the back where two swinging doors led to even more space. He pushed them open and found those lights, as well. It looked as though it had been used as a large storage room, same exposed ceilings and bare walls, except for the floor to ceiling storage shelves on one wall.

"Welcome to my studio," Nick said, his voice bursting with excitement. "What do you think?"

"Nick," Robbie breathed. "This is amazing. But what does this mean? No more traveling? Are you okay with that?"

"It's something I've been thinking about for a while but wasn't going to jump into unless everything was perfect—the finances, the location," he paused and pierced Robbie with his gaze. "The timing." He took her hand again, his thumb brushing over her knuckles. "I couldn't wait to tell you. That's a lot of why I haven't called. I was afraid once I heard your voice, I would spill it all too soon. You have a way of making me want to tell you everything. Like it couldn't possibly be real until I shared it with you."

Robbie's throat went dry, and she was suddenly aware of every nerve ending in her body. "Were you afraid I would blab it all over town?" she teased, needing to diffuse some of the tension that was mounting too quickly.

He shook his head slowly. His voice dropped to a husky whisper that almost got lost in the emptiness of the space. "I don't know what I was afraid of anymore. I'm just a stupid man. I shouldn't have left town without saying goodbye. I should have called. I had just gotten you back in my life. I shouldn't have played fast and loose with your friendship like that."

"The only reason you didn't call was because of this studio?"

Nick's face flushed and his eyes fixed on a point over her shoulder instead of on her, but he didn't drop her hand. "At first, I thought you still wanted Nathan. After that night in Vegas . . ."

Robbie groaned and lowered her head, heat rushing to her face. "It wasn't like that. I shouldn't have blurted his name out. It was just the first time I'd admitted to myself that I didn't want him, and it took me by surprise. I wanted to explain, but—"

"But I acted like an idiot and didn't give you the chance," he finished for her.

Robbie grinned. "I wouldn't say *idiot*."

Nick dragged his eyes back to hers and squeezed her hand. "I didn't want you to feel pressured. I wanted you to make your next plans on your own terms. That's the only way you'll ever really be happy. Doing Robbie Chin, the Robbie Chin way." He arched an eyebrow. "What do you think of my plans?"

"I think . . . It's amazing, Nick. It really is. You're going to do so many great things here. But now I also think it's my turn to take you somewhere." She pulled him back through to the front of the gallery.

"Where are we going?" Nick asked, his tone playful and curious.

"Well, you showed me yours. It's my turn to show you mine."

"Is it wrong that I really like the sound of that?" he asked, winding an arm around her waist while they made their way out to the waiting cab.

Another painful ride later, they stood in front of the bookstore. "Drea's?" he asked.

Robbie shook her head, bending to scoop up a rock that had strayed from the base of the tree on the curb. "Nope. It's mine." She said it. Out loud. Each word revved her heart up to full speed. She would've shouted it while doing a backflip if she knew how to do one. She clasped her hands in front of her chest, waiting for Nick to say something.

"What did you say?" he asked. He stood behind her shoulder, and when he spoke, his breath tickled the top of her ear. His hands rested lightly on her waist, as though he were afraid she would float away on the excitement he had to feel building inside her like a shaken champagne bottle ready to pop its cork.

"It's mine. I'm signing the paperwork on Monday. Drea's retiring and I'm taking it over. She'll work for me for the next six weeks, teaching me everything I need to know while I make some changes and updates. But, yeah," she sighed, tears of joy rimming her eyes, "this is all mine now."

Nick swooped her up in his arms, knocking the breath from her lungs. He twirled her in a circle, setting her back on her wobbly feet, breathless and laughing. "Talk about a new adventure," he said, his hands resting gently on her shoulders to keep her from toppling over. "I'm so proud of you. How are you going to make your updates, though? You didn't sell the green machine, did you?"

"Never," Robbie gasped. "Well, at least not yet. I'm stuck with the Pinto for a little while longer. I had some money saved up for my future, and well, this is it. Besides, what's another road trip without the wagon?"

Nick laughed. "It worked out so well for us the first time. Why tempt fate?"

Squeezing his hands, she looked into his eyes, letting the joy of the moment wash over her. "I couldn't wait to tell you. I've been keeping it in all night," Robbie said, knowing he understood the exact feeling. "I haven't told anyone else either. I was waiting, for you."

"Thank you for telling me."

"Well, you did tell me your secret first. It was fair." More than fair, it was the way it was supposed to be. Now that she'd shared it with him, all the stars had aligned.

"Don't you know?" he asked, tucking a loose strand of hair behind her ear. "You're my best friend."

Robbie's smile stretched beyond normal human limits. "So, I guess you'll be pretty busy now, huh?"

"Yep," he said, a matching grin spreading across his features. "Long hours. Evenings. Weekends. You?"

"Definitely the same."

"But, you're here," he said as she nodded. "And I'm here."

Robbie heard the unspoken promise between them, and her heart leaped in her chest. This must have been what it was like to have one of those telepathic conversations, and if it was, why did people ever use words?

Nick leaned forward, brushing her lips with his. Robbie tilted her chin toward him, wanting more, but he pulled back. "What are we doing?" he asked.

"I don't know," Robbie said. Her hands rested on his chest, and his arms were around her back, holding her close. People walked by them on the street, but Robbie didn't pay them any attention. She had no desire to move from the very spot she was in. Not yet.

"No plans about this?" he asked, his eyes twinkling.

Robbie ran a hand along his chin. "I have several, but none of them involve us standing here talking." She wrapped an arm around his neck and pulled his mouth to hers. Everything about this moment felt right. It was unscripted and messy. It was happening in the middle of a public street with people walking by in all directions. But she didn't care. All she cared about was the man in her arms and the way he made her come alive. This man, who had started as her best friend's little brother and had turned into something so much better.

Robbie pulled away with a breathless laugh. "Ivy told me not to break your heart."

"She told me the same," he said, grinning like a fool.

"She did? When?"

"When I sent her our selfie in Vegas."

"What do you think she'll say about this? Best friend. Little brother."

"We don't have to tell her anything, you know," Nick said before kissing her temple, and then behind her ear while Robbie giggled.

Robbie stood on her tiptoes to be able to reach his lips with a feather touch of a kiss. "She's my best friend. I tell her everything."

"Tattle-tale."

"Brat."

Rerouting

About the Author

Bex Jalise is a mother of three and author of contemporary stories about finding love, friendship, and a bit of yourself along the way. Her other interests include finding new ways to trick her kids into eating vegetables and seeing how tall she can stack her pile of to-be-read books. Bex lives with her husband and three children in Chicago. Her work can be found on Amazon.

www.bexjalise.com

Made in the USA
Monee, IL
07 November 2019

16461101R00178